THE ASSASSINATION RUN

By the same author
The Omega Factor

The Assassination Run

Jack Gerson

Based on the BBC-TV serial
Produced by Bob McIntosh

BRITISH BROADCASTING CORPORATION

To Bob, Ken and the Crew who made it happen.

And to Malcolm, Mary and the Cast who brought the words alive.

Published by the
British Broadcasting Corporation
35 Marylebone High Street
London W1M 4AA

ISBN 0 563 17785 3

First printed 1980

© Jack Gerson 1980

Printed in England by
Hollen Street Press
Slough, Bucks.

Prologue

He was a small man dressed in a well-cut lightweight grey suit, a soft narrow-brimmed hat shielding his eyes from the glare of the hot afternoon sun. To a close observer the only signs of discomfort he revealed were small beads of perspiration on his upper lip under the pencil-thin black moustache.

He walked with a determined stride towards the air terminal, his appearance contrasting with the brightly coloured shirts and casual slacks of the tourists around him. He ignored cries of greeting directed at other travellers from behind a waist-high steel barrier; his eyes flickered briefly over the uniformed police security guard at the barrier. The guard glanced at him briefly and yawned. A typical bourgeois business man, or a minor civil servant; nothing dangerous there. The guard turned his attention to a noisy group of bearded students jostling each other behind him.

The small man passed quickly through immigration after a brief scrutiny of his Libyan passport. Collecting an expensive leather suitcase from baggage control he was passed through customs. It was only when he reached the main concourse of the air terminal that he permitted himself to relax and the determined stride became hesitant. Somewhere here he knew he would be contacted.

Carl-Jan Husig stood at the edge of the concourse, partially screened by a pillar, breathless from the fast run down the stairway from the observation roof. Carl was twenty-three years old, a blond youth, hair lank over his forehead, eyes deep set, skin marred by traces of adolescent acne. He was dressed in a crumpled checked shirt and faded blue jeans. His thin arms, not yet tanned brown, were deep red with unaccustomed exposure to the Mediterranean sun.

He had been following the progress of the small man since he had left the aircraft. Now he peered from behind the pillar, eyes straining across the concourse. Identification had to be positive. Carl dare not approach the wrong man. He glanced again at a crumpled photograph cupped in his hand. The hair of the man in the photograph was longer, curling back and under the nape of the neck; the moustache was thicker, heavier, and turned down at the corners of the mouth. But the features were the same.

Carl smiled to himself. The man had come through customs and immigration under the alert eyes of the Spanish police without being recognised. Only he, Carl-Jan Husig, had identified a man whose face should have been known to almost every police department in the world. The small man standing waiting in the centre of Malaga Airport was Santos Morales, dubbed by the press of the western world as the 'Leopard' and wanted for acts of terrorism and murder in sixteen countries.

Carl moved forward. Then he stopped. Frightened. Frozen.

Two men in slacks and open-necked shirts had approached Morales. This was not meant to happen, Carl knew. Only he was meant to greet the new arrival. His first thoughts were that they were police officials but this was at once dispelled by Morales' actions. He shook hands with each of them vigorously, smiling and relaxed. Even the 'Leopard' would not face arrest so coolly.

The taller of the two newcomers, a thin figure with dark eyes, olive skin and a long nose, gestured towards the main exit of the air terminal. Morales nodded amiably, returning the gesture with one of his own, motioning the thin man to lead the way. The three figures sauntered towards the doors.

Carl had often been told he panicked easily under stress. He clenched small sweating fists. He must not lose control. Something had gone wrong and yet it might not be irreversible. Morales had associates throughout the world;

6

friends, accomplices, many of whom protected him, assisted him in his various activities.

But on this occasion the understanding had been that he worked only with the group of whom Carl was a member. This was the purpose of arranging Morales' flight from Benghazi where he lived in an elegant coastal villa—rumour had it that this was a personal gift from Colonel Gadafy.

Carl came out of the airport, perspiration soaking his shirt. He was in time to see Morales and his two companions getting into a rather battered Simca saloon. The thin, dark-eyed man took his place behind the wheel, Morales at his side. The other man climbed into the rear of the car. Carl looked despairingly towards a telephone kiosk and then, as the Simca's engine started and it moved off, he dismissed any thought of phoning for help. He knew he must not lose sight of Morales. He ran towards a row of taxis.

The taxi-driver drove with one hand, picking his teeth with a matchstick with the other. He evinced complete disinterest in the fact that his instructions were to follow the Simca. He recognised Carl as a foreigner and the whims of foreigners held no surprises for him.

They reached the outskirts of Malaga. The Simca moved at a steady twenty-five miles an hour, its driver obviously in no hurry. Finally it skirted the centre of the town and, turning off the main highway, drew up outside a tall apartment building.

Carl's taxi drove past the parked Simca and pulled up at the next block. Thrusting a handful of pesetas into the driver's hand, Carl jumped out in time to see Morales and his two companions disappearing into the building.

Assuming a nonchalance he did not feel Carl strolled past the entrance to the building unable to resist staring up at the concrete and glass towering above him. Twenty storeys with at least four separate flats to every storey. Into which one had Morales been taken?

The telephone kiosk was on the opposite side of the road. With his eyes still fixed on the apartment block Carl crossed to the kiosk and stood hesitantly outside it. It was as if he was willing Morales to reappear, cross the road and greet him with some excuse for not waiting at the airport. Carl stood shuffling his feet in the dust. Above him the sun shone down, the heat from its rays increasing as it neared its zenith.

Carl knew he should phone Rolf. He knew he should phone at once and report. Yet he dreaded Rolf's reaction, dreaded being blamed for allowing Morales to be spirited away. That was how Rolf would put it, spirited away while he, Carl, did nothing. But Morales hadn't been spirited away; he had gone willingly with the two men, as if he had been expecting them, friendly associates greeting a colleague.

Or had they passed themselves off as Carl's group? The thought frightened him. Nobody outside the group apart from Morales knew of the arranged meeting at Malaga Airport. And yet Morales had been intercepted.

Two minutes passed. A woman came from the block of flats and walked at a leisurely pace along the road leading to the sea front. A beach bag swung carelessly from one hand.

Carl made a decision. He went into the kiosk and dialled a number. As he waited for the number to ring out his fingers drummed on the glass impatiently. At the same time his head was still turned towards the apartment block. He was nervous that Morales might reappear and he might miss him.

The voice that he finally heard at the other end of the line was harsh and angry. Carl became staccato in his nervousness as he explained what had happened at the airport. It wasn't his fault, he had no idea who the two men were, Morales had gone with them willingly; the words tripped over each other as he tried to explain.

Then it happened.

His eyes were still on the entrance to the building, when there was a movement above, activity at the edge of his vision. He looked up. Figures moved at the window of a room on the sixth floor. Then the glass of the window

8

showered outwards, flashing in the sun, and something large arched through the window as if thrown with considerable force. The sound of the smashing glass reached him followed instantly by another sound, a thin, high-pitched scream.

The scream was cut off abruptly as the body struck the pavement six storeys below. There was a third sound as it hit the concrete, a sound Carl tried to shut out by looking away, as if by averting his vision he would stop it reaching him. He babbled for a second into the telephone only to be cut short by the voice at the end of the line, terse and guttural.

Hanging up, Carl turned reluctantly and came out of the kiosk. He walked across the road slowly towards the broken bloody shape on the kerb. Already figures were gathering around it, curiosity overcoming horror. As he neared the body, glass from the window crunched under foot. He looked up at the window. A curtain hung over the sill, lazily swinging in the breeze.

A policeman, running swiftly from across the street, knelt by the body and gently eased it around. The unrecognisable shape that had been the skull was turned away and Carl stared into the contorted dead face of Santos Morales. One eye, open, stared up at him. The other merged into a crimson formless mess. The 'Leopard' had finally been destroyed.

Two hours later in another room in another place Carl faced the man who had been on the other end of the telephone line. And behind him three other pairs of eyes stared up at him.

'Who were they? The men that took him?' he asked. 'And why did he go with them?'

The slim man with the thinning hair and the young old face ground a cigarette out under foot.

'They probably passed themselves off as his reception committee. In other words, as you, Carl.'

'But who . . .?'

'I've an idea. The only people that would be clever enough to find him in Libya and keep an eye on him. Mossad. The Israeli Secret Service.'

'How could I know?' Carl was conscious of the whine that crept into his own voice.

'You couldn't and nobody is blaming you.'

A sense of relief filled Carl. He nodded a nervous acknowledgment of his absolution. There was a long silence in the room broken only by the distant sound of traffic.

Then, from behind the young old man who led them, one of the two girls spoke.

'I suppose that's the end of the operation then?' Her German accent was soft, belying the cold blue young eyes under the short dark hair.

'No!' The voice from the young old face was loud, angry, definitive.

'But without Morales, what can be done?' The question came from the third man in the room, a tall lank youth in a T-shirt and oil-stained jeans. 'None of us could carry out the operation. We're not trained, we haven't the ability . . .'

The young old man, the leader, cut him short.

'Then we get someone else who can! I have an idea who that will be. And how we will persuade him to carry out the operation.'

He smiled, showing his teeth, and turned away, walking to the window of the room. He stared out into the yellowing light of the late afternoon and, when he spoke again, it was almost as if he was talking to himself.

'A professional. An expert killer who thinks he has retired. All we do is convince him he hasn't.'

ONE

A thin grey cloud patterned the midday sun, diluting the warmth of its rays, sending a chill breeze down the sides of the glen and causing a ripple to disturb the surface of the river. The man who had been sitting on the bank stood up lazily and reeled in the line of his rod.

Mark Fraser was thirty-five and looked younger. He was six feet tall with reddish hair thinning slightly at the temples but thick over the centre of his brow from which it fell carelessly over his forehead. He was dressed in corduroy slacks and an open-necked, checked shirt. His skin was tanned, not from the sun but from living in the outdoors through all manner of weather.

Having reeled in the line, he swung the fishing bag over his shoulder and started the walk to the head of the glen and the large cottage in which he lived with his wife, Jill. Three trout were in the fishing bag, enough for a pleasing supper. He smiled to himself. Jill would make a face; five hours on the river and only three fish. But then she was city-bred and, although she had taken to life in the Scottish countryside with a controlled delight, she still made demands on nature which nature did not always provide.

Fraser walked, not fast, but with a measured stride pacing himself to cover the two miles to the cottage without strain but as fast as was comfortable. It was an old habit learned in other places, during longer walks when life and death might depend on arrival at his destination not late or early but at an exact time.

As he walked his eyes seemed downcast but were actually alert, flickering from side to side under his slightly hooded eyelids, taking in everything in front and at both sides of him. Another old habit. Training dies hard, damn it, he

11

thought to himself. A meticulous awareness of surroundings had been bred into him in the old days and the knowledge of it sometimes irritated him. He wanted to forget completely, eradicate from memory and action the old days.

He called them the old days and yet they had ended only two years before, with the return from Holland and the angry words in the dusty Whitehall office. His office, when back in the country, had always been dusty, a square cell with a thin strip of carpeting in front of the desk commensurate with the mystical civil service grading which had been assigned to him. The Civil Service grading always amused him. How did you assess a grade for a man whose duty usually culminated in someone's death? Easy for Fleming to give James Bond a double-o rating. No basis in reality.

The reality had not only been different but at the start almost cosy. A young Scot, doing a post-graduate course at Oxford after two years at Edinburgh University, is approached by a seemingly benevolent don. Again he could smile at that memory. He had been naïve enough to prepare to resist a homosexual advance but it hadn't happened. Instead there had been tea, cakes and jam or honey as if invoking the spirit of Rupert Brooke. There had been questions too about his ability to speak languages, fluent French, German, Italian and a little Spanish by the time he arrived at Oxford and in the first year a working knowledge of Russian. And then the quiet question from the benevolent don, what did he intend to do with his life after leaving university? Fraser had shrugged awkwardly, talked about teaching or possibly journalism. Another question, what about the Civil Service? And another pause for his tea-cup to be refilled.

The don, who was shortly to become Master of his college, pressed the question. Fraser had replied that he did not think he was interested in the dry as dust atmosphere of Whitehall; the corridors of power represented boredom to him. The don pointed out quietly that teaching would be equally boring; the young today had no real desire to learn anything other than how to make as much money

12

aₛ quickly as possible with as little effort. And journalism, while it might have moments of excitement, preferred youngsters who had come through their own inky ranks rather than highly-educated young men who were too old at twenty-three.

So what was the answer? The don replied slowly and carefully. There were branches of the Civil Service that were keen on healthy young men with an ability to speak a number of languages like a native. And hadn't Mark Fraser distinguished himself at Bisley in the University team. His marksmanship had brought him two gold cups. At this Fraser had shrugged modestly. His uncle, who had brought him up since his parents' early death in a car accident, had taught the small boy how to shoot in a dark glen north of Perth. In that glen he and his uncle had lived in semi-isolation, an isolation broken only by periods at a village school and later longer periods at boarding school.

The don had revealed himself at that point as a kind of recruiting officer for certain obscure branches of government activity, intelligence agencies whose code names and numerals had an aura of excitement and romance. Mark Fraser had fallen.

The reality at first was far from romantic. The dusty office in Whitehall where he had worked for months on translating obscure reports from Central Europe became the centre of his life on leaving Oxford. The monotony of this task was broken by occasional periods of training in a variety of skills, all violent. After a year he had been sent overseas on various missions, the earlier of which were innocuous and indeed required only that he act as a courier. However, gradually the missions became more involved and he was sent into what could only be called unfriendly territory. And violence crept into the picture as he came into contact with the dark underside of European and Scandinavian politics, the world of espionage and counter-espionage.

Then the 'Firm', as his department was called, had discovered Fraser's ability with a rifle. The first time he had been used as a marksman, as his superiors called it, the man he had been ordered to kill had been described to him as a former Nazi SS officer with a record of war crimes that was horrendous. This unsavoury character was acting as a double agent for the KGB and the CIA but with distinctly anti-social tendencies towards the Firm.

Fraser had shot him as he stood at the window of an apartment in Prague at a range of five hundred yards. The bullet had entered his chest at the exact centre of his heart. With this Mark Fraser gained a reputation he did not want and grew to hate.

The second killing had been of a black African statesman whose political achievements had been gained by the simple expedience of feeding his opponents either to crocodiles or to equally voracious secret policemen. If Fraser felt the beginnings of a growing conscience about killing people, the reputations of his victims had gone some way in assuaging that conscience. At the same time his abilities with all manner of weapons confirmed his position as the Firm's hit man.

Attempts were made by the other side to kill him. Evading them had at once excited and frightened him. But it was not until the fifth killing that his conscience began to sicken and a realisation that he had become a paid killer forced him to examine that conscience. In the interim his uncle had died leaving him the cottage in the dark glen, five thousand acres of land and a considerable sum of money. And he had met Jill Marshall.

At the time they were married Jill was twenty-six and worked as a secretary in the Firm. She was the orphaned daughter of a former agent who had distinguished himself in the war and died in comparatively poor circumstances some three years before. Her job as secretary had been arranged with a consciousness of making a benevolent gesture by the then chief of the Firm, Sir Alfred Tarrant. Jill had accepted it out of necessity rather than any patriotic desire to serve her country. Indeed her feelings towards the Firm were confused. She had long suspected her father's deteriorating health had been due to experiences both during and after the war, working for the Firm. At the same time a straitened financial situation demanded an immediate remedy. Tarrant supplied that remedy.

It was the same Tarrant who had ordered the elimination of the man who was to be Fraser's fifth and last victim. A minor official in the British Embassy in The Hague, Vincent Hartley, using his embassy position to cover the fact that he was the Firm's man in Holland, had, it appeared, been selling secrets to the Russians. Tarrant had insisted to Fraser that the whole of the Firm's central European network was threatened. The Department did not want another George Blake on their hands. Fraser suggested Hartley might be arrested.

'No evidence, Fraser,' Tarrant had replied, staring vaguely over Fraser's shoulder. 'Nothing tangible, but a certainty that the fellow's selling us out, name by name. He has to be eliminated.'

'Murdered, you mean.'

Tarrant had actually looked at Fraser briefly then looked away again, eyes misted into a distant focus.

'Removed with extreme prejudice is the terminology used by our American friends.'

Five days later Vincent was 'removed with extreme prejudice' in a side street near the British Embassy building in The Hague. On this occasion Fraser was forced to work with a Mauser at close range. He fired twice and between the shots experienced a feeling of revulsion greater than any such emotion he had felt in the past. Hartley had looked pained and surprised as he fell to the pavement.

Fraser had consoled himself with the thought that the killing of Hartley had saved the lives of a number of British agents. A week later in his office he had lost this consolation when Tarrant told him, almost casually, a mistake had been made.

'The leakage was coming from Paris. We caught the man and he will be dealt with. Pity about Hartley. We were so sure . . .'

'So he wasn't involved. His death was unnecessary.' A bleak statement.

'Unfortunately that is so.' The matter-of-fact tones were so lightly uttered that Fraser felt a chill run down his spine.

'However no blame attaches to you,' Tarrant had gone on condescendingly.

The chill was still in him but now he felt something else, a physical nausea. 'You bastard!' he gasped at Tarrant.

'I don't think that is necessary . . .'

'I do. I think it's bloody necessary to tell cold-blooded inhuman bastards exactly what they are. Murderous . . .'

'That's enough, Fraser!' Tarrant's face had flushed a deep red. 'Apart from being your superior officer, I would remind you that you have yourself killed four other people . . .'

'And are you sure they were guilty too? Or were they official mistakes?'

Tarrant walked to the door of Fraser's small, coffin-shaped office and turned. 'I'll choose to ignore what you have said. Perhaps tomorrow you will have reconsidered . . . understood the pressures . . .'

'No!' Fraser was quick and incisive. 'For me there will be no tomorrow with the Department.'

He typed his formal resignation that afternoon. He handed it in and with it, a Mauser and a Walther PK. The actual process of releasing him took a month, during which he sat in his office, a pariah to his former colleagues. It finally ended in an acid interview during which Tarrant insisted that he be reminded that, despite resignation, he was still subject to all the provisions of the Official Secrets Act. He acknowledged this with a curt nod, cleared his desk out and left the building.

His uncle's death had left him financially independent so he had no immediate problems. He had often told himself he would like to live in the cottage in the dark glen, possibly use his land as a tourist attraction, arrange for deer stalks and grouse shooting for visiting Americans and that way he would have a modest income on top of his assets.

That night he took Jill to dinner, told her of his resignation and discussed his plan. During the previous six months, when he was not abroad on operational duties, he had taken her out and indeed two months after they had started to go out together they had become lovers in what Jill described as a rather unsalubrious motel bedroom somewhere off the North Circular Road.

Fraser was nervous of her reaction to his news of resignation but she greeted it with unconcealed delight. Although, as a secretary within the Firm, she did not officially know too many details of the Firm's operations she could deduce much of what was going on from certain reports she was cleared to see. And she was glad that Mark was free of the Firm.

Later that night Fraser suggested with an awkward quality that surprised even himself with its own naïvety that it might be a good idea if they got married. Jill stared at him expressionlessly for a full minute before she replied. And when she did reply she did so with artless simplicity.

'Yes, of course.'

The next day Jill resigned from the Firm and two weeks later they were married.

The honeymoon was in Venice and they passed a lazy, idyllic fourteen days marred only by the awareness that they were under surveillance. This surveillance continued on their return to London. When they finally moved to Scotland and Mark's cottage, which Jill instantly started redecorating, they were conscious of occasional observation by various apparently new faces in the nearby village of Craigallen from which the cottage derived its name. They tolerated this until one evening when, after the visit of various tradesmen who were working on Jill's redecoration plans, Fraser himself discovered a bug on their telephone. Only a trip to London and a short, sharp angry meeting with Tarrant terminated the surveillance. Tarrant murmured various apologia including remarks about the dangers of former members of the Department passing information; about the general suspicion surrounding ex-operatives, and the experiences of other organisations such as the CIA with books of revelations written by former agents.

Finally, however, Tarrant was persuaded to withdraw his observers when Fraser threatened that, if the surveillance continued, he would consider writing his memoirs, risking prosecution and revealing the persecution he and Jill had endured since leaving the Firm. Further, he emphasised that in the event of his death, by accident, purpose or natural causes his solicitors in Edinburgh would instantly make available to the press papers outlining certain activities of the Firm and his own missions on its behalf which might prove sensational and hardly credible to those who believed only in the more honourable actions of British Intelligence.

Tarrant agreed to withdraw from any further interest in the activities of Mark Fraser and his wife.

Yet now, two years later, as he strolled towards Craigallen Cottage he knew he could never completely rid himself of the training and the memories of his years with the Firm. Sometimes in the colder hours of the night he would see Vincent Hartley's face, twisted in the puzzlement of violent, unexpected and undeserved death, intruding on the edge of his dreams, contorting them into nightmares.

Jill Fraser was pulling on her coat as he entered the flagstoned kitchen of the cottage. At twenty-eight Jill was a woman verging on becoming beautiful. Apart from intelligence and a warm, slightly off-centre sense of humour she was, as Fraser never stopped acknowledging, a woman whose beauty flowered and was nurtured by increasing maturity. Her dark hair flowed to her shoulders in a seemingly casual perfection and her eyes, a greenish blue in colour, contained their own honesty.

She looked up as he laid his fishing bag on the heavy whitewood work table.

'I'm glad you're back,' she greeted him with a mock scowl. 'Six hours neglecting me for a damp river bank is not good for my ego. Nor for rheumatics which you will undoubtedly get early in life.'

'I think I've got them already,' he replied, throwing in a slight wince as he perched on the edge of the table.

'Anyway, I'm just popping down to the village. You ate

too much over the weekend and we need groceries,' she
went on. 'And, by the way, Mr McKay phoned to say he's
got a puppy he thinks would make a good gun-dog.'

Fraser frowned. He fished certainly but, although he
would arrange deerstalks for visitors, he had given up
shooting anything when he left the Firm. It was as if he
felt a need in some way to compensate for the death of
Hartley. More than that, for the deaths of the other four
victims. No matter how deserving of death they had been
he had long concluded his part in their deaths was something for which he had to atone. Something to do with the
Scots Calvinistic conscience, he told himself, an inheri-
tance from his uncle, that kindly but stern man who shot
and fished six days a week and on the seventh went twice
to the kirk.

'I told McKay I wanted a dog but not necessarily a gun
dog,' he insisted. A gun dog would be a temptation to shoot
which he wanted to resist.

She smiled. 'Try telling that to old McKay. He believes
dogs have only two functions. Sheep dogs or gun dogs. I
must go.'

'Wait a minute, wait a minute. You might ask me if I
caught anything.'

'Sorry, O mighty hunter. Did you catch anything?'

Fraser tipped over the fishing bag and the three fish slid
out on to a copy of the morning paper which lay on the
table.

'Brown trout!' he indicated with mock pride. Fishing, he
had convinced himself, was different from shooting. And
the catch was for the pot.

Jill stared at them, amused at the three small fish. He
caught the look and added quickly, 'Well, they're not bad
for that stream at this time of the year.'

'Lovely, darling,' she reassured him. 'But hardly enough
to satisfy your gargantuan appetite.'

She kissed him lightly on the cheek and went to the
door.

'See you in about an hour. And don't forget to phone
Mr McKay.'

Outside the cottage she climbed into the secondhand Mini he had bought her when they first came to the cottage. It was parked beside the sleek four-year-old Jensen, Fraser's one indulgence when he had inherited his uncle's money. Jill insisted she would not drive such a powerful beast and had demanded he purchase the Mini, as her one mode of transportation in and out of the glen.

As she drove off Fraser leaned on the lintel of the cottage door and gave a brief wave before turning back into the kitchen. One small task to be done before he relaxed with a large dram; the fish had to be cleaned.

As he scooped them from the now damp surface of *The Scotsman* his eye caught a headline at the foot of the page.

INTERNATIONAL TERRORIST IN MYSTERY DEATH FALL

He glanced over the text briefly. Another assassin from another country had completed another mission. He wondered vaguely if somewhere that day there was a man sitting back, nausea threatening to rise in his throat, hand trembling at the memory of shattering glass and that almost inhuman scream as the body plunged through. Or was he less sensitive, the best kind of assassin, without conscience, without imagination, the ideal killing machine?

Fraser shrugged and turned away to the deep kitchen sink and the culmination of his minor river massacre. For God's sake, he told himself, stop dwelling on the past. He managed to avoid thinking of it for weeks on end, and then suddenly it was with him. One of those damn days. Without cause, he thought.

Five hundred miles away in a Whitehall Office which Mark Fraser had once known, Sir James Mackeson, a tall balding man running to fat, stared down at a report of the death by defenestration of Santos Morales.

'He was a nasty piece of work,' Mackeson growled, frowning at the thin-faced man on the other side of his desk. 'Still, any idea who got to him?'

Frank Lloyd stroked his pencil-thin moustache nervously. He was always nervous when facing his immediate superior. His hands sweated profusely at such moments and he was conscious of it and embarrassed.

'Our man in Spain had no idea when he submitted that report.'

Mackeson frowned again. 'I trust you have some idea.'

Lloyd nodded. 'My reports point to the Israelis.'

'Damn it I don't like the Israelis operating in Western Europe without even a by-your-leave. They might inform us.'

'They *are* doing our job for us when they knock out someone like Morales.'

Mackeson stood, stretching his large frame. When he spoke the acidity was obvious.

'My dear Lloyd, I wish you'd understand I don't like other people doing our job for us. It happens that I may not have felt ready to take out Morales.'

Lloyd blinked, surprised. The pressure to get Morales throughout the Western world had been considerable.

'Anyway it could create problems in Spain,' Mackeson went on. 'Stir up mud. All sorts of creatures crawl out of mud. Who did you say was in charge in Spain?'

He knows perfectly well, Lloyd thought, but he has to ask.

'Bartlett,' he replied.

Mackeson affected a shudder. 'Oh God, those hearty ex-rugger types!'

He walked to the window, affecting the rolling gait he assumed to remind those who knew that he had been a naval officer. After a moment he spoke again.

'If anything blows up in Spain I may need you to go out there.'

Lloyd nodded acknowledgment wondering what on earth could blow up over the death of a terrorist whose demise would be regarded even by his friends as the removal of an international embarrassment. Still a trip to Spain would be a pleasant relief from Whitehall.

'Thank you, Lloyd,' Mackeson's tone indicated dismissal. Lloyd went to the door.

'Oh, and I'm not to be disturbed for half an hour,'

Mackeson added. 'And tell Miss Gorringe to give me a closed telephone line.'

Lloyd left the office and dutifully informed Mackeson's secretary, the ageing *ingénue,* Miss Gorringe, of her chief's wishes.

In his office Mackeson returned to his desk and stared down thoughtfully at the report from Spain. Of course he had known from another source of Morales' death. These things always created a flurry because of their unexpectedness. He gazed at the telephone, decided against the need to use it and looked across the room at the rows of potted plants which lined low tables under the window. These were his own additions to the office since Tarrant's retirement. Of course Tarrant had to go after the Vincent Hartley fiasco. And some of the potted plants Mackeson had brought from his old office in the Admiralty. Indeed one of them, an elderly cactus plant, had even been in the cabin of his last sea command.

The thought comforted him. It gave him a feeling of permanence in a changing world; it was a comfort amid so much that was disagreeable.

TWO

The village of Craigallen was about three miles from the Fraser's cottage. It consisted of ten grey stone houses lining the main road to the north. One of the buildings was the village inn with its three bedrooms and a large public bar which catered to the thirst of the farmers in the district. Another building housed the combined post office and general store. About a quarter of a mile north were three other buildings, the village school, the church and the manse. These lay at the junction of the road that led to the dark glen and the main road. Ten minutes after leaving the cottage Jill Fraser drove around the junction and into the village.

As she parked outside the store and stepped out of her car, string carrier bag in hand, Jill noticed the large Volvo parked across the road. She caught a glimpse of two faces in shadow in the front seats

Inside the store, Mrs McCrae, small, dark and plump, a roll of fat bulging her pullover over the tight edge of her skirt, greeted Jill effusively. After only two years Jill had managed the enviable achievement of being completely accepted by the people of the district. The rareness of this achievement was emphasised after six months when Mrs McCrae confided that one minister had lived at the manse and preached in the church for over eight years without ever being accepted. Jill had been pleased and amused at the compliment, wondering at the time if she would ever be able to accept the locals. After a year she had achieved it. She found she liked the Highlanders.

In the store Mrs McCrae bustled around with her usual excess of energy filling Jill's orders with an unnecessary alacrity. As she did so she chattered volubly. Jill had learned it was never required to take in all that she said.

'Alistair Morrison . . . up at Lee's farm . . . a girl from Perth . . . indeed he'll have to be marrying her . . . not that it'll ever work . . . a town girl and big Alistair . . . no, indeed.'

Behind Jill the bell above the shop door tinkled and Jill's perfunctory glance took in a small, dark girl with short, neat black hair dressed in a tee-shirt and grubby blue jeans. Lifting a newspaper from under a small mountain of morning rolls the girl deposited a ten pence piece on the counter.

'Of course Mrs Morrison'll never accept the lass . . . thank you, dear . . .' Mrs McCrae acknowledged the sale, barely taking a breath in her recital of the Morrison saga. The girl went out. Only when she had gone did Mrs McCrae stare after her, looking up from the block of cheese she was slicing with a thin cutting wire.

'Students!' she said, as if all was explained. 'Nothing against them, mind, but they do dress so skimpy. And they're not like the real tourists, are they? I mean they've barely any money at all, have they?'

She wrapped and handed the cheese to Jill who passed a five pound note over the counter, muttering something vaguely in defence of student travellers.

Collecting her change, Jill checked that she had completed her order.

'Anything else you can get tomorrow morning,' Mrs McCrae beamed benevolently. 'Or if you give me a wee phone I'll get Willie Murchie's wee lad to cycle up to the cottage with it. A grand thing for me, him getting a bicycle for Christmas.'

Outside the shop, Jill hesitated. Had they enough cigarettes at the cottage? If they hadn't, Mark would get edgy. Serve him right. They had both sworn to cut down on their smoking.

'Mrs Fraser?' The voice had a guttural quality, good English but spoken by a foreigner.

'Yes?'

She turned to face a tall young man, early twenties, she

24

reckoned, long dark hair falling over a polo-necked sweater under a thick tweed jacket stained with usage. The man's right hand was buried in a bulging pocket. His left hand reached out and gently but firmly took Jill's carrier bag from her hand. Behind him the girl who had been in the shop stood, a scowl on her face.

'You will please walk over to that car with me.' The young man, whose name was Jurgen, indicated the Volvo on the opposite side of the road.

Jill, astonished, opened her mouth but Jurgen went on before she could say anything. 'Do not say or do anything. I have a gun in my pocket and so has Elisa, under the newspaper. We do not wish or intend to shoot you but we will not hesitate to shoot the woman in the shop or any others.'

'Do exactly as he says,' the girl, Elisa, added, the scowl deepening.

They walked across to the car. The pale, blonde, young man, who had seen Santos Morales fall to his death in Malaga, shifted from the driving seat to the passenger seat. The rear door was opened and Jill, her knees starting to tremble, was pushed gently but forcibly into the back of the car. Elisa climbed in beside her letting the newspaper slip to the floor of the car. Jill saw she was indeed holding a large automatic gun, its bluish grey metal glinting in the light.

Jurgen walked quickly around the car still swinging Jill's carrier bag. As he opened the driving door of the car, he stopped, momentarily aware that he still held the bag. He swung it away from him into the gutter where its contents spilled out on the cobbles. Climbing into the driving seat he switched on the ignition.

The car moved with increasing speed out of Craigallen.

The telephone rang at Craigallen Cottage.

Mark Fraser, legs stretched out, head back on the deep armchair, nursed a tumbler of malt whisky. He had been dozing for an hour after cleaning the trout and putting them in the refrigerator. He had wakened, an itch of irritation niggling in his mind. Why was Jill taking so long? He had determined to await her return before walking over to McKay's farm to look at the pups. Better she come with him and choose the dog herself. Then she couldn't blame him for bringing a puppy into the house.

He'd smiled to himself just then. Jill would be the one to cosset and spoil the dog, enjoying every minute of doing so. He'd switched on the television then and dozed again. But this time, when he became fully awake another hour-and-a-half had passed. He'd poured himself the dram of whisky, the irritation starting. If she'd gone to visit the McFarlane's at Glen Grange to make faces over the cot of the new baby she should have told him.

The phone rang again. Slowly he bent his legs and rose. At least she was phoning. And she would know from his tone of calm ice-cold flatness that he was not pleased. As he went to the phone he tried to prevent himself smiling. She knew, damn the woman, he couldn't keep up the icicle demeanour for longer than two minutes. All she would do would be to start giggling and steel turned to putty. Damn the woman for knowing how much she was needed.

'Hello! Craigallen Cottage.' The aloof tone might irritate her slightly.

The voice at the other end of the line was masculine, hesitant and stammering. The accent was German.

'Herr . . . Mr Fraser? Mr Mark Fraser?'

Fraser concealed his surprise that it wasn't Jill. 'Yes?'

'Mr Fraser, we have your wife.'

Fraser didn't reply at once. He thought he'd misheard. The voice repeated the statement. 'W . . . we have your wife.'

'What's that?' He knew he hadn't misheard, but he thought now it was a joke. 'Who the hell is that?'

The reply was again hesitant. In the telephone box some fifty miles away Carl's hand shook as he spoke.

'It . . . it doesn't matter who I am. This is the Holgar Group of the Red Action Brigade . . .'

'What on earth is that?' As soon as he uttered the words,

Fraser felt a first chill of fear.

'Your wife has been taken by us as . . . as a h . . . hostage.'

Irritation rose to crowd out the fear momentarily. 'Oh, come on you ruddy lunatic, my wife has gone shopping!'

'Your wife is with us. I will p . . . put her on to the telephone.'

There was a scuffling sound at the other end of the line. It was followed at once by a faint gasp and a muttered indistinct sentence. Then he heard Jill's voice, distressed, strained.

'Mark . . .!'

The panic gripped him. 'Jill, what the hell is going on?' Another scuffling sound. 'Jill!' he shouted.

'I don't know, Mark! These people . . . just took me . . . in the village.' The words came between the gasps as if she was struggling to breathe.

'Jill . . .?' He didn't know what to say. The knuckles of the hand holding the receiver were white.

Scuffling again. A high-pitched squeal at once cut off. Then the voice with the German accent. And still the stammer.

'N . . . n . . . now you kn . . . know we've got her you will dc . . .' a pause to draw breath. Like Jill he was struggling but not with others. With his own fears. '. . . do exactly what we tell you.'

'Look, I don't know what you want but if you. . . .' The words seemed weak, ineffectual.

'We want you to do exactly w . . . what we tell you . . . you will listen carefully and p . . . please not to interrupt . . .'

Anger now, with fear. Directed against this stammerer, this frightened boy German. That was the kind of voice, a boy's, a child's, a sick child's voice.

'You will listen to me, you maniac!' The anger rose with bile in Fraser's throat. The anger that killed five men, would have gone on killing but for some civilising safety catch in mind and conscience. Now he had cause, if Jill was threatened, to switch off that safety catch.

27

'You will let my wife go at once . . . !' he went on, shouting into the phone.

A scraping sound and a far protest at the end of the line. Then a different voice, a girl's voice, definitely a girl's as opposed to a woman's; but a girl's voice that was different from the other voice. No stammer, no hesitation. A thin voice but with steel in its tone. And something else. Hatred.

'Tomorrow you will go to London. From Gatwick you will fly to Spain. To Malaga. There is a plane at ten in the morning and a place has been reserved for you. The ticket will be at the information desk . . .'

The bile rose to fill Fraser's mouth. 'Now just you wait . . .'

'Not to interrupt!' The kind of voice that must have echoed in a concentration camp. The sins of the fathers embraced by the children in another name. 'You will go to the Hotel Mijas in the village of Mijas south of Malaga. There you will be contacted. Miss that plane or contact anyone before you leave and your wife will be killed instantly.'

A long pause. Fraser was breathing heavily, irritated now at the calmness of the voice at the other end of the line.

'You understand what I have said?'

An effort of will. Self-control needed now. Anger later, anger and controlled rage when the time came.

'I understand.' The flat statement.

'In case you doubt our intentions look in your newspaper tomorrow morning. There will be a report of an occurrence in a village to the south of your home.'

He waited for the voice to continue. But the next sound was the click as the receiver in the distant telephone box was replaced.

Mark Fraser hung up. His face was a mask, unmoving, controlled. After a moment he reached out for the tumbler which he had placed by the telephone. It still held a sizeable dram of whisky. He drained it in one gulp and stood staring at the bottom of the empty glass. Then suddenly, but with great deliberation, he lifted his arm and threw the glass across the room where it shattered against the fireplace showering the hearth with bright, fragmented splinters. It was as if the sharp needle-like slivers of glass he had brought into being represented the stabbing agony of every thought that was running through his brain. Jill was in danger and he, of all people, understood such danger, could feel it in the body, in every cell in his brain. He had been the hunter too often not to appreciate the feelings of the hunted.

Then the questions came. Why Jill? Why his wife? What could they want of him? He was retired, out of the game, no longer connected to the old life and that nightmare world. Yet these kids, these dangerous children were trying to drag him back into it. Why?

Then another thought. The connections were never quite severed. He still knew some names, remembered faces, had phone numbers. He reached into a drawer of the desk on which the phone was perched, shoved aside a pile of papers, invoices and receipts from tourists who had shot and fished on his land, and pulled from under them a battered address book.

The book contained no names, simply initials against numbers. He ran his finger down the first page, stopped at a set of initials and moved the finger across to the number.

He lifted the phone and dialled the number. A series of clicks was followed by a short whine and then a female voice.

'Lines to London are engaged. Please try again later.'

He swore softly to himself, slamming the phone down. The lines had to be clear shortly. He had to reach that London number.

Darkness had fallen and the dying of the light seemed to narrow the country road, distorting vision. Jill sat in the back of the car staring into the darkness, trying to memorise the route she was being driven. The concentration helped. It took her mind away from the questions that were in her mind, questions of why and where to, questions of what they intended to do with her whenever they reached whatever destination they were moving towards.

Don't think about it, she told herself, don't think at all except to try and recognise the road, commit to mind any landmarks.

Her three captors sat in silence; Jurgen, his eyes fixed on the road ahead, seemed calm and unconcerned. The same could apply to Elisa, sitting beside Jill, head turned towards her captive, hands lying loosely on her lap, almost caressing the revolver that lay there. But it was her very relaxation, the casual quality belied by the open, alert eyes, that gave Jill a feeling of cold fear. This seeming child could lift the revolver, point and aim it and fire into a human body with no more emotion or effort than she expended sitting beside Jill.

Movement came from the third of the kidnappers. Carl twisted and turned in his seat, tense, edgy, a man afraid. There was something else there, something away from the coolness of Jurgen and the icy deadliness of Elisa. The sense of barely suppressed panic Jill felt the boy exuded was mixed with a feeling of regret, of a need in his eyes that was meant to reassure Jill that he was not as his companions.

The car swung round a bend and came to a halt quickly, brakes scraping in protest. In the strong twin beams of the headlights Jill could make out a signpost with the name of a village on it.

ARDSKEAN

She thought, about fifty miles from Craigallen on the back road to Stirling and Glasgow; she had driven through it several times as a change from the main road. Larger than Craigallen, Ardskean had a number of shops, a small group of new council houses, habitation for the employees of a modest factory on the edge of the village; and a police station with one full-time constable.

'D . . . d . . . do we have to?' Carl said, his stammer causing him to splutter damply across the windscreen.

Jurgen glanced at him with a slightly contemptuous

30

smile. 'Not you, Carl. You just have to stay here and look after her.' A curt nod towards Jill.

'What are you going to do?' Jill forced herself to ask the question. She had to find some piece of information, a fragment of fact to hang on to.

Jurgen didn't bother to turn round as he replied. 'Nothing to do with you, Frau Fraser. Time you had a sleep.'

Another nod, this time towards Elisa.

The girl reached down and from below the overhang of the seat produced a small black case. Tucking the revolver into the side of the seat away from Jill she flicked open the case. Jill peered down into the darkness unable to see what she had produced. As if in answer to her questioning look, Elisa cursed under her breath.

'I need some light!'

Jurgen switched on the interior light.

Jill could now see the black case and it was open. The hypodermic syringe lay beside the unmarked ampule. Elisa fitted the ampule into the syringe.

Jill felt very afraid.

Fraser couldn't keep still. He paced the room, the caged creature trying to find an escape route. Adrenalin was high in his bloodstream and his hands were trembling whenever they came to rest. He was chain-smoking, half-smoked cigarettes being stubbed out, new ones being relit.

It had always been like this in the old days, the neurotic hours when considering a new mission. Yet, once started on the mission, he imposed upon himself a seeming serenity, a quality of coolness which to those who knew him, made him appear callous and without nerves. They could never appreciate the rigidity and strength of will he employed to control his emotions.

After numerous attempts to dial the London number he had contacted the local operator who had promised to ring him the minute she made the connection. And so for nearly an hour he had waited, fear and impatience tearing at his nerves.

31

Finally the telephone rang.

His hand stopped trembling the minute he lifted the receiver. The mission was about to start.

'Sorry for the delay, Mr Fraser, but I have your White-hall number now.'

A series of clicks then the connection was made.

'Ministry of Agriculture and Fisheries. Can I help you?' The voice was nasal and jarring. A woman sounding almost like a man.

'I want to speak to Sir Alfred Tarrant.'

Hesitation. The voice at the other end of the line seemed to catch its breath.

'There's no one of that name here, I'm sorry.'

Fraser felt irritation rise within him. They were still playing games in Whitehall.

'Then give me the duty officer in Department Six. And don't tell me there isn't a Department Six. Tell the duty officer Mark Fraser is calling from Scotland.'

Another pause. A little mind making a big decision.

'If you'll hold on I'll make enquiries.'

He held on. Two minutes passed. He hated people who asked him to hold on and then went away forever. The two minutes seemed like forever.

Another series of clicking sounds then another voice, male, clipped, the weariness of education at the right schools in the voice.

'Who is that speaking?'

'Fraser! Mark Fraser. Who am I speaking to now?'

'Duty Officer, Department Six. What can I do for you?' The voice was trying to be impersonal but there was a nervous edgy tone. Fraser thought, at least he had got through to them.

'I want to speak to Tarrant!'

Yet another pause. Then a deep breath.

'You're out of date, Mark. Sir Alfred Tarrant retired about two years ago.'

'Who the hell am I speaking to?'

This time a chuckle at the end of the line. 'Frank Lloyd. It's been a long time . . .'

32

Fraser remembered Lloyd. The thin face and the thinner moustache. They'd got on reasonably well in the old days. Lloyd hadn't been very good, he thought, but at least he tried and he'd always seemed honest.

'. . . didn't expect to hear from you again after you resigned,' Lloyd went on. 'You know they still talk about your row with Tarrant. Gone into legend, that historic event . . .'

'Who's in charge now?' Fraser cut in harshly.

'Sir James Mackeson. Seafaring type. Hello, sailor and all that. Anyway he'll have gone home to his . . . pansies . . . or his tulips, for the night. Keen gardener.'

'Look, I want information!'

Lloyd inhaled sharply at the other end of the line. 'But you're not one of us these days, old man.'

Fraser replied through his teeth. 'Pretend I am for to-night. Tell me what you've got on the Holgar Group of the Red Action Brigade.'

Four hundred and fifty miles away Lloyd fingered his tie and leant back in his desk chair. To sound casual he always believed you had to assume physically a casual pose.

'Funny company, you keep,' he attempted a light laugh. As he did so a figure appeared at the door of his office. Sir James Mackeson could be positively cat-like when it suited him.

'I don't think I can help you, old man. But just a moment . . .' He put his hand over the mouthpiece of the phone and looked to Mackeson with a muttered explanation.

'Fraser. Mark Fraser . . . he used to be . . .'

'I know who he used to be. For that matter still is. The retired instrument, I believe. I've been listening on the other line. Give him what he wants.'

Lloyd was surprised and his surprise showed. Mackeson spoke so calmly and he couldn't have moved so quickly as to have heard what Fraser wanted, hung up the connecting line and walked to Lloyd's office.

As if in reply to Lloyd's unspoken thought Mackeson added, 'And find out why he wants it.'

Lloyd nodded and took his hand from the mouthpiece of the telephone.

'Mark! Hold on, I'll see what I can do.'

He went along the corridor to the records room. Old Ruskin was putting on his coat to go home. It was said Ruskin had been in charge of records since the First World War. Someone had once said the Russians should have kidnapped him and they would have learned more from the old man than Philby, Burgess and Maclean put together. In fact it wasn't true. Ruskin knew names and file numbers but he never read the contents of the files. It wasn't lack of interest. He was simply devoid of curiosity.

'Holgar? Red Action? Oh, yes. It's to hand. You're the second person today,' Ruskin said, producing a folder from a deep drawer. Later, much later, it registered with Lloyd. Who had taken the file out? It should have been date stamped and initialled by whoever had taken it. Even later he studied the file. There was no initial or stamp.

He initialled it himself and took it back to his own office. Mackeson was perched on the edge of his desk staring at the phone. He was holding an extension earpiece to his right ear. He nodded curtly at Lloyd indicating he should go ahead. Lloyd lifted the telephone.

'Here we are. Red Action Brigade. Offshoot of the Baader-Meinhof gang. Originally formed in 1976 by Johannes Kleindorff, later killed by West German Security Forces in Cologne during attempted bank robbery.'

Fraser cut in. 'I'm not interested in the dead, Frank. Tell me about the living.'

'Five known separate cells . . . wait a minute . . . here we are . . . Holgar Group. Last known trace, the Pyrenees.'

'What's known about the group?'

'We believe there could be five or six in the group. But we only have three names.'

Holding the phone in his right hand, Lloyd arranged three photographs in front of him. These were attached to facts sheets overstamped 'West German Security Department.'

'We've got photos to go with the names,' he went on.

'Elisa Toth, aged twenty-three, Carl-Jan Husig, aged twenty-two, and Jurgen Haussmann, aged twenty-seven.'

'Does either of the two men have a speech impediment? A stammer?'

'I don't think we have that kind of detail.'

Fraser could hear him shuffle the documents.

'Wait a minute,' Lloyd came back. 'We do have something. Carl-Jan Husig has a stutter.'

There was a pause. Fraser, hand trembling, made a note against the name he had scrawled on a pad beside the telephone.

'You still there, Mark?' Lloyd demanded.

'Yes. Thanks.'

'Glad to be of help. What's it all about?'

'Personal.'

'Now, look . . .' Lloyd did not press the question. Mackeson was shaking his head to indicate he must not try and compel Fraser to give information.

Lloyd sighed to himself. 'Anything else you want?'

'Yes. I shall be in London tomorrow morning. You'll meet me . . .'

'Now wait a minute . . .'

Fraser's voice was cold.

'Eight-thirty at the old place. Bring copies of any photos of the Holgar Group you have.'

The old place. Lloyd remembered it well; meetings arranged in a hothouse at Kew when it wasn't advisable to talk in the office, agents comparing notes they might not always want others in the section to know about. Those were the days of Philby and Blake when no one knew who to trust. But Lloyd hadn't used the rendezvous for years now.

He decided to protest. 'I'm going out for dinner tomorrow night . . .'

'Not night! Morning!'

'Good God! Look, old man, I can't . . . well I can't just lift photos out of a file . . .'

He covered the mouthpiece with his hand as Mackeson gesticulated.

'You have my authorisation to have copies of the photos made. And you can give him these.'

Mackeson then disconnected the earpiece and rose.

'See if you can find out what he's up to and why,' he said, going to the door. 'And by the way, Frank, not pansies or tulips. Orchids. I cultivate orchids under glass. Goodnight.'

The door closed gently behind Mackeson. Lloyd took his hand from the telephone.

'Yes, all right, Mark, I'll meet you. But I shall want to know something about what you have got yourself into.'

The only reply he got was a click as Fraser replaced his receiver.

The police station in the village of Ardskean was actually a small council bungalow. The hall and front room represented the offices of the law and the rest of the bungalow was the living quarters of Police Constable McIlhenny, a widower in his middle fifties.

The knock came at the door when he was upstairs watching television. Constable McIlhenny was an ardent follower of all police series on television and the knock downstairs caused a grimace of annoyance to cross his face as he abandoned the small screen and the pursuit of a mass murderer through the streets of New York by a large actor with a shaven head.

McIlhenny clumped down the narrow stairway, irritation giving way to curiosity. He was rarely disturbed at night in Ardskean. The local crime rate was practically non-existent apart from the occasional poacher and even that was usually dealt with by a gamekeeper. There was always the hope that some major crime would take place in the district and the thought gave him a momentary thrill of excitement. And yet should such a crime be perpetrated in his patch he knew his first duty would be to phone higher authority in Stirling.

He was not to know of course that, on this particular evening, steps had been taken to isolate him from that higher authority. Below a window at the side of the house the telephone wires had been neatly severed.

So McIlhenny, a large man, dressed only in a shirt and uniform trousers, his jacket having been left over a chair upstairs beside the television set, opened the front door to find himself facing two faces he vaguely recognised.

'What's this then?' he asked, assuming a gruffness in keeping with his profession. As he asked the question he knew where he had seen the faces; two foreign students who had sought directions to some place further north only the day before.

'We are sorry to be of such inconvenience,' the girl said. 'Especially so late but we need help from you.'

'What kind of help would you be needing?'

'If we could perhaps enter . . .' the tall young man suggested with a smile that was almost feminine in its uncertainty.

McIlhenny hesitated. He was going to miss the end of his television programme. Still, a policeman was always on duty, he told himself.

'You'd better come into the duty room.'

He ushered them into the hall, shutting the door behind them. They stood together, nervous, half-smiling, shy as foreigners always seemed shy to him when faced with authority.

'In here!'

He led the way into the small office he always referred to as the duty room. He went round the small desk and turned with a reassuring smile.

It was then that Elisa Toth produced the revolver and shot him twice through the head. The heavy silencer ensured the noise, a dull plopping sound, would not carry beyond the four walls of the room. And although McIlhenny was thrown back against one wall by the force of the bullets, apart from the thump as his body hit the wall he uttered no sound himself. The first of the two bullets had killed him instantly. The second was a completely unnecessary insurance on Elisa's part.

THREE

The girl, to an onlooker, might have appeared to be impatient at having to wait for her companions. She stood at the top of the staircase leading from ground level to the main concourse of Abbotsinch Airport, air terminal for the city of Glasgow, shuffling her feet beside the large haversack on the ground against the wall of the souvenir shop. Occasionally she tugged nervously at the loose sweater which she wore with no sense of style, a garment, like the old denims, that was purely functional.

Gudrun Moller looked like any typical female student travelling light and annoyed at being kept waiting. She was twenty-three, with blonde straggling hair, and far from being a student had been an active member of one terrorist organisation or another since she was seventeen. It was at the age of eighteen, while involved in a bank raid in Hamburg, that she had met Jurgen Haussmann and on the same night as the bank raid, excited and stimulated by the successful foray, she had allowed herself to be bedded by her fellow terrorist. That night she had found a physical passion, an orgasmic exultation she had never before experienced. Gudrun Moller had found what passed with her for love.

Thus her apparent impatience actually concealed a deep fear that something had gone wrong with the mission on which they were engaged. And of course if she was honest she would have admitted her concern was not with the mission but with the safety of Jurgen Haussmann.

Her fears were soon proved ill-founded. He appeared on one side of the woman who swayed drunkenly as they reached the top of the staircase. On the other side Carl-Jan Husig held Jill Fraser's arm with a grip that indicated his own fear. Elisa Toth brought up the rear.

'Jurgen!' Gudrun greeted him without attempting to conceal her relief.

'You've got the passports?' he demanded, ignoring any emotion in her welcome.

She nodded, fumbling under her pullover and producing a thick envelope. 'Passports and tickets.'

'Show me her passport.' He indicated Jill's stumbling figure. Gudrun selected the top passport and flicked it open. He stared at the passport photograph.

'Put her glasses on!'

Elisa complied, placing a pair of thick horn-rimmed spectacles on the bridge of Jill's nose. Jill blinked, her eyes attempting to focus. It was a futile effort. The drug injected outside the village of Ardskean two hours before was in her bloodstream, distorting her vision and confusing her brain.

Elisa surveyed the effect of the spectacles and then produced a beret which she pulled down over Jill's forehead.

'It's close enough to pass if they don't look too closely,' Jurgen pronounced. 'Remember, she has had a little too much of the wine of the country.'

'W . . . whisky,' Carl stammered.

'I hope the passports will pass for all of us,' murmured Gudrun, handing them out.

'They're good passports unless they look at them under a microscope,' Jurgen reassured her. 'Rolf would make sure of that.'

'Did you attend to . . . to the policeman at Ardskean?'

Elisa answered. 'Of course.'

'I d . . . don't see why you h . . . had to . . .' Carl demanded but was cut off by Elisa.

'It was necessary to convince Fraser we are serious!'

Jurgen added a question. 'You phoned the newspaper?'

'Fifteen minutes ago,' Gudrun replied. 'I told them they'd find a dead man in Ardskean police station.'

The statement was made coldly and casually. She had lived with death too long to exhibit any feeling.

'This is a call for all passengers on Flight BA 261 to

Malaga. Please proceed to Gate Number Eighteen. . . .'
The tannoy echoed throughout the concourse. Jurgen
nodded to them, placed Jill's arm around his shoulder and
moved towards Gate Eighteen. The others followed.

Only a slight twitch at the corner of Carl-Jan's mouth
gave any indication of the tension they were under as they
walked towards the passport desk.

It was seven o'clock the next morning as he drove off the
M1 on to London's North Circular Road when Fraser
heard on his car radio of the murder of the policeman at
Ardskean. He knew what it meant and apart from a
momentary feeling of sadness at the futility of the unknown man's death, he felt only fear for Jill's safety.

The years with the Department had taught him to control emotion, to put from his mind anything that would
distract him from his immediate task.

That task had been to drive throughout the night to
London. He had driven steadily, with great care, maintaining a speed of just below seventy miles per hour. There
were occasions when he had driven the Jensen at speeds
over one hundred and twenty; but now he could not afford
the risk of an accident, or the delay of being flagged down
by the police. His timetable was tight.

Yet there had been few moments during the journey
when he had not been thinking of Jill. Had they harmed
her during the kidnapping? Would they harm her while
they held her? And if he did complete whatever scheme
they demanded of him as ransom for his wife's safety,
would they honour the bargain and release her later? He
knew there were no guarantees. And he knew speculation
was pointless. He must follow the orders they had given
him and at the same time remain alert to every possible
lead to where they might be holding her. With his mind
directed only towards this, he would function, he knew, at
maximum efficiency; and he would be ready to act to find
and free Jill when such opportunity arose. The question as
to whether or not the opportunity would arise he dismissed

too from his mind.

There was another factor which preoccupied him during the drive to London. This was the growing certainty that, from the moment he had left Craigallen, he was being followed. If he was right, it was a professional job of work. One car trailed him to Glasgow. There it turned away and its place was taken by another car which followed him to Carlisle. Again this car drove off and its replacement tracked him to the Preston turn-off. Five cars in all were in the game and as the M1 joined the North Circular a sixth took over.

All this gave Fraser some comfort. He had to allow the cars to follow him. When the time came, he thought, it could prove the first opportunity that might lead him to Jill. Nevertheless it puzzled him that they should follow him, presumably to reassure themselves he was following instructions. The fact that they held Jill should be enough reassurance. Unless . . . and another thought intruded . . . there might be another party involved. Or was that merely his old experience reasserting itself? In the days he had worked for the Firm there had always been competing factions in the field; the KGB, the CIA, the French Deuxième Bureau and so many others. Even freelances got into the act, organisations of entrepreneurs with information or services to sell to the highest bidder. But surely not now, not this time, unless someone else had an eye on the Holgar Group and an interest in whatever plans they had for him.

Again, damn it, dismiss the thought. Confusion would be another distraction he had to avoid.

He drove towards Kew.

Lloyd was waiting on a bench in the hothouse. He was sweating profusely, the collar of his white shirt already staining and curling up. When Fraser approached he looked up and Fraser could see the beads of perspiration on his upper lip.

'Well, long time, Mark.'

Fraser sat down, his face impassive. 'It should have been longer. You have the photographs?'

Lloyd produced a large envelope. 'I'm undoubtedly infringing the Official Secrets Act.'

'It'll do you good,' Fraser replied coldly. 'Let's walk.'

Lloyd rose and they walked. Fraser's desire to walk was prompted by two things. He wanted to get back to his car and he had observed, on entering the gardens, that a small dark man had alighted from a car parked nearby. He was certain this was the driver of the car that had fallen into line behind him when he came off the M1.

'What's all this about?' Lloyd asked, patting his upper lip with a white handkerchief.

'I told you. My business.'

'Oh, come on, old man, when it comes to the Red Action people it is our business.'

'Not in this case,' Fraser replied glancing behind him. The small dark man hovered at the entrance to the hot-house.

'Look, Mark, ever since that nasty business with Hartley when you resigned we've kept away from you. At your request. Now you come to us and we co-operate. Surely we're entitled . . .'

Fraser cut him off sharply. 'You're entitled to nothing. This is simply, thank you very much and goodbye!'

Lloyd tried not to look abashed but without success. Fraser thought, there's still something of the little boy in Frank Lloyd, even if he is well into his forties. Fraser decided to press any advantage.

'Have you got a tail on me, Frank?'

The surprise on Lloyd's face was genuine 'Hardly necessary since you arranged this meeting.'

Fraser acknowledged the partial denial with a jerk of his head. 'In case you feel like putting a tail on me and since the immigration people will inform you anyway, I'm flying to Spain this morning.'

It was Lloyd's turn to reveal no emotion. 'Good for you. Wish I could get some sun.'

'Don't come after me. Don't send anyone. Or I'll go right through them.'

'Wouldn't dream of it, old man. You've gone through a few people before in the old days. Very messy.'

'It would be just like that again.'

Fraser stopped suddenly. They had walked in a complete circle and were back at the entrance to the hothouse.

'Time I was away,' Fraser said. 'Thanks for the photos. I probably won't see you again.'

He turned and walked swiftly away leaving Lloyd standing staring after him, utterly nonplussed. Lloyd was so intent on Fraser's receding figure he didn't notice the small dark man scurry past him.

Three hours later Fraser's plane took off from Heathrow.

The sun slanted through the small square window, the rays striking Jill's face. She stirred, tried to open her eyes and turned away, dazzled. A sharp pain shot from the back of her neck across the top of her skull.

'You will have a headache.' Gudrun sat beside the bed in the small room with the whitewashed walls. She sat slumped in a battered armchair staring down at Jill who was lying on top of a large bed that seemed to take up three-quarters of the room.

Jill peered up at the girl. The face was strange. She had no memory of the encounter at the airport, indeed she had no memory of the flight. But the immediate recollection was of being taken in a car from Craigallen. That came back very quickly. She grimaced at the memory and the pain in her head.

'I . . . I have a headache,' she admitted reluctantly.

'It's the injection we gave you. Not harmful but it makes as if you are drunk. That is how we got you through the people at the airport.'

Jill tried to sit up, looking around, puzzled.

'To save you asking,' Gudrun went on, her tone not unkindly. 'You are in Spain.'

'What am I doing in Spain?'

'You are with us for the time being.'

Jill succeeded now in sitting up and she swung her legs over the edge of the bed. The bed, the chair on which

Gudrun sat, and a small cane table were the only furnishings in the room.

'Why? Why am I here?' Jill asked, her throat rough with sleep.

Gudrun gave a slight smile. 'You are an insurance policy, Frau Fraser.'

'Mark? My husband . . .?'

'Friday! You will see him on Friday. After he has done some work for us.'

'What kind of work?' As she asked the question, Jill dreaded the reply.

Gudrun was not however forthcoming in her response. 'Not your concern.'

She rose leisurely, flicked the ash from her cigarette on the strip of torn linoleum at the foot of the bed and walked to the door of the room.

'I will bring you some food,' she said without turning. Then she unlocked the door with a key she produced from the pocket of her denims, opened the door and then glanced back, not at Jill but at the small window.

'The window is locked,' she explained. 'If you should break it open there is still an impossibly high drop.'

Jill glanced at the window. The sunlight was intense, so strong that from the bed she could see nothing beyond the glass.

Gudrun went on. 'Mrs Fraser, please do not try to leave. We all carry these and we use them.'

She held out her left hand. In it Jill caught a metallic gleam. In the outstretched hand was a small revolver. Gudrun smiled and went out of the room. Jill heard the key being turned in the lock.

She tried to get to her feet. The pain shot across her head and she swayed as the floor seemed to buckle. She held the headboard of the bed until the feeling of vertigo subsided. Then slowly and shakily she walked to the window.

The quality of light was dazzling but gradually as her eyes became accustomed to the glare she found herself looking down at a small cultivated garden some twenty feet below. The soil was sandy and, whatever growth there was, was sparse. Her view beyond the garden was blocked by a rising hill, covered with some kind of gorse and interspersed with grey rock.

She turned away, a feeling of nausea taking over. She believed now she was in Spain, a prisoner in some kind of rundown farmhouse. She crossed back to the bed and sat on the soiled brown blanket. A kind of despair embraced her.

The plane landed at Malaga sometime after one o'clock. The delay had been caused at Heathrow by some minor industrial dispute and Fraser had sat with ill-concealed impatience, sweating in the overheated aircraft. He had however been able to get a good look at his fellow passengers during the wait and he had easily spotted the small dark man he had seen at Kew. Sitting at the rear of the aircraft the small man had tried to immerse himself in a newspaper, opening it out and holding it in front of his face. Unfortunately part of it disintegrated, falling at his feet, and Fraser was able to identify him. Fraser also noted for future reference that the newspaper was the London edition of a Greek journal.

Now as he crossed the main hall of Malaga Airport he was aware that the small man was close on his heels. Fraser headed straight for the Hertz desk, a qualm of regret that the Jensen was parked in a multiple garage at Heathrow. His first aim was to be mobile and he was determined that his mobility would be of a nature that ensured speed.

'The fastest car you have,' he demanded of a demure young woman in a black skirt and white blouse.

Forms were speedily filled in, passport and licence shown, and Fraser was directed to a door at the side of the main concourse and told to wait. He turned away towards the door and was aware of the small man taking his place. He hesitated long enough to catch the man's opening gambit.

'Please, you will hire me faster car than that man?'

The two cars arrived outside the airport almost simultaneously. As Fraser climbed into the low-slung grey coupé he had signed for and deposited his suitcase and one bottle of duty-free whisky in the narrow rear seat, he caught a glimpse of the little man peering myopically at him before getting into the driving seat of a blue Simca.

Fraser drove leisurely out of the airport allowing the Simca to fall in behind him. As he was about to turn towards Malaga and Mijas the thought struck him that he was making it too easy for his shadower. He swung the wheel around, turning the car towards the Sierras. The Simca followed.

The airport traffic thinned out. Gradually Fraser increased his speed. Ahead of him he saw a signpost. A road branched off climbing upwards. Again Fraser spun the wheel and, a plume of dust rising from the rear wheels, the coupé roared up the mountain road. The Simca, bucking like some mechanical animal, swerved off the motorway and moved after him.

Once on the mountain road any pretence that the Simca might not be following Fraser was abandoned. The road was narrow and pitted with fragments of rock and patches of sand and loose earth. It twisted through the foothills, curving back upon itself, writhing and dipping only to rise up again.

Both drivers were forced to change gear frequently as the road climbed higher and higher and the yellow and grey of the mountains came nearer and nearer.

And then they were on the side of the mountains, the curves and bends becoming more frequent and they were driving now with brakes screaming protest as they held the cars down. It was as if each car had a life independent of its driver and was trying to leap from the road possessed by a suicidal impulse to crash over the feeble barriers that only occasionally marked the boundary between road and ditch, or road and thin air as the hillside plunged a thousand feet into a narrow gully.

With his foot on and off brake and accelerator alternately Fraser could not help admiring the little man following him so tenaciously. The man could drive and he had courage. That courage was indispensable when driving a saloon car up a road which was fast becoming a mere mountain track at speeds of anything between fifty and seventy miles an hour. Every now and then Fraser would glance at his rear view mirror only to see a cloud of dust thrown up by his own wheels. He peered into the mirror wondering whether or not the Simca had abandoned the chase and then, through the dust, he would catch a glimpse of its bonnet rearing over rock, piercing the cloud, still behind him. The distance between the two cars would widen for a moment as Fraser cleared a bend and swept up into a short straight section. Then it would narrow as he slowed to take another bend and the Simca, taking the straight behind him, roared closer to his rear bumper.

Suddenly the road widened ahead and the shapes of a few stone and adobe houses appeared on either side. A dozing peasant outside the first of the houses jerked awake as the two cars raced past him. Two women, swathed in black bombazine despite the afternoon heat, swung round in surprise at the unaccustomed roar of engines and the scream of brakes. And as quickly as they were into the village the cars were out of it, still climbing higher.

Less than a minute later they were driving through a gorge, rock faces on either side. Sometime in the past the road had been blasted through solid rock and the scars of the blast could be seen in the lighter scars across the surfaces of the stone. Then almost immediately one side of the gorge fell away and only a two-foot-high ridge of stone separated the road from another sheer drop of two or three thousand feet.

Then, ahead of him, Fraser saw that the road bent sharply to the right, turning back on itself. He changed down from top to second gear ignoring the squeal of protest from the gearbox, swung the car as wide as he could, his front wheel barely missing the two-foot ridge, and came around to move up a long straight section. Another half-inch and he knew he would have ripped his tyre apart on the stone. There was a sound above the noise of his engine and again he glanced quickly at his rear-view mirror.

There was no sign of the Simca.

A few seconds before, the little man had made his first and, at least in this pursuit, his last mistake. He had allowed his attention to stray. Coming out of the gorge he had caught sight of the sudden sheer drop which had appeared on his left and he had held it in vision too long. Snapping his eyes back to the road he saw, in front of him, that the road turned sharply out of view. He was coming up on it too fast and he knew there was no time to judge the turn without ripping against the barrier ridge. He did the only thing possible. He slammed on his brakes in an emergency stop and tried to ram the gear lever down into first.

The teeth in the gearbox ground against each other, refusing to come together. But the brakes were sharp, the brake linings new and the tension in the cables held. The Simca's wheels jammed to a stop and, while the impetus of its speed propelled it forward into a skid, the rough road surface brought its speed down until, at the moment the front wheels hit the low barrier ridge, the car was almost at a stop. Rocks from the barrier were thrown into the void below as it ploughed through and came to its shuddering halt, front wheels suspended over the drop, the car itself resting on its own frame under the front doors.

The little man sat behind the wheel for what seemed to him a very long time. He started to tremble and he could feel the perspiration course down the length of his spine under his shirt. His heart thumped loudly. Hands, soaking wet, shook. His right eye misted over and he blinked several times before it cleared. Then carefully he removed a gaudy red handkerchief from the breast pocket of his lightweight jacket and mopped his forehead diligently. Following this he wiped his cheeks and his neck and, putting the handkerchief back in his pocket, he moved his legs.

The car creaked, a protest against its treatment and its position hanging over the edge of a sheer drop. The little man slowly and with infinite care reached out and took hold of the door handle. He depressed it and the door swung open. At the same time it seemed to him that the car swayed forward threatening to plunge over the drop. Still moving slowly he eased himself out of the driving seat and settled his feet outside, inches from the void.

Then, at last, he was out of the car, gulping air with relief. Head down, he moved on to the road as if assuring himself he was on firm ground. Staggering slightly he reached the rear of the Simca and stared at the boot, marvelling at the precariousness of the position in which the car had come to a halt.

He was standing studying this position, still dazed, when he felt a small cold circular piece of metal touch the back of his neck.

'Now just lean gently against the car with your arms wide and your legs spread out.' Fraser said coolly.

'Yes, yes, at once,' the little man replied, another kind of fear taking over his body.

He complied with the instructions quickly and felt Fraser's hands run lightly but expertly over his jacket and trousers seeking a weapon.

'I have no gun, no weapon,' he explained, his accent thickening in his terror. 'I do not like guns and anyway I would not be able to bring one through customs.'

The words poured out, indicative of his panic. As Fraser had searched him he had glimpsed the steel of the revolver in the taller man's hand. A thought crossed his mind, a question; more words but they could only serve to delay anything that might happen, delay a greater unpleasantness than merely being searched.

'You brought your gun through customs, eh?'

Fraser smiled without humour. His suitcase had a false side giving the impression of leather being warped. Customs men might look for a false bottom to a case yet they rarely paid any attention to its sides. The revolver fitted snugly into the leather.

'There are ways,' he replied to the little man's question. 'Now just be quiet and turn around.'

'I am turning, sir,' he faced Fraser.

He was small certainly with a wispy, straggling black moustache and pock-marked cheeks. His hands were

trembling again and his eyes, small and round, like six-
pences, Fraser thought, sparkled with terror. This was the
character that had pursued him from London; no fearful
menacing figure but a small sack-like shape in an ill-fitting
suit, speaking English with an ill-fitting accent.

'Why are you following me?' Fraser demanded.

'Me? Following you? No, sir, not me, sir.' The denial
was outrageous in its delivery as well as its meaning.

Fraser took a step forward, moving with calculated
heaviness, over-emphasising every gesture. It was another
old technique. Give them time to see and worry about the
end result of each action. He lifted the revolver and placed
its barrel against the little man's mouth which gaped
slightly. The metal rasped against his teeth.

'Please sir, not to shoot.' The plea was distorted by the
position of the revolver.

'Listen you, you started following me from Kew Gardens . . . !'

'Yes, sir. From before that. As you came into London . . .'

Fraser frowned. 'Frank Lloyd didn't put you on to me?'

'Sir! No, sir! I do not know Mr Lloyd whoever he may
be.'

This was a comedian, Fraser decided. A comic singer,
to use part of an old Scottish expression. Whores and
comic singers. This little man could be both. The old world
Fraser had worked in was full of whores and comic singers.

Changing his tactics he suddenly shot out his left arm
and reaching into the inside pocket of the little man's suit
he pulled out a slim wallet and a passport. He flicked the
passport open. The little man's face, even more distorted
than in nature, stared up at him from the passport photograph. Opposite, the place of birth was listed as Salonika,
Greece. Yet it was a British passport so he was naturalised.
Fraser closed the passport and read the name, Andreas
Costas. Dropping wallet and passport at his feet he looked
at Andreas Costas.

'Now, listen to me, Mr Costas, I want to know why
you are following me. I want to know right now. And if
you don't tell me it doesn't matter to me whether I pull

50

this trigger or not.'

Costas gulped. His throat was beginning to ache with gulping air. 'I . . . I am hired to follow.'

'Who hired you?'

'At first you see . . . some of us were hired to follow the others. The ones who took the lady . . . but when we knew they were going near you, the plan was changed. We were to follow you.'

A surge of anger went through Fraser. 'You bloody well saw them take her and you did nothing?'

'Not me, sir. A man who works for me in Scotland. You see I have these men . . . friends. We do these little jobs. But we are paid only to watch. And when the man in Scotland phones and says they have taken this lady and I report this, then I am told we are all to follow you.'

Fraser thought, it made a kind of sense But in relation to what? Why follow the kidnappers unless Costas worked for an organisation that was concerned with keeping the terrorist group under surveillance?

'Who do you report to?' he demanded. 'Who pays you?'

Costas gave a twisted shrug. 'Is only a telephone number. A voice on the telephone. Tells us what is required that we do. After we do it the payment is sent by post. No cheques. A cash business.'

He stared up at Fraser. Then he took another deep breath. 'It is the truth, please.'

'Who do you report to in Spain?'

'I follow you to wherever you go. Then I go to a hotel, the Altiza, and they contact me. This is truth, please.'

Fraser believed him. Whether he was telling it all or not, he could not be sure. But what he had said seemed true. The man was in too much of a panic to lie. Only a greater fear might limit his capacity to tell the entire truth. But, Fraser knew, when in a tight situation some of the truth often served.

Costas was standing, a look of hope that he might survive the encounter in his eyes. Fraser removed the revolver from the proximity of the little man's mouth and walked around to the driver's door of the Simca. He noted that despite his shock at nearly driving the car over a precipice Costas had automatically put on the handbrake.

'You are very good driver, Mister Fraser,' Costas suddenly gasped, nervous of the silence. 'I know. I am good too. When I am younger I once drive at Monza . . .'

Ignoring him, Fraser reached into the car and released the handbrake carefully. The car seemed to sway slightly and then settle.

'Actually I was mechanic at Monza,' Costas went on, the words almost running together. 'Only mechanic. But once I drive in test drive so I know I am good.' He added hurriedly, fearful of overplaying his role, 'It is the only thing I am good at.'

Fraser walked back to the rear of the car and faced Costas again.

'Now, push the car!'

The little man looked confused. Fraser indicated the precipice.

'That way.'

Costas stared at him for a moment, turned, looked at the edge of the drop and then looked back at him.

'If I push it that way it will go over . . .'

'Push it!' Fraser ordered again.

Costas ran his hand through his thinning black hair, panic showing in his eyes.

'Is . . . is a hired car! I will have to pay . . .'

'You can always reclaim it from your voice at the other end of the telephone.'

Fraser motioned with the gun. Eyeing him Costas was trying to make up his mind whether or not Fraser was the kind of man who would use the weapon. He decided it was a possibility. He turned and, placing both hands on the rear of the car, he pushed.

His feet scrabbled on small stones. At first the car seemed to resist his exertions. And then, with a scraping sound it slowly slid forward, tipped over and was running, then dropping down the precipitous slope. The bonnet struck a rocky outcrop with a clanging, crunching sound. It veered on to its side, rolled over and was in space again. A wing

52

flew off, following the rest of the car down and out of sight. Then there was a final distant smashing sound and then nothing but the occasional rock bouncing down the mountainside.

Costas stood at the edge of the slope staring after the car. He felt sick. His mind was trying furiously to work out the value of the car in pounds sterling and then convert the answer into pesetas. It was such an unfair, expensive thing to have done to him. At the same time he waited with a kind of anticipation for an explosion from below. In all the films he had ever seen in a lifetime of addiction to the cinema, cars always exploded when they went over cliffs. But, as he waited, he knew he would be disappointed for this was reality and there was no explosion.

The sound of the car engine behind him broke his train of thought. He turned round to see Fraser, now seated in his car, moving off.

'Please . . .!' Costas started to say, but stopped as he realised his plea would only be to the warm mountain air.

Fraser glanced briefly at his rear-view mirror as he steered his car with increasing speed down the road, back the way he had come. He could see Costas take a few steps forward, arms wide with despair. Then Fraser drove around a bend and the little man was out of sight, a minor obstacle removed for the time being, if not for good, and without violence. Now, Fraser thought, he would be heading towards the first round of the main event. He felt a grim anticipation.

FOUR

Jill Fraser stood at the small window staring at the gorse and the grey rock. She had moved between the window and the bed restlessly ever since she had first been locked in the room. There had been only one interruption when the girl, Gudrun, had brought in a battered tin tray on which was a cup of thick black coffee and a plate which contained a thick slice of ham and two hard-boiled eggs. Gudrun had withdrawn with a brief nod and the door had been locked again.

Jill had swallowed the coffee gratefully, assuaging a thirst which had built up from the moment she had become conscious. She had left the plate of food for some time until a sudden realisation came to her that she was actually hungry. The only implement on the tray was a fork, the prongs twisted out of alignment. Presumably they did not trust her with any kind of knife. She made the best of the fork and found herself wolfing the ham and both eggs.

Now, as she turned away from the window, her eyes alighted on the fork. She looked from the fork back to the window. Was it possible to prise the window open with the fork? She dismissed the thought. The window, even if it could be raised, was too narrow and the drop below was a further deterrent. She looked towards the door.

The door had at some distant time been painted but the paint was now peeling off and with it there were cracks and broken ridges in the wood. Around the lock, wood had flaked off as if some kind of dry rot was eating at the surface. Picking up the fork Jill crossed to the door and knelt down, thrusting the prongs of the fork between the door and the lintel at approximately the spot where the bar of the lock held the door.

She felt metal rasp against metal and, moving the fork, she felt pressure. At the same time part of the wood of the door flaked off. She pressed the fork up and down and though it bent slightly an even larger sliver of wood cracked off. Again she moved the fork in, pushing upwards until she felt it grate on the lock. She manipulated it for some time and then paused, finding she had broken out in a cold sweat and was gasping for breath. She relaxed for a moment drawing air into her lungs. Then again she thrust the fork into the crevice and pushed hard. She kept the pressure up until her hand holding the fork started to tremble with the exertion. She was about to give up and withdraw the fork when there was a dull cracking sound and the fork shot upwards gashing her hand against the door.

Ignoring the pain in her fingers she stood up, gulped air again and reaching out she turned the handle of the door. It opened about an inch. She had broken the lock.

Gently she swung the door inwards until there was enough room for her to squeeze through. A slight creaking of the hinges caused her to hesitate and then she eased herself into the corridor.

The floor of the corridor was wood covered by an ancient threadbare section of linoleum. It led past two doors to a staircase that disappeared downwards, out of sight. Above the staircase another small window provided the only illumination in the hall.

Jill took one slow tentative step and, under the linoleum, the wood protested with a loud creak. Reaching down, she took her shoes off and moved forward on stockinged feet. The wood ceased its protest and, with a feeling of exhilaration that she might quite easily escape, she went slowly to the head of the stairs. About twenty stairs led to a door below which she knew would lead to the outside. But there was a door on either side each leading to the rooms on the ground floor of the house.

At the head of the stairs she stopped, listening for sounds, voices of her captors. There was nothing but her own heavy, nervous breathing and, somewhere beyond the door, the cawing of a bird in the distance.

One step down slowly, her foot trembling. Then another, now all the time holding her breath.

The sounds came at once from behind her and they came quickly, so quickly that she had no time to react, no time even to turn her head. One of the doors at the side of the corridor flew open and there were five or six quick running footsteps. Jill was about to turn when the side of the gun cut through the air, down, slamming against the side of her head, throwing her on to the wall. A flashing of light in front of her eyes gave way to a stabbing shooting pain as the metal struck her forehead.

She sank to her knees, one hand clutching the wall to prevent her pitching down the stairway. At the same time her head came up and she saw the girl, not Gudrun but another girl, the one she knew from the car the night before. And this girl had a pistol in her hand and it was rising again to deliver another blow. Jill pulled her head down, shutting her eyes as if by cutting off her sight she would somehow avert the second blow from the pistol.

'That's enough, Elisa!'

It was a man's voice and she opened her eyes blinking in fright to see the girl's hand caught in a firm grip from behind. Then the girl was thrown aside and the same hand was on her arm, helping her to her feet. She rose, dazed, unaware of the scarlet rivulet trickling from her bruised temple.

'For God's sake, Rolf, the bitch smashed the lock! She was on her way . . .'

The man called Rolf steadied Jill against the wall. He was slightly-built, of medium height, with a sallow complexion and thinning black hair.

'She would not have got very far,' he said in a calm voice. 'And you could have killed her.'

Pain was pulsating through Jill's head now and she swayed again. Holding her arm the man called Rolf led her across the corridor and pushed open another door.

'I'm sorry, Mrs Fraser, but since you have broken the

lock over there, we have no choice . . .'

The room was even smaller than the bedroom she had broken out of, a tiny windowless cell, empty but for one wooden chair and an old mattress on the floor.

Jill stared at him, pulling her arm from his grasp. He had a slight smile on his face and his eyes, penetrating and dark, seemed warmer than those of his companions.

'Who are you?' Jill gasped. 'What do you want with me?'

He had an air of authority over the others which prompted her to ask the same questions. But as she did so, her hand brushed her cheek below the aching temple and came away with a warm dampness on it. She looked away from him at her hand and saw the deep crimson of blood.

'My name is Rolf,' the young man replied almost formally. 'And this is Elisa who you have met. You'll have to forgive her . . . she can be carried away by her sense of . . . revolutionary fervour.'

Jill was still staring at the blood on her hand. It held a frightening fascination in the deep richness of its colour.

He noted the direction of her gaze. 'Please sit down,' he insisted. 'Elisa, bring some water and a dressing for Mrs Fraser's face.'

The girl went out. Jill sat on the solitary chair. Rolf stared at her pensively for a moment. Then he paced the small room, turning at the mattress to face her.

'Perhaps some explanation will make your stay easier . . .'

'I've heard an explanation from the other girl.'

'Ah, yes, Gudrun. Not the most articulate of our group. But not quite as dangerous as Elisa. You must be careful of Elisa. She is . . . very enthusiastic. Always, with her, the end justifies the means. Any means.'

Jill's hand strayed to her forehead. She felt again the dampness of the blood and the broken skin.

'And what is the end?' she asked. 'More violence?'

He smiled indulgently. 'We use violence only to destroy the violence of the capitalistic system.'

'Who are the "we" you talk about?'

'A group fighting for a cause,' he hesitated and glanced

at his wristwatch. She noted it was expensive, a thin Rolex Oyster in gold.

'If I had more time I could elaborate. Perhaps during the next few days . . .'

Elisa came in carrying a bowl of water and a lump of cotton wool to which was attached the edge of a small strip of sticking plaster.

'Give it to me,' Rolf stretched out his hand without looking at her. She handed the cotton wool to him at the same time holding out the bowl. She had a scowl on her face as she did so.

Taking the cotton wool, Rolf dipped it into the bowl and then, taking Jill's chin between finger and thumb, turned her head to one side and proceeded to daub gently at the wound on her forehead.

His touch was light, soothing and yet this very soft, almost kindly motion caused Jill to shiver and pull back slightly, a sudden revulsion possessing her.

'Please don't pull away,' he said. 'But turn your head a little, if you will.'

His voice was calm with a hypnotic quality. Jill relaxed a little only to tense as pain shot across her forehead.

'Easy,' he went on. 'It will pass.'

He rinsed the cotton wool and applied it again.

'Your husband was once an operative for the British Secret Service,' he spoke casually now as he continued to daub at her head.

'He finished with that some time ago,' she interjected quickly.

'They are never finished with it!' Elisa cut in loudly. 'They are never allowed to!'

Rolf ignored the interruption. 'Finished or not, Herr Fraser has some special skills which we need. You are here in order to ensure he will provide them for us.'

Finishing bathing the wound he detached the piece of sticking plaster from a dry segment of cotton wool, padded the area of the wound with the wool, and placed the sticking plaster over it. He stood back contemplating the dressing with satisfaction.

'You see, we had another expert but he was eliminated. We therefore need your husband. However on Friday everything will be over and you will be released. Meanwhile you will stay with us.'

He glanced over his shoulder at Elisa. 'Also I will ask Elisa to see if we can obtain some English books so that you may pass the time reading. That should surely not be too unpleasant.'

Turning away he walked to the door.

'Oh, one thing more,' he spoke with his back to her. 'Please do not try to escape again. It is not a deep cut but, next time, who knows . . .?'

He went out of the room. Elisa stared at Jill for a second, a look of contempt on her face. Then she turned and followed Rolf, shutting the door behind her.

The key turned in the lock.

The foyer of the Hotel Mijas was cool and spacious. A modern four star hotel, it stood on rising ground overlooking the sea and the small town. The gardens of the hotel were well kept, immaculately laid out and, below the balconies of the rooms, the blue-green water of a large swimming pool reflected the rays of the afternoon sun.

'Señor?' The receptionist looked up as Fraser approached, small suitcase in one hand and a carrier bag with a duty-free bottle of whisky in the other.

'My name is Mark Fraser . . .?'

'Ah, si, Señor Fraser! You are expected. Welcome to the Hotel Mijas!'

The room was on the first floor overlooking the pool. On the right of the door was a small, spotlessly clean bathroom, a tiled cell illuminated by concealed lighting. The bedroom itself was typical of the better-class Spanish hotel, with two comfortable beds separated by a small table on which was a telephone. A large wardrobe of stained mahogany, the one old-fashioned item in the room, was against the wall at the side of the beds and, facing them, a long dressing table ran almost the length of the room.

Above it was an equally long mirror about four feet in height. Sliding glass doors at the opposite side of the beds opened on to a balcony on which were two lounging chairs and a glass-topped table.

Fraser tipped the page-boy who handed him his room key and departed. It was only then, when he was alone, that an overpowering weariness came over Fraser. He sank on to the bed, exhaustion taking over; a sleepless night and a five-hundred-mile drive had had its effect. Then there had been the flight and the fast drive into the mountains pursued by Costas. And all the time he had tried to avert his mind from any thought of what might be happening to Jill.

Now he found he could no longer stop himself from thinking of her, could not prevent the feeling of despair and of helplessness. He knew from his own experiences the danger she was in as long as she was held by the Holgar Group. The other thought haunted him too; of the times he had been the hunter and others the victims. Dead faces rose in the mind and the old sickness came over him, self-disgust he could never be rid of, the anguish that still came to him in long nightmares.

He sat, head in hands, for fifteen minutes and then gradually the old training took over and he forced himself to avoid dwelling on dark possibilities. He knew he had to be alert, ready for the contact that would be made. He rose, rinsed his face in cold water, changed his shirt and went out of the room.

Ten minutes later he was sitting, seemingly relaxed, a few yards from the swimming pool drinking an iced lager. He was aware of course that he had been under observation since he came out of the hotel.

'Eh, good afternoon!' The voice was English, an assumed jocularity ill-concealing the tentative quality of the greeting.

Fraser looked up unsmiling. The man was in his early fifties, red-faced, sweating in long streaks that ran down the side of his face to disappear into the thick moustache that surely concealed a twitching upper lip. The face was fat, plump, possibly with a degree of self-indulgence that showed in the red-rimmed, uncertain eyes. The lightweight jacket had once been well-tailored but was now creased; and the white shirt and regimental tie were both well-worn and slightly stained.

'English, aren't you?' the man went on.

'Scots,' Fraser insisted calmly.

'Same thing.'

'Not quite.'

A fleshy hand gesticulated vaguely. 'Can always tell. The British stand out a mile among the Dagos. And the Boche, of course.'

'Really.' Fraser was ice cold and disinterested.

'Oh, yes, every year, more and more German tourists. Easy trip. They just drive down. Don't have to fly.'

'Nice for them.'

The man took the short replies to mean some kind of acceptance.

'Mind if I sit down?' he asked, doing so before Fraser could reply. 'The Spanish are much more polite to the Hun than to our people. Of course they know where the real money is these days. Makes you wonder who won the war.'

A waiter appeared at their side.

'Bring me a whisky and soda,' the man ordered brusquely without looking at the waiter who, equally brusquely, departed.

'Yes,' the Englishman babbled on. 'Place is full of German beer gardens and pumpernickel shops. More of them than English Tea Rooms. Of course I blame it all on the trade unions back home.' The non sequitur did not faze him.

He stared at Fraser cheerfully expecting another response. Fraser said nothing. This prompted him to lean forward confidentially

'Lucky you met me, you know. Able to show you the ropes, so to speak. My name's Bartlett.'

'Yes,' Fraser said quietly. Bartlett frowned. There was an element of recognition in Fraser's response.

'You forget,' Fraser went on. 'I was with the Firm in seventy-four. I'd just come back from Austria. You were leaving Tarrant's office. Our man in Spain, I believe they called you.'

Bartlett grinned, an ingratiating movement of the mouth which created valleys around the fat cheeks. 'Oh, well, damn observant of you.'

'They also called you the Bulldog Drummond of the Department.'

The smile faded on Bartlett's face. He wasn't sure how to take this. After a second, however, he decided it was a compliment and the smile reappeared.

'Oh, is that so?'

'They called you Bulldog Drummond because you had the brains and stamina of a tired bulldog.' Fraser enjoyed the cruelty of the remark. He felt a momentary pleasure at striking out, however mildly. And, in addition, he hadn't liked Bartlett's pomposity as far back as the meeting in seventy-four. Also he had an uncomfortable feeling that, due to his meeting with Lloyd, the Department had decided to become inquisitive.

Bartlett was protesting feebly against the insult. 'Oh, I say, look here . . .'

Fraser decided the Department had to be warned off. 'Listen to me, Bartlett, go back to wherever you operate your little crystal set, get on to London and tell Frank Lloyd I told you to keep out of my way!'

The waiter reappeared silently and placed a tumbler of whisky, speckled with soda bubbles, in Bartlett's eager hand. Fraser nodded to the waiter to signify it be added to his bill. The small gesture he hoped might speed Bartlett on his way.

'Oh, thanks, old man,' Bartlett went on, taking the payment of the drink as some kind of acceptance of his presence. 'Listen, Lloyd thought I might be of some assistance.'

Fraser silently cursed himself for mentioning Spain to Lloyd that morning.

'After all, you can't really expect to find your wife single-handed, now can you?'

It was Bartlett's first real mistake and he knew it as Fraser's hand flashed out, gripping his wrist in a hold that caused pain to shoot up his arm. He was forced to put his whisky on the poolside table with his other hand or the pain would have made him drop the glass.

'How did you know my wife was missing?' Fraser demanded, tense with anger. He had said nothing to Lloyd about Jill's disappearance and yet Lloyd had been in touch with Bartlett and knew what had happened in Scotland the day before. How the hell had he known?

'You're hurting my . . . hand,' Bartlett spluttered, flecks of saliva on his lips.

'Tell me!' Fraser insisted. 'I never told Lloyd so how did you know?'

'Two and two, old chap,' Bartlett replied from between clenched teeth. 'Your wife isn't at home. And she isn't with you . . .'

He hesitated, wincing again, colour draining from his face. Fraser's grip increased.

'Go on!'

'You asked Lloyd about the Red Action people. And then a policeman was shot in Scotland . . .'

Fraser had almost forgotten about the policeman's murder. The poor, unknowing sod who had been killed merely to indicate the Holgar Group meant business.

Bartlett continued, pain forcing out the words. 'A check at Glasgow airport found some kids that could have been Red Action had gone through last night. There was a dark woman with them who seemed to be drunk. Answered to the description the Department has of your wife. From when she worked there.'

Fraser released his hold on Bartlett's wrist. The Englishman massaged the white ring around the wrist and then mopped his forehead with the white handkerchief he took from his breast pocket.

'You know we . . . we don't go in for strong arm stuff here, Fraser,' Bartlett assumed a forced indignation. 'Not these days. It's not done . . . unless in a pretty serious emergency.'

Fraser sat back, relaxing. 'Go away, Bartlett! Take your whisky, go away and keep away. If I see you again I'll break your wrist. And if that doesn't stop you, I might even kill you. I was trained to do that, remember?'

Bartlett rose unsteadily. The redness of the sun on his face seemed to have faded. He tried a last nervous riposte.

'You may need me yet, you know.'

He could not meet Fraser's cold stare. He turned and walked away along the poolside, having reclaimed his whisky and soda which he held delicately in his left hand. A young girl clad in the briefest of bikinis rose from a deck-chair and, crossing in front of him, dived into the pool. Water splashed around Bartlett's trousers and he was forced to protect the whisky from falling pool water by clamping his right hand firmly over the tumbler.

Watching him scowling at the swimmer and dabbing ineffectually at his trousers, Fraser allowed himself the ghost of a smile. Apart from Bartlett's obvious discomfiture Fraser could hope that he was rid of the large red-faced man's bungling offer of assistance which would almost certainly create some kind of uncalled-for havoc. Bartlett had long held that kind of reputation.

Fraser sat for some minutes after Bartlett had gone, an uneasy impatience growing within him. If he was to be contacted let them contact him now. Yet he appreciated that they might leave him sitting around in the sun for some time, preparing him for the contact, weakening any resolve he might have to do other than their wishes. Finally he rose and strolled back into the hotel. It was always possible they would contact him in his room.

They had already done so. He entered the room to find himself staring at a large package decorated with a shining pink ribbon which had been placed on his bed. On top of the package was a card on which was printed in large black letters, 'With Compliments. You will be Contacted.'

Gently Fraser lifted the package and placed it, with infinite care, on the dressing table. Then he knelt on the floor beside the dressing table so that the package was at eye level. And, as he reached out and, gently again, loosened the ribbon he was aware of his old training coming into mind. Packages were never assumed to be benevolent in their contents or their purpose. They were always to be regarded as potentially lethal weapons aimed at their recipient. Fear the Greeks bearing gifts was the maxim to be drummed into every novice in the department.

Not that there was any reason, Fraser assumed, for the package to contain explosives. The Holgar Group needed him alive at least for the time being. Perhaps, when he had completed whatever task they intended him to carry out, then he could be eliminated. But not before.

With delicate movements of his fingers Fraser unwrapped the package to reveal a slim, metal-rimmed, black suitcase. He pressed the catch and eased the top open with both hands.

He found himself looking down at the velvet-lined interior in which were a number of shaped sections. The thin barrel was in the longest section and below it were the telescopic sights. The breech and the magazine were beside the sights and below them were the trigger and firing mechanism and the short skeletal butt. The whole was precision made, a weapon that Fraser could only admire. Over each piece was a thin film of oil causing the metal to glint in the sunlight that still poured through the window of the room.

A marksman's rifle, Fraser thought, custom built to order. And now delivered to him; no gift, but a practical weapon made to be used. But to be used for what purpose and against whom?

'Mr Fraser!'

The voice came from outside, from below the balcony outside the window. Fraser closed the suitcase with one quick movement of his arm and looked around the room. Although the case was slim it would not fit into any of the drawers under the dressing table; and he had no wish to leave it lying on the table in full view of any inquisitive hotel employee. Lifting the case he reached up and placed it on top of the large wardrobe. One gentle push and it was out of sight. Then he walked quickly onto the balcony.

The balding young man Jill knew as Rolf stood at the side of the pool looking up at Fraser's balcony.

'*Buenos dias,* Mr Fraser,' he greeted Fraser. 'Shall we take a walk?'

The contact had been made.

FIVE

They strolled through the gardens of the hotel and down into the village of Mijas. To an onlooker they appeared to be two friends, rather solemn foreigners, enjoying the afternoon sun. Their shadows moved across the white walls of the old town, the only sign of tension or impatience was in the occasional sudden hand movement, magnified out of proportion in shadow.

Mark Fraser started the conversation.

'All right! We're walking. So talk to me.'

'You are an impatient man, Mr Fraser,' Rolf replied easily, casually. 'Of course it's understandable.'

Fraser gripped his arm. 'Who are you? A paid messenger boy or one of them?'

A flash of irritation from Rolf. 'We don't use messenger boys.'

'You do your own dirty work?'

The German grinned showing very white even teeth. 'Unlike you, Mr Fraser, in your previous career. You always carried out the dirty work for someone else.'

'Not this time,' Fraser insisted. 'Your people have my wife?'

'She is reasonably comfortable and will not be harmed. Unless . . . '

Fraser nodded. 'I have to believe you.'

'Yes, Mr Fraser, you have to believe me.'

They had reached a tiny piazza overlooking the sea. They stood in silence watching a motorboat weaving out over the water. Rolf Gruner regarded the boat wistfully. Soon, in a few days, it would be over and he would be away, free of it all for the time being at least; but now he envied the occupants of the boat.

Fraser turned away from the sea. Rolf followed and they retraced their steps back through the village towards the hotel. The conversation had been brief, broken by silences, as if each man was assessing the measure of the other.

Fraser took a deep breath. 'All right. What do I have to do?'

Lighting a Gitane from a crumpled packet he produced from his slacks Rolf offered Fraser one as an afterthought. Fraser accepted, taking a light from the other's cigarette.

'You've heard of Alexander Scherer?' Rolf asked softly, almost an aside.

'I've heard of him,' Fraser inhaled from the Gitane. 'West German newspaper proprietor.'

Rolf nodded. 'Publisher of a large number of Fascist rags. A man of great power and wealth. Fingers in many greasy pies, as they say in your country.'

He hesitated and then looked up at Fraser.

'You have an opinion of him?'

'Too close to some of the old Nazi types,' Fraser responded. 'Slightly to the right of Genghis Khan.'

Nodding with a sudden enthusiasm Rolf went on. 'Yes. Yes, that is good. Very good. Scherer, he once called us murderous clowns.'

Fraser couldn't resist the crack. 'So nobody's ever wrong all the time.'

Rolf's expression hardened.

Ignoring the change of mood Fraser went on. 'Anyway, why the hell are we walking around discussing a character who's safely installed in a bloody great Schloss outside Bonn?'

'But he is not, Mr Fraser . . .' Rolf replied glancing at his watch. 'At about this moment Alexander Scherer is arriving at the villa of his old friend, The Duke of Porto Christo. Not far from here. At the Duke's villa Scherer will pass a discreet and anonymous vacation. One of his very rare holidays, I may say.'

So that was it, Fraser thought. Alexander Scherer. A big name. Wealth, looks, a distinguished character in his late forties, Fraser had seen the newspaper photographs. Friend of politicians everywhere. But politicians of the right. As a young man he had visited America, sat at the feet of Senator Joseph McCarthy. Like McCarthy, Scherer had become a Red-baiter, a destroyer of careers, a power force without control or conscience. Fraser had no admiration for Alexander Scherer. Yet he now suspected what was to come and he knew he had no stomach for it.

'So Scherer's on vacation,' he said casually. 'What's it to do with me?'

'We want you to kill him for us.'

A simple sentence. A flat statement of intent spoken without emotion.

They were entering the hotel grounds again. Fraser stopped at the gate.

'Because he called you murderous clowns?'

Rolf ignored this. 'We have decided you will do it on Friday, Mr Fraser. The occasion will provide the maximum opportunity. The Duke is having a garden party for a select group of friends, most of them old-time Falangists, to meet Scherer.'

'I hardly expect to be invited,' Fraser interjected. 'Do I gatecrash?'

'You received your gift package?' Rolf asked.

'I wondered what I had done to deserve it. Or what I would have to do.'

They were walking again now, around the edge of the swimming pool. And, unbeknown to them, they were being observed.

Andreas Costas had obtained entry to Fraser's empty bedroom using a small plastic credit card to force the lock. He stood at the side of the window, back from the balcony, staring down at the two figures strolling between the sun-bathers and the would-be swimmers. And he was sweating again.

He turned away from the window, and wiped his brow with the back of his hand. It had been a long day and a considerable walk down the mountain road until he had finally secured a lift from a battered lorry carrying barrels of cheap wine. He was tired and he had new orders and

69

they had to be carried out. He surveyed the room. Somewhere was a package or a case which he knew had been delivered to Fraser's room. He had to find it and remove it. He started by looking under the bed.

Below at the poolside Rolf considered, not without interest, the bikini-clad body of a young girl as he talked to Fraser.

'You will tomorrow be given photographs of the Duke's villa, where Scherer is staying. The grounds and the garden are overlooked by a high promontory. Ideal for your purpose, I would say. But that is up to you of course. The guests are invited to meet Scherer at midday.'

'I might shoot the wrong guest?'

'That would be most unfortunate for Mrs Fraser. But I don't think you will. You'll have seen Scherer in the newspapers. But anyway we will provide photographs of him. You will collect them at the Hotel Hispano in Fuengirola. We will have them waiting for you tomorrow.'

They had now strolled away from the pool and reached a terrazzo outside the hotel's bar. A line of tables and chairs along the terrazzo were unoccupied with the exception of a young man and woman, beautifully tanned, sipping long drinks between gazing into each others' slightly red eyes and holding hands over the table. Below the terrazzo there was a view of the sea. Again Rolf stopped, staring out at the water with some barely realised inner fascination. Abstractedly, Fraser thought, he'll die by drowning, this young, educated thug. Full fathom five and the world will be a better place. But let me not be his executioner. Five deaths are enough; five deaths are too many.

'I think I have said all that is necessary.' Rolf turned away from the sea, moving from the ornate metal railing, indicating the meeting was at an end.

'I haven't!' Fraser said, stepping in front of him. 'Sit down, you bastard.'

A small smile and a shrug from Rolf. It was immaterial, he was in no hurry. He sat beside one of the tables. Fraser took the other chair and waved the waiter hovering at the edge of the terrazzo over to them.

'Cognac! Two.'

The waiter nodded and disappeared into the bar.

Fraser leaned forward and spoke very quietly. 'You'll have to take my word for it that a Luger is pointing right at your stomach under the table.'

Rolf said nothing but under his tan he visibly paled. Fraser drew comfort from the sight just as he drew comfort from the cool metal of the gun which had been in the waistband of his trousers under the loose shirt. It was the same gun Costas had felt against his neck in the mountains.

'It would make a very big messy hole,' Fraser went on.

'It will not help your wife, Fraser.'

'When the waiter brings us the brandies we'll talk some more about my wife.'

In the room above the pool, Costas had found the suitcase on the top of the wardrobe. He was sitting on the bed now, left hand curled around the case, cossetting it, as if he was drawing strength from the rifle inside. His right hand held the telephone receiver and he was talking excitedly to a listener in another room in the hotel.

'Yes, yes, he was at the pool with this other man. They were walking towards the bar. Of course I will be delighted to avoid him and will take care to do so, I assure you . . .'

The voice at the other end of the line cut in. Costas nodded enthusiastically. The finding of the suitcase with the rifle had pleased him, reassured him that he was still of use to his employers.

'You want I should observe him from the pool. He will have to pass below to return here.'

A thought struck him, and he stood on the bed peering down at the swimming pool. If he should have missed Fraser passing . . .? He dismissed the thought.

'The minute he passes, I will leave the room,' he went on. 'And of course I will bring the gun with me when I leave.'

The voice at the other end of the line seemed reassured. Costas heard the click of the receiver being replaced. He gently put down his own receiver and, still clutching the case, he went over to the window. There, he carefully assumed a position at the side of the expanse of glass where he had a complete view of both sides of the pool below.

On the terrazzo the waiter placed two brandies in front of Fraser and Rolf Gruner. Fraser waved him away with a Spanish currency note of generous value for two drinks.

'Now,' he addressed himself to Rolf. 'When do you release Jill? Exact time and place, please?'

As soon as you kill Scherer we will leave your wife at the Café Dos Palmas in Granada. You will be able to collect her . . .'

'Unhurt?'

'Of course.'

'If I'm not caught committing murder on your behalf.' Fraser took a sip of the brandy. The warmth seemed to scald for a second the back of his throat.

'You have not been caught in the past,' Rolf made the statement as if assuring a business man that his credit was good.

Fraser turned the brandy glass around between two fingers. 'Why me?' he asked.

'We need a professional who would have sufficient motive for doing the job and escaping undetected. You have the experience and the motive is your wife's safety.' Rolf gave a curt shrug, scratching the side of his nose with his index finger. A segment of sunburnt skin flaked off.

He went on. 'To tell you the truth we had another professional gentleman lined up but . . .'

'Somebody threw him out of a high window,' Fraser completed the sentence. 'It was in the British press. Pity. Or was it? So how did you know about me?'

Rolf's hesitation was barely perceptible except to Fraser's trained eye. He recovered quickly however as Fraser noted with interest and an awakening of curiosity.

'You . . . you remember the raid on the German Embassy in Stockholm in 1975?' Rolf asked. 'It was carried out by the Holgar Meinz Kommando.'

It had been all over the world's newspapers. Fraser remembered it too well.

'The Holgar Meinz! Alias the "crazy brigade".'

Rolf affected indignation. 'They were martyrs!'

Fraser remembered too the philosophy the group had spouted to the world. 'Therapy through violence! Bomb for mental health! Isn't it a sick idealism?'

Rolf ignored the question. 'You were a British agent at that time, Herr Fraser. You were also killing people. You were the weapon of British Intelligence in Germany and in Scandinavia. You know, the West Germans were aware of your activities. And they had your name on file in their Embassy.'

Fraser frowned. It was possible that he was known and there had been a dossier on him. He didn't like the thought. All countries had dossiers on known operatives. And those were rarely closed unless the subject of the dossier had been killed. He wondered whether he was still the subject of slim secret folders in locked files in strange embassies.

'Your name was passed on to the Holgar Meinz Group for future reference,' Rolf continued. 'We have now come to the time where we remember that reference. So we knew of you. And now we have made contact and you will kill Alexander Scherer and we will return your wife.'

So saying, he swallowed his brandy in one gulp. 'Thank you for the drink. Now, may I go?'

Fraser watched him, eyes cold. Then he inclined his head in a nod of dismissal. Rolf stood, not without a small sigh of relief.

'One more thing,' Fraser added. 'And listen to me carefully. If my wife is harmed in any way, however minor it may seem to you, then you and your "crazy brigade" can all be sure of one thing. You will all be "martyred" by me. Slowly.'

Rolf hesitated, suppressing a small shiver. He knew Fraser meant exactly what he said.

'I respect your feelings, Mr Fraser,' he gave a slight inclination of the head, then, turning on his heel he walked from the terrazzo down by the side of the pool towards the car park.

Fraser lifted his brandy glass and swallowed the remaining dregs of liquid. Then, as soon as Rolf was out of sight, he moved with cat-like speed. He leaped the last steps from the terrazzo and crossed to the pool on the opposite side from Rolf.

Costas, watching from the window above, stiffened. Was Fraser coming back to his room? It did not seem so from his circuitous route around the pool. And yet this was no time to take chances with a man like Fraser. He could still feel the circle of steel at the back of his neck where the Scotsman had pressed the gun at him on the mountain.

Turning away from the balcony window, Costas took a firm grip on the suitcase and crossed to the door. He threw it open.

Another gun and another tall figure stood facing him. Another man, a stranger, took a pace into the room pointing the pistol at the small Greek's chest.

A flood of panic went through Costas' body. All his life he had been possessed by a fear of guns. It went back to Greece and the war when he had seen his brother shot dead by a German officer with a handgun. That one shot had echoed throughout his life.

He backed away from the stranger until he was level with the door leading to the bathroom. And then in one defiant act he held up the suitcase containing the rifle and threw it at the intruder.

Below, Mark Fraser reached the edge of the car park. The grey coupé was parked in the shade behind a tree, away from the main parking area. It was a precaution he always took. Leave your car at a convenient spot, ready to be driven and away from the possibility of being jammed in by other cars. Also in a position where you could view as much of the parking area as possible.

By cutting around the pool he had short-circuited the route taken by Rolf who was only now approaching a blue car parked in the centre of the area. Standing by the driver's door of the blue saloon, Jurgen, on seeing Rolf, swung himself behind the wheel. Rolf climbed in beside him.

'Okay?' Jurgen asked, the word strangely incongruous in

his German accent.

Rolf nodded. 'Move now. If I am any judge of Herr Mark Fraser he will follow us.'

Jurgen switched on the ignition and the engine came to life with a splutter and then a roar. 'Can't see any sign of him.'

'You won't, not yet,' Rolf replied. 'He is a professional, remember. But once on the road watch for his car.'

Jurgen drove slowly out of the car park. There was no movement behind him. Only when he reached the road did he increase his speed as they moved south. And it was two minutes later when Rolf, half turning in his seat, saw the grey coupé behind them.

'He's following! The grey coupé.'

Jurgen's foot went down on the accelerator.

'No panic.' Rolf relaxed in his seat. 'I'll tell you when we have to get ahead. Carl knows what he has to do?'

'Carl knows,' Jurgen murmured from between his teeth. 'But does that mean he will do it? He's the weak sister. You should have given that job to Gudrun or Elisa.'

'Carl will do what is expected of him,' Rolf smiled icily. 'And it is an expendable task. That's why I did not use Gudrun or Elisa. They're too valuable.'

Two hundred yards behind them Fraser sat at the wheel of the grey coupé peering through the dust thrown up by the car in front. He should have reckoned on the dust, he told himself, especially after the chase with Costas. And he would have preferred a busier road. It was always better to follow a car with another car in between. And something else was nagging at his mind. It would be too easy if he were simply allowed to follow the balding young man and his driver to where Jill was being held. They would either try and shake him off or they were heading somewhere else. Yet they were, so far, his only contact and he had to follow. At least, he told himself, there was one consolation; they needed him, they would not try to kill him.

The black sedan overtook Fraser's grey coupé quite suddenly and manoeuvred itself in between the coupé and the blue car. Fraser felt a mild irritation at what seemed an intrusion but then, he realised it put a car between himself and his quarry. It meant that even if they recognised he was following them, the occupants of the blue car would be unable to take any direct action against him. A bullet aimed at his front tyre was now an impossibility apart from the danger of causing him to crash with resultant injury or even death. Again he clung to the thought. They needed him.

A quarter of a mile ahead on a knoll above the road overlooking the sea, Carl-Jan Husig took the binoculars from his eyes and swiftly slid down a small incline to where a blue sedan was parked on a pathway off the road. The sedan was identical in every detail to the one driven by Jurgen and Rolf with the exception of the registration plate. And that was only one digit different in its number. Both hired from the same company, Rolf had simulated an interest in identical cars when hiring them. The clerk at the car-hire company had been amused at this seeming eccentricity. One had to pander to crazy foreigners.

Carl switched on the ignition. At the same time, less than a quarter of a mile away, Jurgen slammed his foot full down on the accelerator and the blue car shot away ahead of the black sedan and the grey coupé.

Fraser cursed under his breath. He accelerated but the black sedan in front of him obscured the view and the road narrowed making it impossible for him to overtake.

Jurgen sped fast to the bend in the road behind the knoll. He knew that for a few seconds they would be out of sight of their pursuer.

They swung around the curve.

'Now!' Rolf shouted at him.

Jurgen twisted the steering wheel hard to the left and the car bucked as it went off the road on to the track behind the knoll.

At the same time Carl slipped his handbrake and accelerated onto the road. With no acknowledgment the two cars passed each other and Carl was on the road driving fast to the south.

Jurgen did not draw up at the spot where Carl had been

parked but instead steered the car further up the rocky track, the springs protesting as it bounced over unseen stones and rocks. He didn't bring the car to a stop until it was concealed completely from the road by the knoll. Only then did he draw to a halt. He and Rolf sat back, both taking deep breaths.

Behind them the black sedan followed by Fraser's grey coupé had already flashed around the bend and was following Carl in his blue car.

Rolf took out a Gitane, offered one unthinkingly to Jurgen who refused it. Rolf remembered Jurgen rarely smoked and disapproved of the habit. He smiled to himself. A puritan terrorist; he supposed it followed with some people. The coldness of the killer was combined with the self-righteousness of the bigot. It didn't matter. As long as the instrument worked.

'We did it,' he said.

Jurgen agreed but with reservations. 'Where will Carl take them?'

'The mountains. The Sierra Bermeja. He has instructions to lose Fraser up there. And then rendezvous with us.'

'And if he doesn't lose Fraser?'

He will not lead him to us. And if Fraser catches him, what can Fraser do? Carl will deny he even knows us. And even if he did admit he was one of us, Fraser can do nothing. We still have his wife. And we will move her in case Carl is stupid or weak enough to lead Fraser to us.' He drew from the Gitane smugly and then exhaled with pleasure. 'So let's drive back now.'

Carl, despite his stammer and his nervousness, was a good driver. A misguided and doting widowed mother had bought him a fast sports car at the age of sixteen and, for the first time in his life, he had found confidence behind the wheel of an automobile. It had probably been the only good service his mother had rendered to a son whose excessive sensitivity on top of a childhood smothered by female interference had made him ready material for the misguided idealism of the terrorist cause.

Behind him the black sedan pressed forward and, behind

the sedan, Fraser drove, a flicker of hope in his mind that perhaps he might possibly be led to wherever Jill was being held. He was completely unaware that the blue cars had been switched.

At the same time as Mark Fraser was following the blue car into the foothills, Jill Fraser was being forced at gunpoint from the small room by Elisa.

'*Raus!*' The girl commanded harshly. 'Out! Quickly!'

Jill stumbled along the corridor and down the stairs. At the front door of the farmhouse Gudrun stood waiting. As Jill stepped out of the building into the yellowing light of late afternoon she was pushed forward across a small courtyard towards a SEAT saloon.

'Where are you taking me?' she asked, fear rising within her.

'Into the front!' Elisa ordered her, ignoring the question. Jill settled in the front passenger seat and Elisa sat behind her, gun on her neck. Gudrun climbed in the driver's seat.

Elisa spoke as Gudrun switched on the ignition.

'Now you will behave like the good little British *hausfrau* or we will blow your head off!'

She shuddered aware that the girl meant what she said. And now they were moving off to God knows where.

Carl had turned off the main road and was driving into the mountains when quite suddenly the black sedan behind him put on a burst of speed and overtook him in a cloud of dust. Beyond the set frown on his face there was no indication that he was concerned. Fraser's grey coupé was still some way behind and the sedan did not worry him. Strangers or tourists, the occupants of the sedan were nothing to do with him.

He realised his mistake when it was too late. The heavy black car had placed itself in front of him and, veering from one side of the road to the other, had dropped its speed, forcing Carl to slow his blue car down. Carl cursed to himself between tight lips. Fraser was gaining on him and though he had no worries if Fraser did catch up with him, it was too soon for it to happen. He was not deep enough into the mountains. While a confrontation with Fraser could be controlled, since they held his wife, at the same time Carl's task was to lead him as far away as possible.

He was considering all this with some degree of smugness when, quite suddenly, the black sedan shot forward again until it was about a hundred yards ahead of him. Then with a screaming of brakes it swerved, seeming to skid, and came to an abrupt halt, side on to the oncoming cars, blocking the road.

Carl's foot went down on his brakes and his car took up the screaming protest from suddenly abused brake linings.

He came to a halt about ten yards from the black sedan. What the hell were they playing at, he thought? He glanced over his shoulder to see the grey coupé coming up behind him and already slowing down. Assuming the face of an indignant motorist he opened the door of the blue car and stepped onto the road, prepared to demand that the driver of the black sedan clear the way. As he did so he thought with a slight smile that Fraser dare not create a scene in front of strange tourists or for that matter native Spaniards.

His attitude changed at once as two large men stepped from the front of the black sedan followed by a smaller man who came from the rear door. The two large characters were dressed in thick dark suits that seemed slightly crumpled. Both of them had heavy automatic pistols in their hands.

The third man was smaller, neater, dressed in a light-weight tan suit. He had a broad forehead, the eyes of a Slav, thick, black hair and a casual manner only belied by the ice behind the eyes.

Carl panicked. The dark suits and the automatic pistols created their own authority. The men did not look like Spanish policemen but they had an air of officialdom and, as they moved towards him, a determined assurance. He looked around, searching for an escape route. One side of the road was sheer rock face looming over the road. The other side was a sloping field, uncultivated, strewn with rocks. At the foot of the slope were trees and shrub; if he could reach that he might rid himself of any pursuers.

He leaped across a shallow ditch and ran into the field. Behind him he heard a shout. He kept running.

On the road Fraser brought his car to a halt and stepped out in time to see the driver of the blue car running, followed by the two men from the black sedan. The third man from the sedan stood, staring after them, fastidiously brushing dust from his tan suit with meticulously precise movements of his right hand. He glanced briefly at Fraser then turned his attention again to the fleeing youth and his pursuers.

Carl was increasing the distance between himself and the two men when his shin hit the sharp ridge of a large stone. He fell forward, pain stabbing up his leg. The panic became hysteria. Now they would be on to him. He fumbled in his waistband, rolling over onto his back on the grass, and produced his own revolver. Wildly he aimed it at the nearest of the pursuers and fired. The bullet whined inaccurately across the field. The target threw himself to the right.

Swivelling the gun in the direction of the second of the two men Carl fired again. His aim was equally inaccurate. The man did not even bother to take evasive action but instead lifted his heavy automatic pistol, took careful aim and shot Carl in the chest.

The force of the bullet threw Carl back against the ground and his revolver flew from his hand. It was as if he had been punched a tremendous blow just below his heart. At first there was no actual pain but only tremendous force striking him. He forced himself to look down at his chest with some astonishment and saw blood welling up from a hole in his shirt. Then pain spread across his back. He could not see that, despite the comparatively small entry wound in his chest, a hole double the size of a man's fist had been blown out of his back.

He was aware of figures moving towards him and then a kind of twilight came over his view.

Fraser, grim-faced, ran across the field, followed at a more leisurely pace by the man in the tan suit.

'He mustn't be killed!' Fraser shouted, afraid for Jill if his contact should die.

The two men who had pursued the youth were standing looking down at Carl when Fraser reached them. He stared down at the boy's body, seeing blood soaking the once white shirt. He stared without recognition. This was not his contact at the hotel.

'They switched cars on you, Mr Fraser,' said the man in the tan suit, coming up behind him. 'The man you talked to at the hotel is far away by this time.'

Fraser looked up into the ice-blue Slavic eyes. 'Who the hell are you?'

Before he received a reply, Carl groaned and rolled over onto his face. Fraser caught his breath as he saw the size of the wound on the fallen man's back. He should have known what the exit wound from a shot from one of those large automatics would be like, but it had been a long time since he'd seen such an injury and he'd tried to put such memories from his mind.

Callously the man in the dark suit who had shot the youth moved forward, put his shoe under Carl's shoulder and turned him back until he lay again looking up at them.

The tan suit spoke again, as if offering an excuse. 'Oh, he is one of them, Mr Fraser, one of the Group. Probably expendable, not so important, but one of them.'

Fraser knelt by the body. The eyes below him flickered open.

'Where is my wife?' Fraser demanded, aware of his own callousness. No one could live with a wound like the one he had just seen.

Carl stared at him, trying to focus his eyes. Pain was spreading across his back and his chest was beginning to ache. His mouth was filled with the taste of blood.

Fraser's face came into focus. Carl did not actually

recognise the fact but was sure it was one of his pursuers. He was not going to show them fear. He remembered the stories of all the martyrs of Baader-Meinhof and the other groups. He made a final effort and spat upwards at the face looming over him. Then the pain suddenly eased away, darkness came over his eyes and he slid sideways into death.

Fraser stood, wiping the trace of blood and saliva from his cheek.

'Even the nervous ones have an insane courage when they die,' said the man in the tan suit.

Fraser turned to stare at him. 'I asked who you were.'

'I didn't reply, did I?' The man smiled again. He seemed to be always smiling. A smiler not with a knife but with two automatic pistols held by others.

'From the accent I'd say Russian,' Fraser said.

'Very good. I won't ask you to tell the regional dialect. From Novgorod originally. My name is Grigor. Vladimir Ilyich Grigor. Named after Lenin. My mother was a good party member.'

'KGB?' Fraser guessed. It was not a difficult guess.

Grigor nodded. 'I hold the equivalent of your rank of Lieutenant-Colonel.' He turned to the two men in dark suits. 'Remove the body!'

They took their places, one at the head and the other at Carl-Jan Husig's feet and lifted him effortlessly. The ground underneath the body was stained with red and the stain was spotted with scraps of tissue. Fraser turned away. He was not squeamish and he had seen it all before; yet he saw no need to dwell unnecessarily on the extreme unpleasantnesses of his former profession. Grigor and he walked back towards the road.

'We have not met but I have heard of you,' Grigor said affably. 'You eliminated Rasnikov in Vienna, yes, Mr Fraser?'

It had been the fourth killing; a Russian KGB man involved in blackmailing and framing British and Austrian Civil Servants; and not above killing them when their usefulness was over. Fraser had been ordered to eliminate him and had done so with simple professional expertise.

'Self-preservation,' he responded to Grigor.

'Not quite. He was no threat to you.'

'He was a threat to a number of people on our side.'

Grigor gave a lop-sided shrug. 'It's nothing to me. I knew him but I didn't like him. A crude man.'

They reached the road and Grigor walked with Fraser to the grey coupé.

'You knew this dangerous child?' Grigor asked nodding towards the field where his two aides were carrying the body down the incline.

'Carl-Jan Husig.' Fraser acknowledged. 'I didn't know him but I have seen his photograph.'

Grigor smiled again, smoothing his hair which had been disarrayed in the field. 'Yes of course. Your people would have him on their files. But you were retired, were you not?'

'I still am. Anyway what is this business to you?'

The Russian shrugged. 'Let's say an interested party. Go back to your hotel, Mr Fraser. Pack and fly back to Scotland and be retired. And as you really are so, we will have no interest in you.'

'I can't do that,' Fraser said flatly.

'Ah, yes. Your wife. We know these people have taken her . . .'

'How do you know?'

Grigor ignored the question and went on. 'We will get to these people, of course, and when we do, we will release your wife.'

'You can't guarantee that.'

'Who can guarantee anything? But we will try.'

A question rose in Fraser's mind. He put it into words. 'The Red Action Brigade? Aren't they professed Marxists? As you are? Yet you are after them?'

'With extreme prejudice, as the Americans would say,' Grigor replied. 'But, you see, there are Marxists and Marxists. And deviationists, and Trotskyites. And Anarchists and Mensheviks. Such a large spectrum of perverse philosophy.'

With impeccable politeness, he opened the door of Fraser's car and indicated Fraser should climb in.

'If you won't go back to your home, Fraser,' he went on. 'Then at least go back to your hotel. My . . . er . . . colleagues will dispose of the body of Husig so that it will not be found for a very long time. This way we avoid the diplomatic unpleasantness.'

He shut the door of the car carefully and smiled his automatic smile once more.

'If you do not return to Scotland, I shall be in touch with you again.'

Fraser switched on the ignition and started the car. He reversed carefully and drove off on the long road back to the hotel. As he did so, he saw, in his rear-view mirror, Grigor walking back towards the black sedan. His gait was that of a man completely relaxed and unconcerned despite the fact that he had, some minutes before, been responsible for a man's death.

Fraser knew it had to be that way. In his old profession, concern and emotion had to be eradicated from any human consideration. He wondered if he could again subdue and suppress those emotions in his present circumstance. He knew he was capable of killing to save Jill; even, God forbid, to revenge her. But the callous objectivity of the old trade had gone.

It was a dangerous state of mind. Anger, passion, any kind of emotion made misjudgement all the more possible. And with Jill's life at stake he could not afford a misjudgement.

He drove fast but carefully towards Mijas. Around him dusk gave way to night.

SIX

The moment Mark Fraser opened the door of his hotel room he sensed something was wrong. Momentarily he put it down to his meeting with the Russians and the death of Carl-Jan Husig. It had produced in him a quality of tenseness, of being alert to the unexpected; and at first, as he entered the room, the awareness of displacement he attributed to this feeling.

Then he noticed the bathroom door was ajar and the light was on in the bathroom. And his eyes were caught by a difference in colour on the carpet at his feet. He looked down and again saw the colour of blood. It was a darker shade than that of the blood he had seen on Carl's chest; this time, drying fast and turning brown.

He pushed the bathroom door open.

Andreas Costas lay against the bath, sprawled on the marble floor, legs stretched in front of him, both hands clutching his chest. Again, the scarlet of warm blood soaking through the fingers of both hands. And below that the shirt and jacket were stained with clotted blood. The man's face had the paleness of approaching death and indeed Fraser would have presumed he was already dead but for an almost imperceptible movement of the chest and a flutter of the eyelids.

Fraser knelt down, a sudden wave of pity for this strange little man coming over him. As he did so Costas opened his eyes and stared up at Fraser. Deep inside himself the little man made some prodigious effort and focused his gaze.

'Mister Fraser . . . I am waiting for you . . .' The words underlined the effort, forcing themselves from between dry cracked lips, causing him to tense with pain.

'Take it easy,' Fraser said, looking down at the chest wound. Like Carl-Jan Husig, it was a gunshot wound squarely in the centre of the chest. From the amount of dried blood he had certainly been lying in that position for some time and, with the wound and the blood loss, was almost certainly close to death.

'It doesn't . . . matter,' Costas gasped, as if reading Fraser's thoughts. 'I lied to you today . . . on . . . on the mountain. I know who I work for. Colonel Grigor . . . that is the name . . . he is the one I phone to for instructions. You . . . you will speak to him . . . please . . .'

'I already have,' Fraser replied.

The little man gave a small twisted painful smile. The effort was too much. The smile was forced aside. He gasped once and then died.

Fraser remained kneeling beside him for some seconds. In the distance he could hear the strains of dance music from somewhere below in the hotel. The music seemed to underline the futility of the little man's death.

Then there was a small, clicking sound behind him in the bedroom.

Someone had switched the light on in the room.

Fraser drew his revolver from the waistband of his trousers and swivelled around, standing erect. The smell of cigarette smoke drifted from the door of the bathroom and he could see the smoke itself wreathing in the air at eye-level ouside the bathroom door.

A figure stepped into the doorway and Fraser brought his revolver up in line with the intruder's chest.

'Friend, old man, friend. No need to use the gun!' Bartlett said, with a nervous smile that denoted in this case near panic.

'I could have shot you!' Fraser exclaimed angrily. 'What the hell are you doing . . .?'

Bartlett looked over Fraser's shoulder at the body on the floor. 'Good God, I thought he'd died hours ago when I first shot him. Can't trust these foreigners . . .'

Before he could finish speaking Fraser had moved, cat-like, out of the bathroom, gripping Bartlett by the lapels,

86

forcing him back into the bedroom and against the wall with considerable force.

'You bastard . . . !'

'Hang on a minute there, old man!' Bartlett protested. 'I caught him trying to steal your property.'

Feebly he indicated the gun-case now lying on the bed. Fraser paid little attention, still pressing the large man against the wall and still gripping the gun in his right hand threateningly. Bartlett wriggled awkwardly under his grip and forced a ghastly semblance of a smile onto his face.

'I'm on your side, remember,' he choked out the words at Fraser.

'That poor sod didn't know which side he was on,' Fraser responded indicating with a jerk of his head the bathroom and the body of Costas. 'And you shot him.'

Finally, with a look of contempt, Fraser released his grip on Bartlett and turned away. Moving to the dressing table he lifted the bottle of duty-free whisky and opened it. Turning again he went into the bathroom and, skirting Costas' body, lifted a tumbler from the wash-hand basin. Back in the bedroom he poured himself a large dram.

Bartlett watched him, wide-eyed, still nervously propped against the wall. 'I could use a nip myself.'

Fraser did not look at him. 'Forget it. You need a clear head. You'd better bring the rubbish squad in to get rid of the body.'

'Actually, I haven't got a rubbish squad,' Bartlett replied awkwardly. 'I did tell you we don't have much of this kind of . . . activity around here.'

Fraser took a gulp of whisky and glared at him angrily. 'Listen, you bastard, you terminated his contract, so you get him out of here!'

Bartlett flushed. 'Yes, yes, of course. I'll lay something on. One or two of the local lads do odd jobs for me. But, look, Fraser, why don't you clear out. Leave this to me. After all you are heading south . . .'

Before speaking Fraser gave him a long hard look. 'How the hell do you know where I'm heading?'

Only the terrorist contact should know he had to move

to the Hotel Hispano in Fuengirola, a few miles to the south, to collect photos of the villa Scherer was staying at. He had assumed part of their plan was to keep him moving until the time for the assassination. That way he would have little opportunity to look for Jill. But how did Bartlett know he was moving south?

Bartlett's answer was unconvincing in its nervous delivery. 'London heard the Red Action people might be around this part of the world. Frank Lloyd thought I should help you.'

'Why?'

'Frank's idea,' Bartlett shrugged. 'Old times' sake. Friend of yours, isn't he? Anyway I passed the word to some of my people here . . .'

Fumbling in his breast pocket, Bartlett produced a handkerchief and started to mop his brow. He seemed always to be sweating profusely and always mopping his brow.

'Go on,' Fraser insisted.

'My people gave me the word. They were around Granada. The Holgar Group. Three of them we know about.'

'I know about them too. Thanks to Lloyd. Jurgen Haussmann, Elisa Toth and Carl-Jan Husig. I saw Husig two hours ago. And he wasn't in Granada.'

Bartlett's brow furrowed. 'Where then?'

'Lying dead in a field. He'd been shot by the KGB!'

It took a moment to sink in. Then astonishment spread over Bartlett's florid features.

'What the hell are the Russkie's doing here?'

His surprise seemed genuine.

'I was hoping you could tell me,' Fraser replied.

'London had better know about this.' At once Bartlett was London's man in Spain, doing the routine thing.

'Tell them,' Fraser responded casually. 'But before you do, tell me where your . . . people . . . think these kids are going.'

Another shrug. 'They don't know.'

Fraser took one step towards Bartlett but the manner of it indicated a threat and Bartlett backed away.

'They knew enough to spot the kids,' Fraser insisted. 'I want to know exactly where they're going.'

'Can't tell you what I don't know. But I can put you in touch with one of my people, friend of ours, who might be able to help. An old boy called Rocas. Runs a shop in Granada. He was anti-Franco. Didn't like the cut of the old Generalissimo's jib. Admired our Labour government, the Lord knows why. Anyway he helps us and he knows most of what goes on in this part of Spain . . .'

'Write down his address while I pack,' Fraser said. He had come to a decision. It suited him as much as the terrorists to keep on the move. Especially with one dead body in his bedroom, and the KGB involved. Not that he understood their involvement.

Taking his suitcase from the side of the bed he placed it beside the gun-case. He hadn't had time to unpack, come to think of it, except for the bottle of duty-free whisky. What was left of that, he would sacrifice to Bartlett's obvious need. Also he had to keep a clear head.

'When I'm gone you can get rid of your handiwork,' he told Bartlett with a last brief look at Costas, still sprawled on the bathroom floor. The dead, he thought, look not only very dead, but ugly in death.

Bartlett handed him a piece of paper on which he had scrawled an address.

'There you are. Leather-work shop, Rocas has, in Granada.' He was affable and businesslike now, very much our man in Spain. God help us and Spain, Fraser thought.

'You can leave the body to me to dispose of,' Bartlett went on.

Fraser picked up the two cases and walked to the door. 'You can settle my bill too, Bartlett. One half-day and no meals. I expect you'll have to pay fully for one night.'

The florid-faced man missed the irony in his voice. 'Yes, I expect I will have to,' he replied seriously.

'And, Bartlett . . .'

'Yes, old man?'

'If you've misdirected me, I'll kill you. No matter whose side you're on.'

Bartlett blinked as Fraser went out, shutting the door silently behind him. Perspiration broke out on his forehead. The handkerchief came out again as he looked around the room. He had to phone first and get a couple of his helpers around to get rid of the body. Wouldn't look good if he were found near it. Nasty international incident would ensue.

His eyes lit on the whisky bottle. There was time, before phoning, for a restorative to calm him. That last remark of Fraser's was a piece of damn cheek. Kill him, indeed. He'd stopped the little Greek from stealing the gun-case. And more he'd been careful not to ask Fraser why he was carrying a sniper's rifle. Damn fine mechanism too.

He poured himself a large whisky. His hand shook as he brought it to his lips.

This time it was no old farmhouse but a completely dere-lict villa. Parts of the roof in the entrance hall had fallen in and the room beyond in which they had settled was empty, thick with dust, and seemed to Jill to smell of dampness and decay.

There was no electricity working and Gudrun had brought a candle in a bottle from the car. Elisa had car-ried in two sleeping bags, one of which she had reserved for herself and the other she had handed to Gudrun. Jill was provided with two dusty blankets which were, fortun-ately, thick and provided some warmth in the night. Elisa had, on depositing the sleeping bags, gone outside leaving Gudrun alone with Jill.

Gudrun settled on top of her sleeping bag and produced from a haversack a packet of sandwiches. She looked thoughtfully over at Jill who was sitting on the blankets. Then, taking one sandwich from the packet she offered it to Jill. Jill shook her head in refusal.

'Hunger strike?' Gudrun said hoarsely. 'You won't be with us long enough. And even if you were . . .' She shrugged callously.

'I'm just not hungry.'

'So!' Gudrun started to eat the sandwich herself.

It was Jill's turn now to stare thoughtfully at the German girl. What went to make up a female terrorist, she asked herself. What kind of woman was this young, big-boned Teuton with the untidy hair and some degree of humanity compared to her companion?

'Why?' Jill asked.

Gudrun misunderstood the question. 'I thought Rolf told you. So as your husband can carry out a task for us.'

'No, not that. Why do you live like this?'

As she spoke Elisa re-entered, her hard little face moving from one to the other. Gudrun's only reply to Jill's question was a shrug.

'Don't ask her,' Elisa cut in. 'She's only here because of Jurgen.'

Gudrun objected. 'That is not so!'

Elisa turned to Jill. 'You should ask me.'

'All right,' Jill replied evenly. 'I'm asking you.'

'Someone has to fight against the filth of your society.' The girl's eyes shone in the candlelight as she responded vehemently. 'It has to be destroyed root and branch by political action!'

'Your idea of political action is with guns?'

'The only true political action is violence!'

'And afterwards,' Jill pressed on. 'When you've destroyed our society, what do you put in its place?'

Elisa hesitated. There were answers but she had never sorted them out, never arranged them logically in her mind. The need for an answer was however avoided by the sound of a car drawing up outside the derelict building.

Elisa became alert. 'They're here.' She glanced at Gudrun. 'Stay with her.'

She went, leaving Gudrun and Jill staring at each other.

'You must not believe what she says about me,' Gudrun said, feeling some need to explain. 'It is true I love Jurgen. There is nothing wrong with that. It is natural. But one has to fight the violence and corruption of your system.'

'By killing people?'

'In a war there have to be casualties.'

91

Outside the villa Elisa greeted Rolf and Jurgen.

'You're late.'

'So we're here now,' replied Rolf with a trace of irritation. He was tired, still sweating despite the coolness of the night, and he envied the unconcern of Jurgen, who seemed to have little imagination. It was something he had noticed over the past months. The large young man rarely showed emotion or stress. Probably he was the same when alone with Gudrun; sex was a mechanical operation that stilled a pressing need.

He stared at the edifice of the crumbling villa.

'Not exactly a comfortable billet. We'll stay the night and move on in the morning.'

'Why the need to keep moving?' Elisa asked, watching Jurgen locking the car doors carefully. 'Why can't we just stay in the one place?'

'Better to keep moving. Then if Fraser is on to us for a time, we will always be sure of losing him. However our next stop we will remain until the job is done.'

A thought struck Elisa. 'Where is Carl-Jan?'

Jurgen came up behind Rolf and it was he who replied. 'We waited at the rendezvous. He didn't turn up.'

'Fraser must have taken him,' the girl replied angrily.

Rolf looked irritable. 'Then Fraser would have released him rather than risk us harming his wife.'

'But if he has not done so . . .'

'Fraser wasn't the only one following Carl,' Jurgen explained. 'There was another car, a black car . . '

Elisa looked from Jurgen to Rolf. 'Who?'

'How do I know!' Rolf growled, irritability now in the open. 'I am tired and I don't care. Whoever they were, Carl has rid us of them!'

He went into the villa. Jurgen moved his shoulders in a slight shrug and followed him. Elisa stared after them. Questions were forming in her mind, too many questions. There was Fraser, of course, but who else. Fraser would not dare to bring in his old friends in British Intelligence. To do so he would be risking the safety of his wife. But who else was involved?

Mark Fraser paid his own bill at the reception desk of the Hotel Mijas. He had decided that to walk out carrying two cases and leaving the bill to Bartlett might cause comment. He muttered an excuse to the rather bemused clerk at the desk about having received an urgent message; and, collecting a receipt for payment, walked out to the car park.

The thought of the body of Costas in the room with Bartlett had, however, made him careless. He did not notice the tall man in the dark suit who sat in the hotel foyer ostensibly reading a Spanish edition of *Time* magazine and actually observing him leave.

Once Fraser was out of the main door the tall man strolled over to a house telephone, *Time* magazine neatly tucked under his arm, and dialled a room number.

'Peter here,' he said in Russian when the phone was lifted at the other end of the line. 'Fraser has just gone. Carrying two suitcases. And there is no sign of our man.'

At the other end of the line Lieutenant-Colonel Grigor hesitated only for a fraction of a second. 'Stay with Fraser and do not lose him. We will take over here. Phone us when the bird has settled in a new nest.'

The Russian called Peter hung up and walked quickly out of the hotel. He reached the edge of the car park and stopped, waiting. He could just make out the figure of Fraser placing the two cases in the boot of the grey coupé. Slamming the boot shut Fraser swung around the side of the car and got into the driving seat. The Russian still waited, a coiled spring, ready to move to his own car once the grey coupé was past him and out on the road.

Fraser, still oblivious of his observer, turned the car onto the main road and headed south. He told himself that he was at least on the move and he needed that movement. It gave him the feeling, possibly the delusion, that he was coming closer to Jill. But, as he drove, he began to realise that fatigue was taking over.

Cars drove past him going in the opposite direction, headlights flashing across his vision. He rubbed his eyes with his left hand and peered up at his rear-view mirror.

There were two or three pairs of headlights on the road behind him. Yawning, he thought, if he was being followed, there was little he could do. He was too tired to consider evasive tactics.

And then he found, if he relaxed his grip on the steering wheel of the coupé, his hands were starting to tremble. He gripped the wheel determinedly. He had learned long ago to cope with fatigue but now his eyes were starting to blur. Despite the strong beam of his own headlights, he found he was beginning to steer erratically. He determined to find a place for the night, a small roadside hotel, as inconspicuous as possible, where he could snatch a few hours' sleep.

Jill stirred under the blankets and peered over them across the darkened room. The candle in the bottle had long since died and the only light coming into the room was from a pallid moon's rays struggling through clouds to cast distorted shadows through the cracked windows of the villa.

The light struck the opposite corner of the room and Jill could make out the shapes of Jurgen and Gudrun, lying together, spoonlike. Jurgen was snoring gently and Gudrun was breathing easily in sleep.

Dimly, a few feet from her, Jill could see Elisa, back against the wall of the room, pistol hanging loosely in her hand. She was supposed to be on guard but she too was asleep

There was a chance now, Jill told herself, one slim opportunity. She eased herself from under the blankets and stood, swaying unsteadily, fighting for a second not to lose her balance. Finally, steadying herself, she took a step towards the door of the room.

A floorboard creaked underfoot.

She froze. Gudrun stirred in her sleep, nestling closer to Jurgen.

Reaching down Jill took off her shoes and took another step towards the door. There was no sound this time. Reaching the door she pushed gently and it swung open with a slight thud. Again she stood motionless but there was no sound other than the low snoring from Jurgen.

Jill sidled into the hallway. The front door of the villa loomed ahead, a heavy wooden door shut and, though not locked, a formidable obstacle. To open it would create a noise which would undoubtedly awake her captors.

Jill stared into the darkness at the rear of the hallway. A lighter oblong indicated another door and this one was open. She moved quickly and silently to it.

Now she was in what had been the kitchen of the villa. The floor was stone and cold on her stocking feet. But this time there was a rear door, broken, hanging on one remaining hinge. And beyond the door she could make out in the light of the moon a strip of grass.

The cool night air brought with it a feeling of exhilaration, and the grass felt soft underfoot. But, as she stepped forward, the moon disappeared behind a patch of cloud and in front of her a heavy blackness fell.

She moved forward tentatively, at once afraid of the dark void before her.

Then she was off the grass and sharp pebbles were biting into the soles of her feet, tearing her stockings. And the ground suddenly dipped in front of her and she was falling, sliding down a stony, pebble-strewn slope. Her arms went out, hands clutching air, trying to find something to stop the terrifying slide into darkness.

Then the incline ended, the ground became even, and her body came to a halt, pebbles and loose earth sliding down beside her. Gingerly she tried to rise and, stumbled. Then, regaining her balance, she stood erect, gulping air, her body trembling.

The light flashed directly into her eyes.

The shock went through her body with what seemed physical pain. She swayed backwards, again almost losing her balance.

'Good evening, Frau Fraser!' said Rolf from behind the flashlight. 'Now that you have had your walk, shall we go back into the villa?'

She was unable to reply. She stood staring above the

light trying to make out the figure behind it. As if out of politeness Rolf averted the light to what she had thought would be solid ground. But instead she found they were both standing on a narrow ledge. Beyond the ledge was a sheer drop of some thirty or forty feet and she could dimly make out the shapes of boulders below.

'You are very lucky I was here, Frau Fraser,' Rolf went on. 'If I had not stopped you, one more step . . .'

He indicated the drop in front of her with an expressive flicker of the torch.

'We can't afford to lose you, you see. Now please come . . .'

Reaching out he grasped her arm.

'I can manage,' she replied with what little dignity she could muster.

They scrambled up the slope and reached the door of the kitchen. Only then did Jill realise that in her fall she had let go of her shoes.

'Please not to move,' Rolf said and retrieved them.

'You see, I knew you would try to escape,' he continued as she struggled to put the shoes on again. 'You are a resourceful woman but I knew. Just as I knew the others would fall asleep. You will know of course that they are amateurs.'

'And you? What are you?'

He smiled and, the torch in his right hand, ran his fingers through his thinning hair. The moon reappeared from behind the cloud and the young old face was confident, assured of its own ability.

'Let's say I am professional enough to consider all eventualities. You will not try to escape again. Because I would have to kill you and I do not want that.'

They stared at each other in the moonlight in silence for a moment. And Jill knew he was deadly serious.

Then he broke the silence.

'Again I tell you to go in. And this time, try to sleep.

She went into the villa.

SEVEN

Bartlett, whose first name was Victor, so christened by a patriotic father after the old queen, came out of the bathroom in his shirt sleeves, carrying a bloodstained towel. He had succeeded in removing all bloodstains from the walls and floor of the bathroom after moving Costas' body into the bath. Sweating profusely with his efforts, he threw the towel back into the bathroom, and with some sense of relief, lit a cigarette. His eyes found Fraser's whisky bottle and he poured himself a liberal measure into a glass. Then, with a sigh, he sat on the edge of the bed and took a gulp of the amber liquid.

He was still smarting inwardly over the manner of his treatment by Fraser. The man seemed to think he was incompetent. And more, his attitude to Bartlett's shooting Costas was stupid and unpatriotic. The Greek obviously worked for the opposition, whoever that opposition might be. Yet Fraser had shown no gratitude, no appreciation. No wonder the man had left the department. Probably was forced out. That was the trouble with the post-war period, especially during the Labour governments. They let all the wrong types in. Fraser was obviously one of the wrong type.

Bartlett looked at his watch.

Where was his hurriedly organised rubbish squad? When Fraser had left he had phoned two of his Spanish contacts, two rather unreliable characters, Bartlett had to admit, but not unreliable when a specific sum of money was involved. In this case he had mentioned a sufficiently large sum to ensure that they would come and they would bring with them a large cabin trunk. That way Costas would disappear from the Hotel Mijas without a trace. The trunk, heavily weighed down, would disappear into the sea some miles out.

Bartlett smiled and wiped the perspiration off his moustache with the back of his left hand. He would show Fraser, indeed he would show London, that though there had been no activity, no violence in his area of operations for some years, when it did occur Victor Bartlett could cope efficiently.

Another look at his watch. Damn it, they were taking their time. It was over an hour since he'd phoned and although the initial response from the Spaniards had been lethargic to say the least, the money he had mentioned had instantly dispelled the lethargy. Of course they were probably having trouble getting hold of a trunk of sufficient size to hold the body. Still, they shouldn't be this long.

He lifted the telephone and asked for a number. He was speedily connected and a woman's voice answered the phone in Spanish. He grimaced, replying in English. He knew Julio's wife spoke fluent English and he bloody well wasn't going to speak Spanish.

'This is Bartlett,' he growled. 'I phoned Julio an hour ago, and I'm still waiting.'

The woman at the other end of the line replied lazily that they were long gone.

'Then they should have been here,' Bartlett insisted. 'Exactly what time did they leave?'

He knew these foreigners. You said hurry and they took their own time. Everything was Mediterranean *mañana* with them.

Before she could reply, there was a discreet tap on the bedroom door.

'Oh, never mind, they've arrived,' said Bartlett, slamming the phone down.

He took a quick gulp of whisky which seemed almost to burn the back of his throat; and then he crossed the room and opened the door.

The gun that was thrust into his sagging belly seemed enormous, not unlike an American Magnum 45. But the man holding it was no American. He pushed Bartlett into the room with the sheer force with which he thrust the gun forward. And behind him, a smaller, neater man in a lightweight suit stepped into the room and shut the door.

The second man turned and glanced into the bathroom, checking to see if there were any other occupants in the room. What he saw in the bath caused his face to tense. He took two steps into the bathroom, stared into the bath at the body of Costas for a second, then turned and came back into the bedroom.

Bartlett, pressed against the wall, the Magnum still at his stomach, was perspiring again. If only Julio would arrive and take these two strangers by surprise. And yet he knew deep down that Julio and his partner would not arrive now, that they had already been intercepted.

The man in the lightweight suit, who was Lieutenant-Colonel Grigor of the KGB, looked back into the bathroom again and a fleeting trace of regret crossed his face.

'Andreas Costas,' he said quietly staring at Bartlett. 'He carried out small assignments for us, Mr Bartlett. But he was not important enough to deserve this.'

The gun eased away from Bartlett's stomach but its direction of fire did not change. It did however permit Bartlett to take a deep breath.

'Who the devil are you?' he forced himself to make the demand.

Grigor ignored the question. 'Did you kill him?'

Bartlett did not reply but looked from one man to the other, as if seeking a way of escape.

'You will tell me eventually,' Grigor persevered.

The man holding the gun, whose name was Alexi, prodded the weapon in the direction of Bartlett's stomach again.

Bartlett winced. 'Fraser! Fraser killed him!'

Grigor moved silently to the whisky bottle. He topped up Bartlett's tumbler and handed it to him. Bartlett's hand trembled as he took the glass.

'You are telling me a lie, Mr Bartlett,' Grigor broke his silence.

'No!' Bartlett insisted quickly, nearly spilling the drink.

'Costas came here when Fraser was away,' Grigor insisted. 'To bring me a gun-case.'

He looked at Alexi who moved away with a cat-like motion and opened the wardrobe. A glance was enough to see that it was empty. Alexi stood on a chair and looked at the top of the wardrobe. He jumped from the chair with a brief shrug in Grigor's direction and then he expertly searched the room and the bathroom. Bartlett, sipping whisky with his still shaking hand on the glass, watched the search. Grigor watched Bartlett. Finally Alexi shrugged again.

'No gun-case,' said Grigor. 'Costas, you see, should have been in and out of this room in two minutes. But he wasn't. Because he was shot. And during the time he must have been shot Mr Fraser was not here. He was under our observation. So you lied. You shot him.'

Bartlett tried to think quickly. But his mind was filled with anticipated terrors. Still he had to say something.

'The man attacked me!'

Grigor gave a small cold smile. 'Such a little man. Still it is some kind of reason. And now Mr Fraser has gone, presumably with the gun-case. Leaving you to tidy up?'

Bartlett nodded.

'Ah, well,' Grigor went on. 'Now you will come with us. Out of harm's way, eh?'

Alexi picked up Bartlett's jacket from the bed and threw it over to him. Bartlett caught it neatly with his free hand and swallowed the rest of the whisky. Putting the glass down he donned his jacket, surprised at its weight. And then he remembered. There was the revolver in the pocket. And the idiot with the Magnum hadn't even felt it. There was hope there; but he must be careful. He must choose his moment.

Alexi slipped the Magnum into his pocket and motioned Bartlett towards the door.

'Don't worry, Mr Bartlett,' Grigor said, still smiling. 'Our people will tidy up Mr Costas. Now, if you please . . .'

They came out of the hotel and walked along the side of the swimming pool. Bartlett was ahead of the two men when

100

he became aware of Grigor, directly behind him, obscuring the view of the one with the gun. Now there was a chance. He reached into his jacket, twisting around as he did so and presenting the barrel of the revolver at Grigor's chest.

'Now I think the situation has changed,' he said, unable to conceal the exultation in his voice. 'You'll please tell me who you are.'

Grigor stopped but his bland expression did not change.

'Lieutenant-Colonel Grigor, Mr Bartlett.'

Bartlett smiled. 'Thought so from the accents. KGB, eh?'

The second Russian drew level with Grigor and stopped. His hands were deep in his coat pockets and Bartlett couldn't help thinking the Russians were crazy wearing coats in this climate, even light raincoats.

'Careless of you not to search my jacket for the old revolver,' Bartlett was enjoying himself. 'After all I needed something to kill your little messenger boy with. Costas, was that his name?'

'Perhaps we omitted to search deliberately,' Grigor replied icily and took one step to the left.

Bartlett's reactions were slow and apart from stepping to one side Grigor made no other movement. But while Bartlett's eyes were distracted by this movement the other Russian's arm moved almost imperceptibly and the right-hand pocket of his coat bulged suddenly.

There were two shots, dulled by some device on the muzzle of the Magnum and further muffled by the coat itself. The first shot hit Bartlett in the neck causing his head to jerk back and at the same time cutting through his vocal cords. The second shot hit him in the upper chest throwing him backwards into the pool. A cascade of water rose in the air and fell, splashing the turn-ups of Grigor's trousers. Bartlett disappeared under the water to rise a moment later, floating face downwards. Then slowly, as the water around the body turned crimson, he sank again. But he was no longer aware of this. He had been dead before he struck the water.

Grigor walked to the edge of the pool and stared down.

'He gave us the excuse to kill him,' Grigor sighed. 'Yet now I suppose it evens things up.'

He glanced at his tall companion who was examining with some distaste the hole in his coat.

'But tell me, Alexi,' Grigor asked. 'Why does a British Agent aid a man who is being forced to work for terrorists?'

The question went unanswered. Alexi never made guesses. Indeed he never made decisions. He merely took orders.

'Leave him there,' Grigor went on. 'It will give his London people something to think about when he is found.'

They walked quickly away from the pool.

It was six o'clock in the morning when Alexi and Grigor drove up to the small hotel just off the main road. The Russian called Peter was waiting for them beside his own car. As they climbed out of their car he came over.

'We received your phone message,' said Grigor. 'He's here?'

'Ground floor. Room 21.'

Grigor considered for a moment. He himself was tired and he knew Fraser must have been exhausted. Even now he could only have had a few hours' sleep. It would be a good time to face him.

'We'll say good morning to him,' he said and looked around. 'His car?'

Peter pointed to the grey coupé. 'There!'

One always had to be ready for all emergencies, Grigor thought. Fraser could be watching them even now; he could be preparing to leave via the patio window the moment they entered the hotel.

'Do a little work on the car,' he ordered Peter. 'You have something you can do in case he eludes us . . .'

Peter nodded. As Alexi followed Grigor into the hotel he crossed to his own car and took from it a small suitcase. This was his working kit in case of emergencies. He walked slowly towards the grey coupé. From somewhere nearby came the insistent sound of cicadas intruding on the dawning light of day.

Mark Fraser was not asleep. He had managed a few hours stretched out on the bed, hovering on the verge of sleep. But the thought of Jill had brought the feeling of desperation again, of helplessness; and his mind was alive considering the possibilities of action should opportunities present themselves. At five minutes to six he had risen, stripped off his shirt and trousers, and showered. He had followed this by shaving and was in the process of donning a clean shirt when the door of his room was kicked open by Alexi.

The tall Russian entered, gun in hand, followed by Grigor.

Fraser finished buttoning his shirt, succeeded in showing no reaction to their breaking in. It was an old trick to control obvious reactions. Just occasionally, when dealing with non-professionals, it threw them off guard.

'Very noisy,' he said calmly. 'You'll disturb the other guests.'

But the Russians were professionals too and his lack of reaction had no effect on them.

'I'm not feeling humorous this morning, Fraser,' Grigor said with an assumed scowl. 'I didn't sleep last night. And my friend Alexi here was forced to kill another man. One of your people.'

'Bartlett?' There was little regret in Fraser's voice. He hadn't forgiven Bartlett for killing the little Greek.

As if echoing his thoughts Grigor went on. 'He did kill our friend Costas. And then he attempted to shoot us . . . he would have done so too.'

Grigor sat on the one chair in the bedroom and lit a long Russian cigarette.

'We don't like killing people in another country,' he continued, his eyes moving around the room to settle finally on the gun-case which was lying on the dressing table.

'It's never stopped your people in the past,' Fraser replied.

With a sigh Grigor inhaled and then blew the smoke out, pursing his lips as he did so.

'Have you never heard of *détente,* Fraser?' he asked, eyes still on the gun-case. 'Anyway it's an old story we both know. You kill one of ours, we kill one of yours. Where does it end? Who will be left to do the work and collect the information if we get again into such a spiral?'

'You tell me.'

'It is not good. No, not good. Now yesterday I told you to get on a plane and go home.'

'I'm afraid of flying. I need my wife with me to hold my hand.'

Grigor gave a relaxed shrug. 'Smoke a cigarette, sit on the bed and we will talk.'

Fraser reached over for his jacket but Alexi moved faster. The tall Russian grabbed the jacket and expertly rifled through the pockets. With a mild expression of triumph he produced Fraser's revolver, showed it to Grigor and then put it in his own pocket.

'Alexi is a very careful man,' Grigor explained.

Fraser smiled slightly, took the jacket and drew out a packet of Gitanes and a lighter. Lighting the cigarette he sat on the edge of the bed.

'That is better,' Grigor nodded. 'Now, you see, I do not want any more killing.'

'How do you feel about killing terrorists then?' Fraser asked.

Grigor considered for a second. 'That is different. One destroys sick animals. But, Fraser, I am already worried about how your London people will react when they learn about Bartlett.'

Fraser had to admit to himself that worried him too. Mackeson and the Department could not ignore the death of their man in Spain. And they would react in some fashion. That reaction could affect his search for Jill. It could more than affect it, it could cause dangerous problems, dangerous particularly for Jill. He wondered vaguely how and where Bartlett had died.

Grigor broke into his thoughts. 'I am concerned, Fraser, as to why Bartlett, a British Agent, seemed to be helping you.'

104

'For old times' sake?' Fraser replied unconvincingly.

'Did he know you *have* to be working for these terrorists?'

'You have a point He didn't know. I didn't tell him anyway.'

Grigor looked pensive for a moment. 'And I suppose you are wondering why we are trying to stop you doing what this Red Action Brigade wants you to do?'

The thought had crossed Fraser's mind, he admitted.

'Nothing seems to be what it should be, is that not so?' Grigor asked quizzically.

'The time is out of joint,' Fraser replied.

Grigor contemplated the nails on his right hand. 'And yet you will fire the gun these people put in your hands?'

Fraser was suddenly alert. 'You know what they want me to do then?'

There was no answer. The Russian gave a slight shrug.

Fraser formed the question he wanted to ask. 'Why should you protect a man whose politics make the Czar of Russia look like a liberal?'

'Again, perhaps, *détente*,' Grigor replied, looking up at Fraser. 'We could have killed you yesterday, you know. But we are really not interested in you. We want the Red Action people. And we will take them soon. But now you must quietly go home.'

'And my wife?'

'I have told you . . .'

'Not good enough!'

Grigor shifted uneasily in his seat. 'What else can I say? There are no guarantees.'

He suddenly leaned forward and tapped the gun-case heavily. 'But I tell you, Fraser, you will not need this any more.'

Fraser stood staring down at him for a moment. Grigor's determination to stop him would, he was sure, not be weakened by argument. Nor would the condition of Jill's being held prisoner sway the Russian. Therefore he knew he had to go on, but without the formidable opposition of the Russians.

He shrugged, allowing his shoulders to sag, and stood up, as if in acceptance.

'May I get my suitcase?'

'Proceed, Mr Fraser. I am glad you are seeing sense.'

Throwing open the wardrobe, Fraser reached up. The suitcase was on a shelf at the top of the wardrobe. He moved it aside, stretching towards the back of the shelf. He felt the metallic grip of the rifle. Of course they had not taken into account that he might assemble the rifle, a first attempt to familiarise himself with a weapon he hoped he would not have to use. And it was there, where he had placed it for the night, behind the suitcase. Had Grigor lifted the gun-case he would have known it was empty and been alerted. But he had not done so and Fraser was about to take advantage of the fact.

Behind him, Grigor frowned and stiffened, suddenly aware that all was not as it appeared; perhaps sensing what might ensue.

Before he could do anything Fraser had pushed the suitcase from the shelf. It fell heavily thudding onto the polished wooden floor. Alexi, gun in hand, followed the case to the floor with his eyes. This gave Fraser his opportunity.

Gripping the assembled rifle by its stock he pulled it from the shelf and twisting around he raised it. With animal grace he brought the muzzle of the rifle down as hard as he could on Alexi's gun hand. There was a sharp crack of bone and a short scream from the Russian. His large automatic fell onto the bed as he slumped to the floor, right hand hanging uselessly, and left hand waving in an unsteady movement as if to avert a further blow.

Grigor leaped to his feet but Fraser had spun the rifle around in his hands so that it pointed straight at Grigor's face.

'I wouldn't try and move, Colonel. Although this rifle is more effective at long range it still does the job it was designed for at a few feet!'

Grigor froze, his eyes angry. Fraser leaned forward and took the Magnum from the bed.

'I couldn't resist assembling the rifle,' he explained. 'I have to become familiar with the weapon I may have to use.'

With the Magnum now pointed at Grigor and the rifle cradled in his arm, Fraser leant down and retrieved his own revolver from Alexi's pocket. The tall Russian half sat on the floor leaning on the side of the bed. He was trying gently with his left hand to hold his sagging right arm. At the same time, his face contorted with pain, he was making low moaning sounds. Fraser pushed past him, still watching Grigor.

'You would go through with killing Scherer?' Grigor asked, as if not believing in the possibility of such an act.

'Colonel, I would even kill you if I was sure it would save my wife.'

The Russian shook his head dejectedly.

'At least you admit you know what they want me to do.' Fraser went on.

'Yes.'

'Then why didn't you kill me yesterday?'

'Because they would only find another assassin.'

Fraser decided the Russian was speaking the truth. Yet he still could not understand why the KGB should wish to protect a right-wing anti-communist. But now there was no time for further questions. He had to keep moving, keep active; and try and delay if not rid himself of the Russian interference.

He moved closer to Grigor. 'Whether I assassinate anyone or not, there is one thing I have to do just now. I'm sorry.'

With a kind of delicate precision achieved only by training Fraser leaned forward and brought the muzzle of the Magnum down at a precise spot on the back of the Russian's neck. Grigor slumped forward unconscious.

Enough to keep him quiet for some time, but not enough to kill him, Fraser thought. Then nimbly he dismantled the rifle and placed its components back in the gun-case. Shutting the case he pocketed the two guns. The moans from Alexi had ceased and a quick glance told him the tall

Russian had lapsed into unconsciousness.

The sun was coming up as he reached the car park. The open space appeared deserted as he made his way quickly to the grey coupé. And it was only after he had driven on to the road and was moving away from the hotel that the third Russian, Peter, appeared from the shadow of the hotel patio and stared after him with a small enigmatic smile.

EIGHT

The girl was in her late teens, slim, with a narrow waist line that was the envy of older women. Her fair skin had, under the Spanish sun, at first reddened and then turned to a deep brown, darkened even more by freckles. She was English and on holiday, staying at the Hotel Mijas, and she had been at a party in the village. It had been a long party and was still going on as she left with her Spanish escort, a young man whose anticipation of further favours outran the reality which he was to meet at the gates of the hotel.

She permitted one fleeting kiss, a brief brushing of lips against each other and, when he had reached out with assumed charm to embrace her, she had slipped away from his questing arms and ran towards the hotel. The trouble was they were so charming, she thought, the Spanish boys, but they expected far too much. Or perhaps their expectations were fulfilled by other girls; but they would not be by her.

She reached the swimming pool as the dawn light filtered through the trees and she was aware that she was warm despite the thinness of her dress. She looked around the pool and up at the balconies of the hotel building. Nothing stirred. She giggled to herself, a giggle induced by several glasses of dark Spanish wine. Then with one swift movement she pulled the dress over her head and let it fall to the ground. Apart from a small pair of panties, she stood naked at the edge of the pool anticipating the coolness of the water in front of her.

The dive was almost flawless, the result of much practice at municipal baths in a far-off English town. She cut through the water cleanly enjoying the sensuous chill against her skin. She surfaced quickly and struck out towards the steps at one side of the deep end. As she approached them she swam underwater for the last few yards and surfaced again at the edge of the pool.

She found herself staring at dead eyes, water lapping ashen cheekbones. And she became aware that the colour of the water had changed, was stained a darker hue. And then she heard a scream and knew it was coming from her own throat.

Within twenty minutes the Spanish police had arrived at the hotel and an hour and a half later a weary-eyed radio operator in a small room in Whitehall was decoding a message from the British consul in Malaga.

In this way the Department learned of the death of Victor Bartlett.

The air was cool on Fraser's face as he drove towards Fuengirola, with both side windows rolled down. Despite the few hours of shallow sleep he felt refreshed and his mind was alert. Although he had seen no one in the car park he was only too aware of Grigor's professionalism. The man would cover any possible avenue of escape and Fraser was sure that he would be followed. He glanced in his rear-view mirror. Nothing. But then if Grigor knew from Bartlett that his destination was Fuengirola there would be no need to keep him in sight; at least not until he reached the town itself.

There was a chance now to confuse the Russians, give them a run for their money. In a few minutes he would be in Fuengirola and he would have to find the Hotel Hispano. But it was early and if he took off into the Sierras and came into the town from the south he might just create a degree of confusion.

He swung the grey coupé off the main road and drove along what was little more than a track. The car bounced over hidden rocks and he was forced to drop his speed down to twenty miles an hour. But after a few miles the road surface improved and the lower slopes of the Sierras rose before him. On each side of the road stretched rolling spaces, sandy shrubland, spotted with rocks. The road suddenly dipped and he found himself driving down a fairly steep incline into a small valley.

It was then that it happened.

There was a dull, muffled explosion from under the bonnet of the coupé, followed by an agonising sound of metal rattling against metal. But Fraser had no time to be concerned about sounds The bonnet of the coupé rose up in front of the windscreen, blown by the force of the explosion of a small charge of *plastique* from below. And he found himself slamming his foot down on brake and clutch in an attempt at an emergency stop.

Nothing happened. The charge had obviously severed the brake cables and demolished to some degree both engine and gearbox. A cloud of smoke rose and was blown around the edges of the bonnet. Fraser, however, barely noticed this as he struggled with the steering while leaning out of his side window, trying to see the road in front.

He was only partially successful. He could keep the car from the left-hand ditch and try and centre it on the narrow road. But he could feel the wheels on the right lurch over rock, dip into the ditch; and he could feel the side of the car scrape against stone, scoring the rocks of a low wall.

The speed of the car increased although the engine had cut out and Fraser knew he was freewheeling fast down the incline.

Panic gripped him.

Sweat poured from his brow, and his hands, twisting the wheel more by guess and by God than by anything he could see of the road ahead, were soaking and sliding over the plastic curve of the wheel. He knew at once the precautions that Grigor and his men had taken to prevent him getting any distance away from them. The small lump of *plastique* explosive flattened onto a vulnerable part of the engine would be triggered off by a tiny detonator embedded in its surface. It would either have a tiny timing device or, as the engine heated, the detonator would trigger

111

off the explosive. There wouldn't be enough to kill him by the force of the explosion but the sudden destruction of the engine could cause him to crash the car, perhaps even ignite the petrol. It had been a comparatively new trick when he had left the department but one with more subtlety than simply blowing up the entire car and its occupant.

But he was now only intent on trying frantically to slow the car down and at the same time to control the steering wheel. He thanked God the wheel still responded; the steering mechanism had not been sheered away.

As he struggled for control, the car bucking wildly as it struck rocks on the right-hand verge of the road, he could feel the taste of fear in his mouth. He knew that one unseen bend on the slope would finish the car and with it he would be lucky to escape without serious injury. The speedometer had moved quickly up as the downhill gradient had become steeper, and it was now passing fifty miles an hour. He thought, if only they had used a little more explosive the bonnet might have been blown completely off the car and at least he would have had the road in vision.

Then he felt the slope lessen and a small sense of relief, instantly lost as he became aware that the road was curving. There was a crashing, cracking sound from in front of the bonnet and he realised the car had smashed through a wicker fence and was ploughing into a field. A small explosion denoted the bursting of a tyre as a sharp rock ripped into the rubber.

The vehicle was lurching now from side to side and, at the same time, was finally slowing down. He could only pray that there was no gorge or cliff in the field that the car might plunge down. This time his luck held. The field, uncultivated, ended with a gentle hill rising at the far end.

The grey coupé finally rolled to a stop a few yards up the side of this hill.

Fraser sat for a moment, waiting. And then the shaking started in the hands and then in the spine and he was at once cold with the iciness of delayed terror. He lay back in the seat, savouring the stillness, the absence of motion. He squirmed imperceptibly as he felt the dampness of his shirt against his back.

Then his nostrils were assailed by a pungent smell. Petrol! He opened the door and threw himself outwards, hitting the sand and stubble of the field and rolling over until he was some yards from the car. He stood up shakily and stared at the weird outline of what had been a sleek grey coupé. The bonnet was up against the windscreen and was twisted and scored by the explosion. The car sagged to one side, the remains of one of the front tyres shredded so completely that the car rested on the metal wheel.

Despite the smell of petrol there was no fire and he approached the wreck carefully, staring first at what was left of the engine. The metal was bent and cracked and wires, broken, reared up like small snakes.

Quickly he retrieved his keys from the ignition and opening the boot he removed his suitcase and the gun-case.

'Señor? Accidente?'

The voice was indistinct and he realised that his ears were still ringing from the explosion. He spun round to find himself facing a small man in denims, a ragged shirt and a large broad-rimmed hat. The man was staring with an expression of infinite sorrow at the remains of the car. He muttered something in Spanish which Fraser could not make out, and then looked away from the car into Fraser's eyes.

'American?' he asked.

'British,' Fraser replied. 'Inglese.'

'Ah. I speak English good,' he glanced back at the car. 'Once, señor, automobile was the servant of man. Now man is the servant of automobile.'

Fraser thought, I'm not in the mood for homespun wisdom. I have to get out of here. 'Can you tell me where I can hire another car?' he inquired in a matter-of-fact-tone, as if accustomed to automobiles exploding under him.

Some considerable distance away, in the hills beyond

113

Granada, Jill sat in the back of a car, Gudrun at her side. In the front, Jurgen was driving and beside him, smoking the inevitable Gitane, sat Rolf, eyes on the road ahead.

'Don't be alarmed, Frau Fraser,' he said, breaking a long silence. 'We are merely moving to our final sanctuary.'

He turned, giving her what passed as a smile.

'It will be much more comfortable, this new destination. And you will not be moved until you are returned to your husband.'

Jill said nothing. There was nothing to say. She was still in their hands, at their disposal, whatever method they might choose in which to dispose of her. She tried to avoid the thought that after it was all over, even if Mark did what they wanted him to do, they might find it too risky to actually release her. The thought kept creeping back into her mind. She half turned to stare out of the window; anything to distract her from depressive thought.

They were climbing through shrubland and rocky outcrop, the foothills of the sierras. Below were stretches of rolling land, some segments cultivated where any possibility of growth could be exploited. Ahead grey, brown hills filled the front windscreen.

Rolf spoke again. 'You will notice Elisa has left us for the time being.'

Before they had departed from the ruined villa, Elisa had driven off on her own in the other car after a muttered discussion with Rolf.

'To keep you in the picture, she has gone to deliver some photographs to your husband,' Rolf explained expansively. 'Of course she will not make direct contact but will watch him collect the material. When you see her again she will reassure you that Herr Fraser is fit and well.'

Jurgen shot him a look from behind the steering wheel. 'Why bother telling her?' he demanded in German.

Rolf ignored him, continuing to address himself to Jill 'You will excuse the callousness of my companions. They lack charity. I, on the other hand, believe it is sensible to give assurances to those involved innocently in our affairs.'

Jill returned his gaze with an icy glare. 'If I'm supposed

to thank you for your consideration, you can forget it.'

'I appreciate your feelings. I only wish you could have some understanding of our aims. Perhaps later, before we release you, we will have an opportunity to talk. I will then explain the need to use your husband as a weapon in the struggle to rid society of a man like Scherer.'

Scherer? It was the first time he had given the victim a name. She had heard it before but her memory was vague. A German, she remembered, some kind of big name, but not a politician. She said nothing but filed the name in the back of her mind.

'You tell her too much.' This time it was Gudrun who came in, supporting Jurgen. 'Why do you need to tell her anything?'

Rolf turned to Gudrun. His smile showed the row of gleaming teeth.

'This is my operation! I am in charge. I say what I want to say and I do not need you to echo Jurgen here.'

The girl's only response was a petulant glare. Jill wondered, were tensions beginning to show? The strain of keeping her from escaping combined with the planning of the operation must be taking its toll. These people, despite being of the same generation, were an ill-assorted group, Gudrun and Jurgen might be together before and after such operations but Rolf was a loner; and more than that he had a quicker intelligence than the others, and could succeed on his own.

Jill was relieved too that Elisa was not with them, for the time being anyway. The small dark girl frightened her much more than the others. There was not simply a callousness there but something else; a potential for enjoying, delighting in violence, even in killing. Jill knew she might of course be over-imaginative but there seemed in Elisa to be the signs of incipient paranoia.

The car bumped and rattled as it climbed higher and higher, and the air seemed to grow distinctly cooler.

That morning, back in England, Frank Lloyd arrived late

115

at the Whitehall offices of the Ministry of Agriculture and Fisheries. He passed through the main hall at each side of which were the actual offices of the designated ministry. He showed his pass for a second time and was permitted to enter the special elevator which took him to the upper floors which housed the Department.

Lloyd's lateness had been caused by a delay on the southern region line from Weybridge due to small boys having placed a large wooden sleeper across the line. Fortunately it had been spotted in time otherwise Lloyd might have been the victim of a rather nasty train crash. However the delay had allowed him time to finish the *Daily Telegraph* crossword (he felt he was not yet ready to graduate to *The Times* crossword) and to meditate on the flurry of excitement had he actually been killed or injured in a train smash. Would the Department have suspected a more sinister kind of sabotage engineered perhaps by an unnamed foreign power? In other words would Mackeson have believed the Russians had actually derailed a train in order to destroy an important operative of British Intelligence. Reluctantly he concluded that Mackeson would assure everyone that Lloyd's demise could be of little value to any such power. The thought had depressed him.

By the time he arrived at his office, he was in a better frame of mind. Frank Lloyd enjoyed his work despite the mundane scope of activity in which he was permitted to operate. At least he knew he was a good desk man; and he was in touch with areas and activities throughout the world which excited and stimulated him.

On his arrival, Miss Gorringe, Mackeson's secretary, directed him to proceed at once to Sir James's office.

Mackeson was on the telephone when he entered.

'. . . thank you for being so prompt in informing us,' Mackeson spoke into the phone. 'Yes, of course. I shall make alternative arrangements.'

Mackeson hung up, the darkening cloud of a frown growing on his forehead.

'Morning, Sir James,' Lloyd ventured tentatively.

'Damn it, don't twitter inanities!' Mackeson barked at

116

him without bothering even to glance in Lloyd's direction. 'That fool Bartlett's got himself shot!'

'Dead?'

'Found floating in a hotel swimming pool in some place near Malaga. Two holes in him. One in the chest, one in the neck. And we'll probably have to foot the bill for cleaning out their damn swimming pool.'

Lloyd felt a shiver of anticipation. He knew the personnel file backwards and he was only too aware of the fact that the Department's manpower was stretched to the limit.

'Shall I pack?'

He had been in the field occasionally, serving mostly as a courier, but the prospect always excited him. And he knew that Mackeson needed someone in Spain to keep an eye on whatever Mark Fraser was up to out there.

Mackeson did not answer directly but continued half talking to himself or so it seemed to Lloyd. 'Bloody trouble is we don't know exactly where Fraser is just now . . .'

'We have a number of local contacts. Of course if we only knew what Fraser was up to . . .'

Mackeson silenced him with a look. 'Whatever Fraser is up to will be my concern. If you go out to Spain you will go to ensure Fraser's safety.'

'I'm surprised the Department still cares about an ex-agent . . .'

Again Mackeson silenced him. 'We don't! We have no connection with Fraser's activities whatsoever! But should anything happen to him at this time reflections might be cast upon the Department. He must be looked after for the time being.'

He studied Lloyd pensively for a moment. The younger man stood, allowing his chief's gaze to embrace him, waiting. Mackeson glanced at his watch.

'You can fly out this morning. We'll have a further briefing before you go.'

Lloyd restrained the smile of pleasure that threatened his features. He thought, a lightweight suit. It would be hot in Spain just now.

Mark Fraser arrived in Fuengirola at the side of the small
Spaniard whose name was Luis. Luis drove an ancient
Simca van from the rear of which came a strong smell of
liquid fertiliser mingled with various animal odours. He
dropped Fraser outside the local office of Hertz.

'When you get new car you find Hotel Hispano is round
corner to the right.'

A small bundle of peseta notes changed hands. The little
man beamed with gratitude. 'You are lucky you met me,
señor, and me, I am lucky I meet you, *si*?'

Fraser spent an hour with an attractive, olive-skinned
young woman in the Hertz office. He pretended to be unable to offer any explanation as to why the grey coupé
hired at Malaga airport had exploded. He pointed out that
as he had taken out full insurance the matter was now
solely the business of Hertz. He described the whereabouts
of the car and she assured him she would make arrangements for its recovery. In the meantime the fastest automobile she could offer him was a Ford Capri, low slung,
two doors and of metallic golden hue. He took delivery of
this, assuming the pose of the grudgingly placated tourist.

Once in the car the pose disappeared. He was unsure
whether or not the Russians had meant to kill him but he
was certain they had intended to slow him up. Fortunately
the appearance of Luis on the scene had ensured that he
had not lost too much time.

His two cases safely deposited in the boot of the Capri
he drove to the Hotel Hispano. Parking the car near the
hotel entrance he strode into the foyer and up to the reception desk. It would seem to any casual bystander that in
his progress to the desk he had exhibited no interest in his
surroundings. In fact, as he entered, his eyes had covered
every corner of the hall and reception area. He had taken
in the small group of American tourists loudly arguing as
to whether they would spend the morning on the beach
or touring the surrounding countryside. He had noted the
two Spanish page-boys leaning against the wall of an
alcove, smoking cigarettes and avoiding the keen, if preoccupied, eye of the reception clerk. He had registered the

elderly English couple, the man escorting the woman to the elevator, insisting that the proprietary drug he had in their room would cure Mediterranean stomach troubles. And lastly he had observed the dark girl sitting beside a pillar seemingly deeply-involved in a fashion magazine.

The face of the girl was at once familiar. In his wallet were the photographs given to him by Frank Lloyd in London the day before. The second of the photographs was of Elisa Toth, aged twenty-three, member of the group calling themselves the Red Action Brigade, Holgar Group.

His eyes flickered imperceptibly over Elisa Toth for a second time as he spoke to the reception clerk.

'You have an envelope or package for me,' he said. 'To be collected. The name is Mark Fraser.'

'Ah, *si*, Señor Fraser.' The clerk twisted around gracefully, lifted a large manilla envelope from behind him and twisted back to face Fraser in one elegant movement.

'Thank you,' Fraser said, taking the envelope. And without any further glance at the girl he walked out of the hotel.

She sat for fully five minutes before putting down the magazine and rising. Then casually she walked across the foyer and out. It was just as she emerged from the hotel entrance that she felt the hand grasp her wrist. Pain shot up her arm.

'Do you know I haven't had any breakfast?' Fraser spoke casually but the firmness of the grip belied his tone. 'I think perhaps you should join me, Fräulein Toth.'

She glared up at him without replying.

'I have a gun in my pocket,' Fraser went on. 'And I won't hesitate to use it. And that would spoil your plans for Herr Scherer.'

She finally spoke. 'I . . . I don't know you . . .'

'But I know you. A gentleman from British Intelligence gave me a not very flattering picture of you.'

'If you harm me you will not see your wife again,' Elisa burst out defiantly, eyes cold with hatred.

'Now don't spoil my breakfast. I want to have a little talk with you, that's all.'

Lieutenant-Colonel Grigor, despite a throbbing head, had with the help of Peter found Fraser's abandoned car. It had been at Peter's suggestion that, having driven to Fuengirola without seeing the car, they should drive back along the main road and cut up the side track towards the mountains. Ten minutes later they were standing beside the wreck of the grey coupé.

'No sign of Fraser,' Grigor murmured more to himself than to his companion. 'So he is still in the picture.'

Mentally he cursed Mark Fraser. It would have been more sensible to kill the Scot rather than reason with him. After all he had put Alexi out of action for some time. The man was now being driven back to hospital in Malaga nursing a broken wrist. And one could not account for the behaviour of a man whose wife was being held by those people. Yet if he did kill Fraser the Holgar Group would hire someone else with whom he had no contact, or even try and eliminate Scherer on their own. They were not professionals and as such would be less predictable. Furthermore he was not convinced that Fraser would actually carry out the mission to kill the German newspaper proprietor. Despite his record, Grigor did not believe Fraser was a natural killer. Unless Fraser was forced into a corner – which was exactly where he was – for as long as the terrorists held his wife.

Looking around the field past the grey coupé, Grigor sighed. 'So where is he now?'

Peter shrugged his broad shoulders. He was not employed to theorise. Grigor paced around the car, staring at the ground as if trying to find some indication of the direction in which his quarry had taken off. All he could see was hard, arid, brown soil.

The sound of a car engine on the road caused him to look up. Peter's hand strayed to his pocket in which was the customary heavy revolver. Grigor glanced at him and shook his head.

'No guns!'

The ancient Simca van wheezed to a halt by the break in the wicker fence and a small figure climbed out from behind the steering wheel.

'*Señors!*' Luis called, peering across the field. 'You look for your friend who had the accident?'

Grigor smiled and, followed by Peter, walked across to the road. 'We have been looking for him, yes.'

More foreigners, Luis thought, more English or American tourists certainly. Yet these two looked different and the one who had replied to his question in English had done so in a different accent from the man he had taken to Fuengirola.

'Can you tell us where Señor Fraser is?' the smaller of the two men asked.

'What his name is I do not know but I take him to Fuengirola to hire another car,' Luis replied. 'And I direcct him to the Hotel Hispano . . .'

Another flashing smile from the smaller man who reached into his pocket and extracted a large wallet from within.

'You will take us there, please,' Grigor said amiably. 'We are very fortunate to have met you.'

The cup of coffee in front of Elisa Toth was untouched. She sat facing Fraser, her face immobile, her eyes staring at him coldly. They were on the patio restaurant of the Hotel Hispano overlooking the hotel gardens, the temperature rising as the morning sun climbed in a cloudless sky.

'More coffee,' Fraser asked with a twitch of his lips. 'Your cup must be quite cold.'

Her expression deepened into a scowl. Fraser pulled his ear lobe meditatively.

'I don't think I'd like the world after you people had your revolution. Everyone would be much too miserable.'

To this he received no reply but an increase in the depths of the scowl.

'All right,' he continued. 'We've had breakfast. Now it's time to talk. Where are they? Your group?'

'You are just another pig,' she replied, pushing her coffee cup away.

'One of us isn't kosher,' Fraser smiled. 'But I don't think it's me. Now I am asking you nicely . . .'

'And when I don't tell you, what will you do?' She tossed her head defiantly. 'Beat me up? Here? Over the English breakfast. Or perhaps kill me?'

'Not here. Too many people around. Of course we could drive to a nice quiet spot.'

For a moment he thought he detected a flash of fear behind her eyes.

'I told you . . . if you want to see your wife again . . .'

She had left the end of the sentence unsaid but he could feel now she was on the defensive. And she was not aware she had made a tactical error in mentioning Jill. His expression became cold, the smile disappearing.

'Your friends will not harm her at least until I do the job they want me to do! No matter what happens to you.'

She knew he was right but was not prepared to face the fact. Defiance crept into her voice again.

'We are comrades. If I am harmed they will take action.'

'Have they taken action about Carl-Jan?'

She caught her breath. 'He will join us . . .'

'He won't, I'm afraid. The last I saw of him he was quite dead. With two Russian bullets in his back.'

He could feel her begin to tremble across the table. An elderly tourist at an adjacent table stared across at them curiously. Fraser, assuming a nonchalance he did not feel, sipped his coffee. He was uncertain as to whether her trembling was a reaction simply to the death of Carl-Jan or to his reference to the Russian bullets.

'Oh yes, Russian bullets,' he pressed home the advantage. 'Two gentlemen from the KGB killed him. And this morning they tried to put me out of action. Now why would they do that? After all you're all on the left politically, aren't you?'

She stared across the table at him and she was still trembling. He turned and waved the waiter over. The man came with a slow lackadaisical air, as of someone bestowing a privilege on the underprivileged.

'Bring me another pot of coffee and a couple of rolls,'

Fraser ordered without looking up. 'I have to make up the meals I missed yesterday.'

The waiter slouched off.

'You might think about this, Fräulein Toth,' Fraser went on. 'Why are the Russians, who might be thought to have some sympathy for your plan, trying to kill us all off?'

In the girl's eyes he read only a genuine puzzlement. She seemed confused for the first time since they had met. She looked down at the table top, reached out and taking up her cup of coffee, sipped the tepid liquid.

He continued. 'If you can't answer that, then at least tell me why I have to kill Scherer.'

This was a question she could answer simply. 'Do I have to tell you why we want to kill a Fascist?'

'Elisa, you must stop answering my questions with other questions.'

'It is obvious surely,' she replied with a degree of exasperation. 'Scherer controls a large part of the West German press. He demands persistently that we all be hanged. At the same time he would bring back Nazism and many of the old Nazis into power. Even you would hardly support that.'

'Hardly,' Fraser responded meditatively. 'Bring back the fathers and kill the children. A bleak philosophy. Not that there's much to choose between you.'

The waiter returned bearing a tray on which was a fresh pot of coffee, two rolls and a small pot of indeterminate fruit *confiture*. This he placed in front of Fraser with a scowl and departed.

The girl suddenly leaned forward, calm again and the tone in her voice was not, for once, aggressive.

'Mr Fraser, you and I both know that you will have to let me go.'

Fraser did not reply. He was staring over her shoulder at the doorway to the patio.

The familiar figure approached.

'Señor, señor,' said Luis with a broad smile of satisfaction at having found him. 'Señor, I bring your friends to you!'

123

The little man underlined his pleasure with a small bow and Fraser found himself looking up at Grigor and his companion.

'Should I congratulate you on your efficiency in finding me, Colonel?' Fraser asked ruefully.

NINE

The castle stood on a high promontory overlooking a vast plain that stretched to the foothills of the Sierra Nevada. It was an old castle, its origins stretching back to the ages when Spaniard fought Moor and the struggle flowed like a sea-tide across the mountains and plains of southern Spain.

As they drove along a narrow road across what seemed to Jill a plain of sand and scrub, a small desert between the sierras, she received her first sight of the castle and was fascinated by the dominant edifice looming above the plain.

Rolf glanced at her, saw her expression and smiled. 'It is owned by a rather poverty-stricken Spanish nobleman. Much of it, I believe, is shut up and semi-derelict. But part of it is habitable. And it is our destination.'

Some minutes later they drove up a steep incline onto a cobbled surface and through an arched entrance into the outer courtyard of the castle. Jurgen applied the brakes and the car came to a halt.

'A place this size?' questioned Gudrun, unable to keep a sense of awe out of her voice as she peered from the car window.

'But suitably isolated,' Rolf responded smugly.

'Servants?' asked Jurgen, caution in his voice.

'Two,' said Rolf. 'Both ancient. I told you I carried out a very detailed reconnaissance.'

He opened the car door and stepped onto uneven cobbles between which weeds were fighting a winning battle to get through. He turned to Jurgen.

'You and I only! Gudrun, you will stay here with Frau Fraser until we tell you. And you will keep her quiet.'

Jurgen and Rolf crossed the outer courtyard and into a small square inner yard. Here the architecture showed a mixture of influences. The design of the courtyard betrayed its Moorish influence and yet surrounded as it was by ornate narrow pillars in front of a shaded walk, there could be detected the hand and eye of the Italian renaissance.

The main door, large and of heavy panelled wood, was sheltered under a small arch. A heavy brass bell-pull obviously of later origin, probably Victorian, protruded from the side of the stone next to the door. Rolf pulled it and there was a distant clanging sound.

Back in the car, Jill peered out at the two figures in the inner courtyard.

'Where is this place?' she inquired of the blonde girl beside her.

Gudrun shrugged, without interest. 'Rolf discovered it. We will stay here until everything is over.'

The door of the castle swung open and Rolf found himself staring into a yellowing, lined face, a contour map of years under a hot sun. The servant, whose name was José, was wearing a dark jacket, creased and ill-fitting, black trousers and a white shirt buttoned to the neck but lacking a tie. The man peered at Rolf and then at Jurgen without speaking, waiting for them to break the silence.

Rolf spoke in Spanish with a thick gutteral accent. 'Good-day. May we use your telephone? I am afraid we are having mechanical trouble with our car.'

The man replied in a slightly hoarse voice. 'Ah, yes. Please enter. I will ask the Marquisa.'

The entrance hall of the castle was enormous if rather chilling. An inlaid marble floor of some antiquity was unmarred by carpeting. Light slanted through high narrow windows illuminating the shadowy emptiness of the chamber. Apart from a figure in medieval armour and two highback chairs it was devoid of furnishings. Across two of the walls were tattered tapestries, frayed and dusty. And on another wall was an outline where there had once been another tapestry, probably, thought Rolf, long removed and sold.

José led them across the hall, footsteps echoing on the marble, and through a door on the right. They found themselves now in a pleasant airy room dominated by an enormous fireplace which, despite the heat, had a fire burning within its blackened metal brazier. This room at least was furnished; two deep leather armchairs, one on each side of the fireplace, were matched by a long sofa. On a table by the window was an ancient-looking telephone and on the walls were a number of paintings of Spanish grandees. The impression was of comfort fighting a battle against time. The leather on the chairs, though highly-polished, was cracked, the paintings were dim with the dust of ages.

'Please wait,' said the manservant and left them alone, carefully shutting the door behind them. Jurgen walked to the window and ran a finger over the surface of the table. The tip of his finger came up covered in dust.

'The dust of decaying nobility,' Rolf said by way of explanation. His eyes lit on the telephone.

'Disconnect it!' he went on. 'But make sure you can reconnect it later.'

Jurgen followed the telephone wire to a small junction box on the skirting board. He expertly unscrewed the top of the box and with some care detached the wires.

'Who owns this place?' he asked, straightening up.

As he spoke the door opened and a tall woman entered. She was in her forties, attractive but with an air of weariness which emphasised the strong lines on her forehead. She was dressed in a dark skirt and light-coloured sweater. A single string of large pearls was around her throat and on her left hand was a single thick band of gold.

Rolf, staring at her, answered Jurgen's question. 'It is owned by the Marquis de Triana . . .'

'And I am the Marquisa de Triana,' The woman said in English with no trace of an accent. 'Louisa Huerta . . . good morning, gentlemen I gather you wish to use the telephone.'

Rolf did not reply but slowly drew a revolver from the inside pocket of his jacket. The woman stared down at the weapon, eyes widening slightly.

127

Rolf then spoke. 'I am afraid that was a pretext, madame. Please try not to be alarmed and make no sudden movements.'

'I am afraid,' she replied, 'you will find little to steal here.'

'We are not thieves,' Rolf smiled, showing his teeth. 'Rather we are taking over the castle as a sanctuary for a short time.'

The bedroom at the Hotel Hispano was not unlike the room at the Hotel Mijas. It had two single beds, a large window, this time without a balcony, and two upright rather uncomfortable chairs. It had been booked by Lieutenant-Colonel Grigor on his arrival, before he had faced Fraser and Elisa Toth at the breakfast table.

Now Elisa sat sullenly on one of the chairs facing Grigor on the other. Behind Grigor stood Peter who had so expertly placed the *plastique* under the bonnet of Fraser's grey coupé. Fraser himself stood facing the wall beside the door while a third Russian ran his hands expertly over Fraser's body and produced the two guns which he placed on the nearest of the two beds

I hope I didn't hurt your colleague this morning,' Fraser tried to sound affable.

'Alexi will survive a broken wrist. As you see I have found a replacement. The gentleman searching you is Joseph. And you haven't met Peter who was responsible for the unfortunate accident to your car,' Grigor seemed to be matching Fraser's affability. 'You may turn around and relax now.'

Fraser turned and sat on the bed. Carefully Joseph moved the guns onto the dressing table.

'Joseph is very careful,' Grigor remarked. 'And quite ferocious when roused. He may not frighten you, Mr Fraser, but, by God, he frightens me. Now who was it who once said that?'

Fraser surveyed Joseph with interest. He was at least six feet four with shoulders so massive they threatened to burst

128

out of the heavy dark jacket he was wearing.

Grigor turned his attention to the girl. 'So this is Fräulein Elisa Toth. We have records of her enterprises. And now she will tell me where her companions are.'

It was less a question than a statement. Elisa stared into the middle distance without answering.

'She's not the easiest person to talk to,' Fraser remarked.

Grigor gave an expressive wave of his hand. 'I may not have your scruples about how to handle these people.'

He stood up and faced Elisa. 'I have no desire to injure a female . . . particularly a mere child . . . but you will understand this is a matter of preventing an assassination. That is a criminal act in any country in the world.'

Fraser could not resist a question. 'How does it feel, Elisa, to be face to face with the future you and your friends are killing people to create.'

The girl scowled at him but remained silent.

'You will tell me where Fraser's wife is being held,' Grigor went on.

She transferred the scowl to him and this time spoke. 'Pig!'

'But a Marxist pig, Elisa,' Fraser broke in again.

'You will please answer,' Grigor made the request quietly. He received no reply. His right hand rose suddenly and with considerable speed and struck her hard across the face. She was knocked sideways from the chair and sprawled on the floor. But, as she fell her hand moved under the waistband of her jeans, scrabbled there for a fraction of a second and then reappeared clutching a small revolver. In falling she had twisted away from Grigor and before he could see what had happened the revolver was pointing at him.

The explosion was not loud but the bullet struck Grigor in the left shoulder throwing him back across the bed, a look of astonishment on his face.

Elisa then swivelled around on her knees and aimed at the largest target in the room, the man Joseph. This time, as she fired she lowered the muzzle of the revolver slightly. Whereas Grigor had fallen in silence Joseph gave a shrill scream as the bullet struck the centre of his right kneecap. He doubled up, hands flaying in the air, trying to reach the knee from which a red stain was gushing over the dark material of his trousers.

The third Russian, Peter, was taken completely by surprise. Fraser was never sure whether it was the speed of the girl's assault that caused Peter to hesitate or the sheer astonishment that a slight female figure could be responsible for such instantaneous violence. But hesitate Peter did before fumbling for his own weapon.

'You won't make it!' Fraser said, almost laconically.

Peter decided Fraser was right and he ceased to fumble as Elisa's revolver turned towards him. She stood up slowly the weapon still levelled at his chest, ignoring the moans of Joseph huddled against the skirting board beside the door.

Fraser glanced across at Grigor. He was lying on the bed, face down, breathing heavily, gulping air as if excess of it might lessen the pain from the wound on his shoulder. Fraser looked back at the girl.

Coldly, with great deliberation she again lowered the revolver and pressed the trigger. This time it was Peter who cried out, not a scream but a dull, hopeless moan as the bullet struck him on the right kneecap. His knee buckled and he fell forward at Elisa's feet. This time, too, the coldness and the deliberation shocked Fraser.

'For God's sake!' he cried out, the thought that Jill was in the hands of such characters in his mind.

Elisa turned to him but now the revolver was lowered.

'You are lucky, Fraser, that we need you. Otherwise I would do the same to you. You will stay here for a while now and not attempt to follow me. Then you had better move on quickly.'

'Don't worry. I'm too fond of my kneecaps.'

She stepped over Peter's body which was shivering with pain and crossed to the door. Joseph seemed to have mercifully passed into unconsciousness and, with her right foot, she eased his body aside and opened the door of the room. She gave one brief glance back at Fraser and then went out, shutting the door behind her.

Fraser scooped his two guns from the bed and stood up. As he did so Grigor, on the adjoining bed, turned over and stared up at him.

'I think you'll all survive though it'll be painful,' Fraser said, with mild regret in his voice. 'Meanwhile I'm going to see if I can follow that young woman. She may just lead me to my wife.'

To his surprise Grigor gave a brief nod of agreement.

The bedroom the Russians had taken was on the second floor and, with some experience of Spanish elevators, Fraser chose the staircase and ran down the two flights. As he reached the foyer of the hotel he hesitated for a moment, glancing around. The girl was nowhere in sight. He crossed the foyer and out.

A car was disappearing out of the car park and he caught a glimpse of Elisa's profile as the car turned into the main road. Good. He could follow her at a safe distance. He moved towards his own car parked at the foot of the hotel steps. Yet as he did so, he frowned. The girl would surely not make it easy for him. Still she had to rejoin the rest of the group eventually.

He reached the golden Capri and at once knew the girl had not made it easy for him. His two front tyres had been neatly slashed and the car sagged forward resting on the wheel hubs and squashed rubber.

He cursed silently to himself. Then he retraced his steps back into the hotel.

When he re-entered the bedroom, Grigor had pulled himself onto a chair and was attempting to staunch the flow of blood from his shoulder with one of the hotel towels. Joseph was still unconscious, breathing heavily and Peter, propped against the wall, was obviously close to following his comrade into a painless if temporary oblivion.

Grigor looked up questioningly.

'She slashed my tyres,' Fraser explained. 'But then you were careless too, Colonel. Your men searched me but forgot to search her.'

'I know it.'

131

'That kind you don't slap around. Perhaps you have to kill them before they kill you.'

Crossing to the chair Fraser gently eased the towel from the Russian's shoulder. Grigor had his jacket half-off and Fraser carefully ripped the shirt away from the wound.

'Painful, I should imagine. But not fatal,' he said. 'I shall have to leave you now but at least I've time to phone for an ambulance.'

'No!' The Russian protested. 'No ambulance. Must . . . must be our own people. I can give you a telephone number in Malaga.'

'Otherwise we create diplomatic problems, is that it?'

Grigor nodded weakly.

'Sorry, but I really don't mind creating diplomatic problems for you,' Fraser said coolly. 'It may just keep you off my back. Anyway by the time anybody gets here from Malaga you'll all have bled to death. Sorry but it's got to be the local hospital.'

He crossed to the telephone and lifted the receiver. The voice at the hotel switchboard sounded lethargic until Fraser spoke.

'You have some guests in Room thirty-two who require a doctor and an ambulance urgently.'

Before the operator could reply Fraser replaced the receiver. He gave Grigor a tired smile and went to the door.

'Fraser!'

'Yes?'

'You will not assassinate Scherer?'

Fraser hesitated before replying. 'I was trained as a killer, Colonel. By men very like yourself. I gave it up because I didn't like it. Patriotism was not enough reason, you might say. And it struck me that the act of killing a man was an awesome responsibility for some abstract political philosophy. But this is different. This is my wife whose life's at stake. To save her . . . yes, I've told you I would assassinate Scherer!'

A stab of pain shot through Grigor's shoulder and he winced. Fraser quietly stepped from the room.

At the reception desk in the foyer a telephone call to

Hertz assured him that his two front tyres would be changed within an hour. He settled in the same seat in the foyer that Elisa had occupied and opened the envelope he had collected. It contained a number of photographs of a large villa from various angles. One of these showed a large garden at the rear of the villa and beyond the garden a slope upwards to a small flat hill. He stared at this for some moments, he eyes caught by a tall edifice to the right of the hill. Gleaming in the sunlight was a round metal silo about twenty-five feet in height with a flat roof.

He turned from this to a neat typewritten note which was attached.

'The villa is to the north of Marbella and is marked on the attached map. A room in your name has been booked at the Hotel El Rodeo, Marbella. On Friday the Duke of Porto Christo will hold a small garden party commencing at 12 noon. The purpose is to introduce Scherer to local notables. You should be able to carry out your mission at around midday. The rifle we have provided is ideal for this mission. Once we are assured Scherer is dead your wife will be released.'

The note had no heading and no signature.

A flurry of activity from the reception desk caused him to look up. A small, neat, balding man was gesticulating at the receptionist. The word 'ambulance' in Spanish was being repeated over and over again. The doctor had obviously discovered the occupants of Room thirty-two. Forty-five minutes later Fraser drove away from the Hotel Hispano.

For a man facing the prospect of committing murder to save his wife; a man who had slept but five hours in the last forty-eight and been sustained only by a snack on an aeroplane and coffee and rolls, Fraser felt amazingly alert. He knew at once his next move before heading for Marbella. Bartlett's voice had come into mind while he sat in the hotel foyer.

'. . . friend of ours who might be able to help. An old boy called Rocas. Runs a shop in Granada . . . he knows most of what goes on in this part of Spain.'

Fraser drove out of Fuengirola, heading north to Granada.

At the time Fraser was leaving the hotel, Jill sat in one of the leather chairs beside the large fireplace. She felt exhausted, dispirited and had to force herself to an awareness of her surroundings. Behind her stood Gudrun, blonde hair in a kind of purposeful disarray. Next to Gudrun, Jurgen leant against the wall eyes alert, betraying the careless attitude he had assumed. But the dominant people in the room were Rolf and the woman Jill was to know as Louisa, Marquisa de Triana.

'My husband is a sick man,' the Marquisa informed Rolf. 'The result of a serious stroke. He must not be agitated. So if you have not come here to rob us I suggest you leave.'

Rolf contemplated the toe of his right shoe for a moment before looking up to answer her. 'You speak good English, madame.'

'I am English,' the Marquisa replied. 'Or was until my marriage.'

She was interrupted by the door opening. The elderly servant who had answered the door entered pushing a wheelchair. In the chair was a man who could not have been older than his early fifties, although once dark hair was streaked with grey, a once firm jaw-line sagged loosely, and a useless left hand hung over the edge of the arm of the wheelchair. The man was dressed in a corduroy jacket and open-necked white shirt, and his legs were covered by a thick woollen blanket. Jill thought to herself that at one time he must have been a man of striking looks and some dignity.

'My husband,' Louisa explained. 'He can neither walk nor talk.'

Nonetheless the eyes were keen, active if slightly puzzled at the intrusion of strangers into his home.

Louisa continued. 'You have now seen our entire household, except for the cook, José's wife. And you will perhaps have gathered from our circumstances that my husband's

134

ailment has not exactly enriched the family or the castle. So will you please now tell me what you want here.'

'I thought I did,' Rolf replied. 'Sanctuary. We wish to stay here until Friday.'

The woman looked baffled. 'Why? Why here?'

Then she suddenly stared over at Jill and a realisation came to her that this young woman was not as the others.

'The castle is . . . isolated,' explained Rolf. 'Suitable for us at this time. I believe part of the castle can be locked off. That is so, isn't it?'

His eyes fell on José who looked away. The old servant's hands were trembling. The man in the wheelchair sensed José's fear and he glared at Rolf, a look of frustrated ferocity.

'There's no need to frighten my servants!' Louisa stepped in front of Rolf. 'You will address yourself to me. And . . . eh . . . it is true, part of the castle, the upper rooms and the south wing can be . . . locked off.'

'Good!' The German nodded, satisfied. 'You and . . . this young woman will be kept there.'

Jill's eyes met Louisa's. Understanding was beginning to dawn on the older woman.

'But . . . my husband . . .?'

'He will remain with us. As a hostage to your good conduct. Your servant can look after him. If you try to escape or create trouble we'll kill him. Otherwise after Friday we'll leave you in peace.' The words were uttered in such a matter-of-fact manner that their full import did not at first strike the Marquisa. When they did her body stiffened and she drew herself up to her full height.

'How dare you . . .!'

Rolf cut in, ignoring the protest. 'Your husband's ancestors picked an ideal defensive position,' he remarked almost conversationally.

Strolling over to the window he stared out across the plain.

'You can see anything approaching miles away,' he went on and then twisted around to face Louisa. 'In case you doubt my words regarding what we can do to your hus-

135

band, Frau Fraser will assure you we are in deadly earnest.'

Twenty minutes later a door at the end of a dusty corridor was slammed shut and locked. Beyond the door a stairway led to an upper room and beyond the room onto the battlements of the castle. As the key was withdrawn from the lock, on the other side of the door, Louisa, white-faced and shivering with anger, turned to face Jill. Hair awry and hanging over a face smudged with grime, Jill leant wearily against the wall of the corridor.

'I think you'd better have a wash, Mrs Fraser, is it?' Louisa gave what she thought was a reassuring smile.

'Yes. Jill Fraser.'

'There's a small bathroom off the bedroom. I am afraid, thanks to those people downstairs we'll have to share both. After you've washed perhaps you can tell me what all this is about.'

Later they stood on the battlements of the castle, flanked by two circular towers, staring across the yellow plain towards the Sierras. Jill, washed and with her hair pinned back, related the story of her kidnapping to the Marquisa.

'You have no idea what they want your husband to do?' Louisa asked.

'I have some idea.' Jill hesitated.

'Can you tell me?'

'They want him to kill someone.'

Louisa's face darkened. 'Yes, I believe that. The leader, the one called Rolf, he has the look of a man who could kill.'

Jill reddened. 'My husband once worked for British Intelligence. He . . . he had to do things like that. That's why, in the end, he resigned. It was before we were married.'

Louisa paced across the cobbled gutterings of the roof. 'I see. Well, there are wars, even in peacetime, and sometimes people are killed. Anyway the British don't do things like that unless they have to.'

Jill smiled. The tall woman had an honest naïvety possibly wrong-headed, but with an old-fashioned patriotism that under other circumstances might have been laughable.

136

Yet now, to Jill it was reassuring.

'Do you know who they want him to kill?' Louisa went on.

Jill nodded but before she could reply Louisa was suddenly alert, staring intently across the battlements down onto the plain below.

Across the plain above the ribbon of road a thin cloud of dust was rising.

'What is it?' Jill asked.

'We're not so isolated after all. It's a car and it's coming to the castle.'

They gazed down in silence for some minutes as the plume of dust grew nearer until they could finally make out the shape of the car. They were both tense, hopeful that some form of deliverance might be on the way. Jill found herself gripping the ancient stone that ran around the roof, her nails digging into it. Then as the car came up towards the archway into the outer courtyard and disappeared under the arched entrance, she turned away, disappointment on her face.

'It's another of them,' she explained to Louisa.

The Marquisa relaxed, her forehead furrowed. A thought was troubling her and she hated putting it into words. But she knew it had to be said.

'You realise, after Friday, whether your husband carries out this murder or not, they may well kill you,' she paused. 'They may well kill all of us.'

'I know. But I decided I wouldn't think about that.'

Louisa crossed the roof and leant against a shaded section of wall next to the door down to the bedroom. The stone, hidden from the sun, was cool to the touch.

'Did I tell you I was born in Cumberland?' she said, a trace of defiance in her eyes. 'Near the Scottish border. We're very stubborn people in Cumberland. We don't take things lying down. We take action.'

'The Scots are like that. My husband's a Scot.'

'And you?'

'I was born in Devon,' Jill gave a wan smile. Devon and her childhood seemed very far away.

137

'Devon! Good!' Louisa replied gruffly. 'Touch of the Celt in both of us. We'll make quite a team.'

'But the Marquis . . . your husband . . .?'

'Wouldn't like me to take things lying down. Anyway after Friday we may all be killed. Think about their killing us! Think about it a great deal. It will make you angry. Determined too. Determined not to let it happen.'

A small wisp of a cloud passed over the sun and for a second Louisa's face was darkened.

Below, in the hall of the castle Rolf greeted the new arrival. Elisa had driven fast from Fuengirola and she was tired and dusty. Her face, where Grigor had struck her, was marred by a purple bruise.

'You're late!' Rolf growled, noting the bruise and deciding to ignore it.

She scowled back at him. 'I was detained. Unavoidably. I have a lot to tell you. And you may have to provide some answers for me.'

TEN

The town was dominated by the beauty of the Alhambra. The Moors who had fought their way from North Africa across half of Spain had left its ornate, oriental grandeur, its cool gardens, gentle fountains, as a reminder of their power, a gift to posterity. For all its beauty it had still been built as a fortified palace and stood above the city of Granada, dominating everything below.

Fraser drove under its shadow in the heat of the afternoon, too concerned about Jill to give it more than a passing glance. Yet, even with that brief look he caught his breath at the sheer dominance of the concept of the Alhambra.

The address he had been given by Bartlett was of a small leather-work shop on a busy narrow street. Parking his car as close to the shop as he could, Fraser had to cross the street to stand staring into a window packed with ornate wallets and elaborate shoulder bags. There was, however, in the centre of the shop window a sign that real craftsmanship in leather had not been reduced entirely to pandering to tourists. A saddle in the Moorish style, elaborate in its design, yet practical in its concept, the leather polished until it reflected the sunlight like glass, stood on a wooden pommel as if defying the twentieth century and the noise of its mechanical transport.

Above the shop doorway was the name 'Rocas'.

Fraser entered and the dim light was almost painful after the brilliance of the sun on the street. He peered round, through festoons of leather bags and satchels which hung from the ceiling, and his eyes finally focused on a shop counter behind which was a small shadowy figure.

'Señor?'

Fraser stepped forward and a thin ray of light, breaking through between the goods in the window, struck the face of the man behind the counter. It was an old face, a contour map with deep valleys and prominences of flesh above the valleys, a face wrinkled into yellow paper; and yet the eyes seemed to gleam at Fraser, shining coins on furrowed sand.

'Bartlett sent me,' Fraser said simply.

'Ah, *si*. You will be Fraser.' The small figure hesitated. 'You know Señor Bartlett is dead?'

'I heard.'

Rocas looked at his watch. 'Time to shut the shop for siesta.'

He crossed to the door, locked it and lowered a black blind reducing even further the light in the shop.

'I am Rocas,' he announced facing Fraser. 'We will now talk.'

He cleared an upright chair which had been covered in leather satchels. 'Please sit.'

Fraser sat, trying to readjust his vision to the lessening of the light again.

'You will of course want me to try to find out where these people have taken your wife,' Rocas said, moving again behind the counter.

'You know about it?'

'Before Bartlett was killed he had spoken to me on the telephone.'

Fraser cleared his throat. The dust from the shop and the smell of leather seemed almost to choke him. 'This has nothing to do with Bartlett's people,' he insisted and Rocas nodded his head like a small oriental idol.

'*Si, si* . . .'

I'd appreciate any information you can give me about my wife and where she might have been taken. Then I take it from there. On my own.'

'I have people in many places with their eyes open, alert. They will look for strangers . . . Germans who are not vacationing . . . young Germans with the look of murder in their eyes. Like some of our own young Basques. My people will look, they will find and they will whisper to me.'

Fraser nodded. 'I suppose I'm asking the impossible . . .'

'No! My friends will find her. You should know, Mr Fraser, in every country somewhere there is always a man like me who hears all the whispers,' Rocas chuckled like a young boy. The sound was incongruous coming from the old man. 'In Spain since the Civil War many survived by listening to whispers. By being one step ahead of the Falangists.'

'I've met such men.'

'Of course you have. I, Rocas had to be like this. You see, I am socialist. Not communist . . . socialist. One time before the wars I met your George Lansbury . . . and Major Attlee who became a great man, *si?*'

'*Si!*'

Rocas ran his hand along the top of the counter and Fraser imagined he could see a small puff of dust rise even in the dim light.

'Of course,' Rocas continued. 'What you wish to know will take a little time.'

'How much time?'

A movement of the shoulders in the darkness. More dust. 'Perhaps Friday . . . Saturday . . . maybe little longer . . .'

'Friday is too late!'

'Tomorrow is already Thursday. Two days. Is hardly possible. But I will try. Where will you be staying in Marbella?'

Fraser was suddenly alert. 'How did you know I was going to Marbella?'

'More whispers,' Rocas replied.

Warning signals were sounding in Fraser's head. The reply wasn't good enough; there had to be more than the throwaway hint from Rocas.

'Not good enough,' he said, his voice cold.

Rocas stared over his shoulder, eyes vainly trying to focus.

'Mr Fraser,' he said wearily. 'My people have heard that these terrorists brought a man into Malaga . . . a notorious man . . . Santos Morales, whose purpose was to carry out

141

a mission in this part of the world. We learn too Morales was booked into a hotel in Marbella. But he never arrived there. He fell out of a high window in Malaga. It was no loss.'

Pausing momentarily, Rocas abstractly studied a small leather wallet that lay on the counter.

'Go on,' Fraser urged him.

'Now you are here and I am told these same terrorists are holding your wife. There is no talk of ransom so their aim is not money. But your past career, of which Mr Bartlett told me some details, would fit you for the task Morales was unable to carry out. Thus we deduce you will go to Marbella, as he was to do.'

Fraser relaxed. It sounded plausible. The Department would been able to deduce all that Rocas had said. And Bartlett, before he had been killed, before even he, Fraser, had arrived in Spain, could have contacted Rocas.

'So I have to know where to contact you in Marbella,' Rocas pressed the point.

'El Rodeo Hotel. There's a room been held in my name.'

'Don't take up the booking. They will have plenty of rooms at this time of the year. Book another one. Use a different name. Gerrard. Use the name of Gerrard. I have a passport in that name I can give you,' Rocas hesitated again peering at him. 'It is of a man about your age. The photograph will pass for you. Anyway the hotel people never look at a photograph.'

'Why the different name?'

'I have heard more whispers. Something on the radio news about three injured Russians found only a few hours ago in a hotel in Fuengirola. Were you near Fuengirola?'

Fraser nodded.

'I do not know whether they were connected with you and I do not wish to know. But they could easily find out where you are staying if you register under your own name. Some of our police are susceptible to money.'

'I take the point,' Fraser assented.

'Good. Go to Marbella now and wait until you hear from me,' Rocas gave a dim smile. 'I will do all I can to find where your wife is being held.'

'By Friday?'

The smile wavered. 'And if I was not able to tell you by Friday, what then?'

It was Fraser's turn to smile dimly. 'Then I might have to do something I don't want to do.'

Rocas came in quickly, words falling over themselves. 'I do not wish to know that . . . I do not wish to know anything about what you might have to do . . . it is not to be my concern. Now go and I will alert my contacts.'

'The passport?'

'Ah, yes,' Rocas turned on his heels and disappeared behind a small mountain of cases and through a door leading to the rear of the shop. Fraser waited, his mind racing. Rocas knew a great deal but he did not seem to know the mission set by the Holgar Group. Fraser could understand too his aversion to be told anything about that mission. The small man was, after all, a Spanish citizen. A deeper involvement, a deeper knowledge, could be dangerous to him.

Rocas reappeared and handed Fraser an envelope.

'The passport is inside. When you are sure you have finished with it, please to burn it. False passports can be sometimes traced to their source. Now, go, Señor Gerrard. You will hear from me by telephone though I would rather we never actually meet again.'

Outside the shop the glare of the sun nearly blinded Fraser. He climbed into his car and sat for a full five minutes until his eyes were adjusted to the brightness of the afternoon. Then he started the car and drove back out of Granada, heading south again towards the coast and Marbella.

Jill, curled up on the counterpane of the ancient four poster bed, was wide-awake staring up at the ceiling. Outside the window the bright glare of the day had turned to yellows and browns and the afternoon was dying. Louisa was moving from the window to the door and back again, a seemingly endless pacing while she chain-smoked American cigarettes of which she appeared to have an inexhaustible supply.

Earlier she had excused herself with a muttered explanation. 'I think better when I'm moving. So just pay no attention to me.'

Jill, trying to think too of a plan of escape, found a great weariness had overcome her. She had lain on the bed hoping she might sleep but, despite physical fatigue, her mind was too active and she simply lay making the attempt to relax.

Then, from the foot of the staircase outside the room, they heard the door being unlocked and footsteps climbing towards them. The door opened and Gudrun came in carrying a tray on which were two plates of cold chicken salad, two glasses and an open bottle of red wine.

'Your cook prepared this for you,' the German girl explained, setting the tray down on a table by the fourposter. 'Red wine does not go with chicken but we had not time to concern ourselves.'

'How is my husband?' Louisa asked, concern in her voice.

'He sits and stares at us with such hatred in his eyes,' Gudrun replied. 'Perhaps it is as well he is paralysed. The old man, José, is looking after him.'

Louisa had stiffened with anger at the casual mention of her husband's disability. Now she used her anger, her voice filled with contempt.

'You believe it is right to keep us here while you arrange to murder an innocent man?'

Gudrun glanced at Jill. 'So she has been listening and talking. Well, innocent, who is innocent? You, Marquisa, living in this mausoleum, this monument to a class system that is dead. In your system you are all guilty.'

'If you want to change the system there are other ways than murder,' Louisa protested.

'We don't want to change the system!' Gudrun exploded with rage. 'We want to destroy it!'

Jill swung her legs off the bed. 'You may be destroyed

by it.'

Gudrun shrugged, suddenly calm again. 'Perhaps. We accept that possibility. But we will go on.'

She realised at that moment that Louisa was on one side of her and Jill on the other. She took a pace back towards the door, looking from one to the other.

'There will be no point in attacking me,' she went on nervously. 'I do not have the key of the door below. I am let out by Jurgen as I was let in.'

She now backed all the way to the door of the bedroom.

'And after Friday you will kill us all?' Louisa asked coolly.

Gudrun shrugged. 'If we are told to.'

'By whom?'

Another shrug. 'Rolf! It is immaterial to me.'

She glared at them for a second and then went out of the room. They stood in silence until they heard the door at the foot of the stairs open and close.

'They are not people,' Louisa insisted. 'They are . . . animals.'

Jill turned away and walked over to the window. Gathering darkness was rapidly obscuring the view of the plain below.

Fraser dined alone at the El Rodeo Hotel in Marbella. The large dining-room was three-quarters full of chattering holidaymakers but he ignored them concentrating on his meal. It occurred to him that it was the first full meal he had eaten in three days and yet he found he had little appetite.

After dinner he ordered a half bottle of whisky to be sent to his room and there, glass in hand, he sat at the edge of the bed, the photos that he had collected at Fuengirola spread out on the bed in front of him. Sipping his whisky he studied every aspect of the villa in which Scherer was staying.

In addition to the pictures of the villa there were a number of newspaper clippings of Scherer himself. In his forties, the German newspaper proprietor was a good-looking man, brownish hair tinged with grey at the temples. In each clipping he appeared to be smiling, even laughing as he greeted some dignitary or posed obviously for the press photographer.

Beneath the various clippings Fraser found a map of Marbella, a line in red ink drawn from El Rodeo to the villa, some short distance beyond the town, in which Scherer was residing. After studying this for some time, Fraser swallowed the whisky, poured himself a second dram and, undressing, climbed into bed.

After a time he slept.

The girl, Elisa Toth, was there, standing beside him, and they both held revolvers in their hands. In front of them was the long dead black African statesman, now alive and grinning inanely at them both. Next to him was the German ex-SS man and next to him was Vincent Hartley. And they were smiling and laughing, pointing at Fraser and Elisa Toth. Then the girl turned and looked at him and nodded and they both fired shot after shot at the three figures until the figures seemed to dissolve in a kind of mist and in their place there was only Jill standing smiling at them. And Fraser knew that he and Elisa were going to fire again and this time they were firing at his wife. Behind them stood Bartlett and the old young man, Rolf, and these two were egging him on to fire and he knew he was going to do just that . . .

Fraser woke, drenched in perspiration. He had forced himself awake as the dream had become too unbearable. He switched on the bed light and glanced at his watch. It was barely midnight. He had slept for less than an hour. Shivering, despite the perspiration, he switched out the light and lay for some time as if afraid to sleep in case the dream should return. Finally he again slipped into oblivion and the next thing he knew it was seven-thirty and the sunlight slanted through the window of his room onto his face.

By nine o'clock, Fraser had showered, shaved, dressed and breakfasted. Finishing his coffee, he strolled past the

146

hotel swimming pool, ignoring the bikini-clad bodies stretched out in attitudes of sun worship, to the car park and climbed into the Capri.

Driving along the side of the marina, the Mediterranean on his left, he finally turned inland, following the red line on the map he had picked up at Fuengirola. Fifteen minutes later he drove into a lay-by and, leaving the car unlocked in case he had to move off quickly, he walked along the main road until he came to a narrow lane on his right.

The lane curved away into a cluster of thin leafless trees, obviously suffering from a lack of moisture. The right side of the lane was lined by a high stone wall, shards of glass embedded along its top. Fraser strolled casually along the lane passing a heavy wooden gate, aware that the wall marked one of the boundaries of the villa of the Duke of Porto Christo.

At the far side of the trees the lane degenerated into a sandy track which gradually merged with the stubble and sand of a field. The field curved upwards to a promontory instantly recognisable to Fraser from the photographs he had studied the night before.

His eyes scanned the ridge of the promontory until he found what he was looking for. The silo stood on the edge of the ridge, a tower of shining silver metal gleaming in the sun. At the side he could see a metal ladder running from the ground to the top of the tower.

Ten minutes later, sweat covering his forehead, soaking the back of his shirt and almost liquifying the palms of his hands, he had scaled the silo. Slowly he edged his way around its circumference and lay, peering down over the rim of the tower. Under his body he felt the metallic surface heating up under the rays of the morning sun. Ignoring this he looked down at the villa below.

The silo was ideally sited, he knew at once. The entire rear of the villa was open to his gaze. A long shaded patio ran the length of the building and steps from the patio led down to a green sward of grass surrounded at its edges by bushes of lilac and bougainvillaea. The profusion of colour almost effectively concealed the boundaries of the garden and a tall wire fence which, at the rear of the property, had taken the place of the stone wall.

Fraser climbed thoughtfully back to earth. The silo was an ideal vantage point and indeed perfect for a sniper. The metal rungs of the silo were ridged and wide enough for a quick descent. And because they were at the side away from the villa anyone descending was effectively hidden from the garden. Once on the ground he could take off in various directions depending on where he chose to conceal his car.

As he reached the ground Fraser realised that what had seemed an academic exercise, an unreal return to his old and hated profession, was actually much more than that. Just over twenty-four hours from now, if he was unable to find Jill, unable to free her from the young lunatics of the Holgar Group, he would have to climb again to the top of the silo and, this time, he would be armed and forced to commit murder.

He found himself unmoved by the thought of killing Alexander Scherer. From all he had read of the man, his work and his politics, his character was abhorrent to Fraser. A Teutonic version of the late Senator Joseph McCarthy, a man who did not hesitate to destroy the careers and reputations of many sincere liberal-minded men, Scherer was also tinged with darker attributes. It was said that he was behind much of the resurgence of the Nazis in West Germany, that it was Scherer's money that financed many of the underground Fascist groups which were beginning to surface in the larger cities of West Germany.

And yet, despite all this Fraser did not want to kill Scherer. He did not want to kill anyone again. His dis-illusionment with the politics of destruction and murder had long since grown into the very marrow of his being. Murder and war, he believed, were no longer solutions to today's problems. When you killed a man like Scherer it was as if you took over a part of him; as if you absorbed into yourself some of the evil you sought to eradicate.

Fraser smiled to himself. Perhaps he was getting religion;

certainly he was developing a morality he would have dismissed years before. It was, he told himself, a conversion born of hard experience and five killings. And then he thought of Hartley and he felt sick, nauseous at what he might have to do.

He walked down the slope of the promontory, taking deep breaths to rid himself of the uneasiness in his stomach. At the foot of the rising ground he came up to the wire fence and, carefully picking his way around rocks and stubble, he followed the fence until he reached a section of it obscured from the villa by a large spreading clump of bougainvillaea.

A crooked tree, the wood dying for lack of moisture in the soil, reached up towards the top of the fence on the outer edge. Fraser made a sudden decision and, reaching up, grabbed a part of the trunk and, with a minimum of effort, pulled himself up until he was level with the top of the fence.

Thrusting himself forward he cleared the fence and fell between it and the bougainvillaea. He landed awkwardly on his heels and fell back against the fence. As he did so a sudden stab of fear that it might be electrified was stilled when the metal wires of the fence merely groaned back at him. Straightening up, he moved silently around the bush towards the villa.

There was no one in sight as he walked across the lawn, no movement behind the windows or on the patio. He hesitated, looking around. Something was worrying him. It was all too easy to enter the grounds and there seemed nothing to prevent him reaching and entering the villa. Surely there should be guards, security men, at least a servant.

He started to move forward again when he heard the sound. At first a padding sound, a rustling in the grass at the side of the villa, it seemed to be coming closer. Turning to face whatever might appear, Fraser reached into his pocket and took out his revolver.

It appeared around the stone wall of the villa, moving now at speed. A lean, brown body behind a flattish head from which alert ears rose, the dog's mouth was half open, the lips curled into a ferocious sneer as it loped towards Fraser. He stood motionless pointing the revolver, only too aware of the strength behind the slim shoulders; the slashing, cutting power of the teeth of the Dobermann Pinscher.

He was bracing himself while he took aim when he heard the voice from the patio.

'*Halte!* Rudi, *halte!*'

The dog came to a stop, almost skidding across the grass. It stood, still snarling and trembling slightly, ripples from its muscles causing its body to twitch under its sleek coat.

His hand shaking slightly, Fraser turned towards the patio. The tall slim figure at the top of the steps was instantly recognisable to him. The cream shirt, open at the neck was spotless and matched the cream-coloured slacks, impeccably tailored, the creases razor-edged. The silk scarf at the throat curved under the narrow chin, cosseting it. The dark hair, slicked back and shining, was discreetly greying at the temples.

'He could have killed you,' Alexander Scherer said softly, lips curving into a small smile. Yet there was no humour in the eyes which looked Fraser up and down, in some way assessing him.

'Perhaps,' Fraser replied. 'Or I, him.'

The stare was held for a moment. Then the German relaxed. 'My money would be on the dog. Join me for morning coffee.'

It was a statement, not a question. Fraser nodded and moved forward. The dog growled. A glance from Scherer silenced it. Fraser climbed the steps until he stood facing Scherer. The man turned and gestured towards a small table on which was a spotless white table cloth, cups and plates. Three chairs were arranged around the table.

'Please,' said Scherer and Fraser sat down. The German lifted a small handbell and shook it.

'Mr Fraser?' he inquired. 'It *is* Mr Mark Fraser?'

Before Mark could reply the door leading into the villa opened and a manservant, a tall, lantern-jawed Spaniard, came out.

'Coffee, please, Miguel,' Scherer ordered without turning away from Fraser.

The servant inclined his head and disappeared back into the villa silently.

'Grigor?' Fraser questioned. 'Lieutenant-Colonel Grigor of the KGB?'

Scherer's eyebrows rose.

'I beg your pardon?'

'The man who told you to expect me?'

Scherer neither assented or otherwise. 'A Russian?' he said, seemingly amused. 'Why would a Russian call me friend, Mr Fraser? I and my newspapers have been instrumental in exposing a great many Communists and their sympathisers in Germany.'

Fraser nodded. 'Alexander Scherer, the high priest of West German McCarthyism.'

'I'm glad you recognise me. And I would not be ashamed of such a title, if it were not a little *passé*. But why therefore should I receive such sympathetic treatment from the Soviets?'

'That's what I've been wondering,' Fraser retorted.

Scherer gave an enigmatic shrug. 'Regarding yourself, I have my own sources of information. When Santos Morales arrived in Malaga and was thrown out of a high window by the Israelis, there had to be someone else to take his place. These homicidal children, once they get an idea in their minds, don't give up. And they are astute enough to look for the experts. Information therefore led to you.'

'Why me? There are others.'

'I was informed you were in Spain. But I presume you are not here to kill me today?'

It was Fraser's turn to shrug. 'Why that presumption?'

'It would not be spectacular enough for these young people. They must have an audience when they kill . . . even by proxy. And I hardly think you would stroll across my lawn so casually if you intended to kill me just now.'

'It might be the ideal way.'

Scherer laughed. 'Oh, no, I don't think so. But why have you come to see me?'

151

'I think, to warn you,' Fraser said quietly.

The manservant appeared again, carrying a silver tray on which was an ornate coffee pot and a jug of milk. He placed it in front of Scherer.

'Thank you, that will be all,' Scherer dismissed him with a wave of his hand and the man disappeared into the villa once more.

'Black or white, Mr Fraser?'

'Black will be fine.'

Scherer poured two cups of black coffee, handed one to Fraser and then looked up at him. It was a piercing look, the forehead creased questioningly.

'You have come to warn me? Most considerate. I should be surprised, but then you are no longer a professional assassin, I understand.'

'You're well-informed.'

'And of course they have your wife as a hostage!'

Fraser should have felt no surprise this time. Too many people knew what only he and those holding his wife should know. First it was Bartlett, then Grigor and the Russians. Now Scherer, the intended victim, knew. But who had told him? And if he knew so much, he might know even more.

'Your information services wouldn't know where they are holding her?' he asked, a spark of hope in his mind.

'Unfortunately, no,' Scherer replied, a note of sincerity in his voice. 'If I knew I would most certainly tell you. More, I would help you to . . . rescue her. As it is I cannot help. But I must say I am relieved you have come to me before, shall we say, you took any further action.'

Fraser took a sip of his coffee.

'I wouldn't be too relieved, Herr Scherer,' he said calmly. 'You see, if I can't rescue my wife, then I'll have to do exactly what these people want. And of course you won't know when or where.'

Scherer seemed unconcerned. It struck Fraser that, sitting on the patio of this large, luxurious villa, they were like two chess players, each carefully choosing his move.

'And if I had you arrested now?' Scherer questioned.

152

'What could you do?'

'Expedite the task I have been given. You'd be dead before you made a move.'

Scherer's gaze was steady. 'Of course I could inform the police once you had gone. They would pick you up . . .'

'They might pick me up. On the other hand I might kill you before they were able to pick me up.'

Scherer smiled. 'You have a point. I shall not call the police. Instead . . . another cup of coffee, Mr Fraser?'

'Thank you, Herr Scherer.'

ELEVEN

An hour later Mark Fraser left Scherer and, returning to his car, drove back to his hotel. The heat of the day and the amount of coffee consumed with Scherer had taken away his appetite for lunch. And so, deciding to cool off, he changed into a pair of swimming trunks he purchased from the hotel boutique and dived into the pool. The coolness of the water was stimulating after the heavy midday heat and, having covered several lengths of the pool, he relaxed completely and lay floating on an air-bed, trailing his arms on its surface.

The fear of what might happen to Jill still filled his mind and was complicated by the many questions to which he had no answer. Scherer had been unable to satisfy his curiosity as to why the Russians were trying to protect the German newspaper proprietor. And where did British Intelligence fit into the picture? Bartlett, in his own way, before he had been killed, seemed to have tried to help him in his progress. And Bartlett would never have done anything without the knowledge and, indeed, the connivance of the Department. He could hardly believe London was assisting him out of some feeling for an ex-operative; especially an operative who had parted not without rancour from their employment. He lay back on the air-bed and closed his eyes. He was still a puzzled man.

Some eighty feet above the pool the man stood staring down at Fraser from the balcony of a fifth-floor room. Dressed in a lightweight dark suit, collar and tie, the man was feeling the heat. A trickle of perspiration ran down his spine, and his hands, gripping the rail of the balcony, were damp.

Still staring down at Fraser, he mopped his hands

with a handkerchief, produced a small pair of binoculars from his pocket, and focused on the man on the air-bed in the centre of the pool. He then permitted himself a smile.

Thanks to information supplied, Frank Lloyd had at last made contact with Mark Fraser.

Mackeson would be relieved and pleased, Lloyd reckoned. As long as the department was out of touch with Fraser, the Scot represented a danger. They had no control over what he might or might not do. But now he was under the eye of Frank Lloyd and could be controlled.

From the air-bed, Fraser eventually retreated to a sun couch under a large striped umbrella. Here, after sipping a small malt wisky in a large tumbler, he dozed off for an hour. Then, waking with a start and feeling a flood of guilt that he should be able to relax while Jill was still held captive he went quickly up to his bedroom and, lifting the bedside telephone, dialled Rocas' number in Granada.

After a moment Rocas' voice came through. '*Si?*'

'This is Gerrard,' said Fraser.

'Ah, *si*. Yes, Señor Gerrard.'

'Have you got anything for me?'

Rocas seemed to hesitate before replying. 'Eh . . . not yet. They were in a farmhouse above Malaga the first night. But they are clever. They move on. As yet we do not know where. Perhaps tomorrow . . .'

Fraser found he was holding the telephone receiver in such a tight grip that his knuckles showed white and bloodless.

'I have to know before midday. Otherwise it will be too late.'

At the other end of the line it seemed as if Rocas took a deep breath. 'I will do my best.'

Fraser hung up. It seemed as if his best was not going to be good enough. And now Fraser was not afraid of the planned assassination. He was more terrified over what would happen after the assassination. The Holgar Group could release Jill as they had promised. But although two of them were known to Whitehall, the one whom he surmised was the leader, the young man with the old face whom he had met at Mijas, was not known to anyone. Yet, now, Jill would know him and that knowledge would be enough reason for their not releasing her alive. Fraser felt sick at the thought. She could even be dead already, but he did not think this likely. She was still an asset to them in case Fraser had second thoughts.

He dined alone in a secluded corner of the dining-room that night. He ate sparingly and drank only a half bottle of light wine. Tomorrow he would need his strength and his reactions would have to function without a flaw. Yet, as he ate, small tantalising thoughts played around at the back of his mind; ideas, at first shapeless, began to take form. There had to be solutions to all his questions and now he felt he was beginning to perceive those solutions.

After dinner he took a short stroll. The glaring light of the yellow sun had been replaced by a blue-black darkness broken only by the cold glare of each street lamp. Back at the hotel he went to his room and went to bed. It was just after ten o'clock. The next day was Friday when he was expected to kill a man. And it was also the day the Holgar Group would have no further use for his wife.

For the first time since he had left Scotland he slept deeply. There were no dreams. Simply an oblivion into which he sank with gratitude.

At five o'clock in the morning he awoke, aware that he was not alone in his room. There were minute sounds, the creak of a floorboard, a feeling of movement in the air beyond the bed. Fraser tensed, forcing away sleep, preparing himself. Through the sides of the closed curtain the beginnings of daylight filtered through into the room; and between his vision of the light there interposed a darker shape moving slowly and carefully.

Fraser threw himself upwards, casting aside the solitary thin sheet that had been his only cover. As he did so, his hands came forward, open and ready, grasping out at the darker shadow. They closed just below the neck of the figure, fingers digging into the cotton of the shirt and the thin wool of a light pullover. Pressing forward, Fraser pinioned the man against the wall beyond the bed. From the man came a gasping exhalation of air and a surprised, protesting moan.

At the same time as he had thrust the man against the wall, Fraser brought his knee up with some force digging into the crotch. The moan became a cry of agony and the figure slid to the floor.

Fraser switched on the light and turned to peer down at the shocked, agonised face of Frank Lloyd.

'You . . . haven't . . . lost your . . . touch!' Lloyd forced the words out, his hands clutching at the pain between his legs.

'Frank!' Fraser was genuinely surprised. 'What the hell are you doing here?'

'If . . . if you'll give me a second I might be able to tell you.'

With an effort Lloyd eased himself on to the only chair in the room. He lay back in silence for two minutes, Fraser standing staring down at him. Finally Fraser lit two cigarettes and gave Lloyd one. The thin Englishman took a long draw from the cigarette. He was deadly pale and his hand shook.

'I had stopped smoking but I'll make this an exception.'

'Well?' Fraser repeated his question. 'What are you doing here?'

'I got here yesterday. Been keeping an eye on you.'

'Oh, that makes me feel wanted,' Fraser replied with ill-concealed irony. 'So you stalk into my bedroom in the small hours . . .'

'Didn't want anybody else who might be watching you to see me,' Lloyd explained, taking another puff at the cigarette. Colour was now returning to his face. 'And I suppose I couldn't resist a touch of the old melodrama; I merely intended to wake you and give you a bit of a surprise.'

'You could have got yourself killed.'

'Just the point,' Lloyd went on. 'Bartlett *was* killed. I don't know whether you knew that. Poor old Bulldog Drummond. All he was doing was trying to help you. I've taken over. To see you come to no harm.'

157

'I've been wondering about Bartlett,' Fraser frowned. 'And now I'm wondering about you, friend. What was he playing at?'

'Told you. We told him to look after you.'

'Why?'

The question seemed to echo around the room. Lloyd blinked, took another draw from the cigarette and cleared his throat.

'You're a British subject and all that . . .'

Fraser cut in angrily. 'Don't give me that crap, Frank! Your people don't give a tosser for me! But they seem to know why I'm here.'

'We know you're trying to find your wife.'

'Rocas, Bartlett's man in Granada, could have told you that. But he worked for Bartlett so he is working for you . . .'

'Spot on, old man,' Lloyd was looking more cheerful. 'I think Rocas probably told London you were here. They passed the word on to me.'

Fraser, who had been sleeping in his shorts, lifted a pair of trousers and slipped them on. Then he looked back at Lloyd and this time spoke quietly.

'All right! Now the truth. Why are you here?'

'I keep telling you, Sir James thinks you need looking after.'

'How nice of him. I don't believe a word. Apart from my wife, does he know anything else about my being here?'

Lloyd blinked. He seemed genuinely puzzled. 'I don't think so. We presume you're up to something but we just don't want you in trouble. Oh, for God's sake, Mark, you did work for us . . . for the Department . . .'

'And got out when I was sick of it all. The Department has no cause to love me!'

Standing up unsteadily Lloyd looked around for an ashtray. Finding one by the bed he stubbed out his cigarette. He then went into the bathroom.

Fraser heard the sound of running water and then Lloyd came out of the bathroom, drying his face with a small towel.

'I needed that after your athletics,' he explained. 'Look, Mark, you're here creating trouble. I understand why, when your wife is missing. But I'm here to see you create no more trouble until we find your wife.'

'We?'

'I told you, I've orders to help.' He sat down.

Fraser thought it over for a minute. Lloyd was here. He could be useful or he could be a handicap. And if necessary he could be got rid of.

'Look, I'll see you at breakfast,' Fraser said finally.

Lloyd seemed for once to be alert, almost as if he could read Fraser's thoughts. 'I should stay with you.'

'I assure you I intend to do nothing until after breakfast.'

It was Lloyd's turn to think it over. Then he nodded. 'Nine o'clock.'

'Nine o'clock.'

Lloyd rose.

'Oh, and Frank,' Fraser went on. 'No need to crash in on me at night. It's too melodramatic. You could have phoned.'

His face reddening, Lloyd left.

Fraser spent the next hour and a half assembling and reassembling the sniper's rifle. He tested all the moving parts and lightly oiled them. When everything was functioning to his satisfaction he studied and checked the sights. Then he turned to the ammunition which had been supplied. He selected three bullets and produced a pocket knife.

It was past seven o'clock when he was finally satisfied with his work. He took a quick shower and lay on the bed, relaxed, smoking a Gitane, and then, when he had stubbed it out, he dozed for a while.

At nine o'clock he was at the breakfast table finishing his coffee when Lloyd rejoined him.

'Morning!' Lloyd said with an assumed air of cheerfulness.

'I thought we'd had all that,' Fraser replied pouring him a coffee. 'So now you're here to help me, what do we do?'

Lloyd blinked. 'Wait here until Rocas gets some information as to where your wife is.'

'That's all? Just wait here?'

'Nothing else we can do.'

'In that case I should be back in my room. Waiting for
Rocas to call.'

'If you like,' Lloyd responded with some relief. The sun
was getting warm despite the early hour and Lloyd was
beginning to discover he did not like the sun. 'And I shall
stick with you.'

They finished breakfast and returned to Fraser's room.
Fraser had deliberately left the gun-case open beside the
bed, the assembled rifle lying on top of the case. Lloyd's
eyes settled on it. Fraser waited for the reaction. He had
determined in his mind that Lloyd's reaction might indicate the Englishman knew more than he had admitted.

But Lloyd's reaction seemed genuine. 'Good God, that's
a lethal little toy. What is it? A relic of the old days?'

'Hardly. I couldn't have brought it into Spain if it was.'
Lloyd nodded. 'That's true. Be taking an awful chance
anyway. They're pretty hot on firearms with their Basque
terrorist people around.' A thought struck him. 'You mean
you got it here?'

Fraser took a deep breath. Lloyd was studying the rifle
with what seemed like an academic interest and nothing
more. But there had to be something more; there had to
be curiosity at least, if not knowledge.

'Frank?' Fraser said. 'You have never asked me why
these kids kidnapped my wife and why they brought me to
Spain?'

Lloyd regarded him, a wary look creeping into his face.
'Ours not to reason why, old man,' he replied. 'Mackeson
seemed to have no interest in that question. I assumed
these kids, as you call them, were getting back at you for
one of your past exploits.'

It was a weak answer, so weak as to be possibly the truth.
And Frank Lloyd was never one to ask questions. He did
exactly what he was told; he had been trained to do just
that and no more. Initiative in the field was something you

left to others in Lloyd's scheme of things, something only permitted to those with higher grades in the operational pattern of the Department. If Mackeson wanted Lloyd to know more, then he would tell Lloyd. So the question now became, how much did Mackeson know? And Fraser was sure he would not learn that from Frank Lloyd.

Fraser glanced at his watch. It was past ten o'clock. Less than two hours until the deadline. How appropriate that word seemed. And even if Rocas phoned with information it would be too late. He knew he had to put the operation into motion now. And that meant getting rid of Lloyd.

'Frank, come here,' he said, stepping onto the balcony. As he did so he studied the glass doors separating the balcony from the room. The glass was thick, heavy, unbreakable. Outside on the balcony too there was an eight-foot separation between the balconies on each side. Impossible to cross from one to the other without considerable risk of falling five floors to the concrete below.

Lloyd joined him on the balcony.

'I want you to take a good look over there,' Fraser said, indicating the furthest building he could see at the edge of Marbella. Lloyd stepped to the rail of the balcony peering into a haze of heat, towards a massive oblong building, a new hotel thrusting its way into the sky.

'What is it?' he asked. 'I don't see . . .'

The glass doors of the balcony were slammed behind him. He turned to see Fraser on the other side of the glass turning the lock on the inside of the doors.

Lloyd stepped to the glass, shouting, but in the room, Fraser could barely hear him. Lloyd battered on the glass with the palms of both hands. All he succeeded in doing was rattling the frame which held the glass.

With a slight smile, Fraser nodded to him, and wrapping the rifle in a towel, walked to the door of the room. From the handle at the back of the door he took a card which hung on a string and opening the door he stepped into the corridor. He hung the card on the outside handle and closed the door. On the card in four languages was a firm instruction not to disturb the occupant of the room.

161

Over an hour later Fraser had circled the villa in which Scherer was staying and climbed up the promontory to the foot of the silo. The gold Capri was parked off the road at the entrance to a field on the far side of the villa. It stood shaded under wild bougainvillaea, hidden from the road. Fraser had calculated that, from the foot of the silo, he could reach the car in just over sixty seconds at a run and the entire length of the run would be invisible from both the villa and the lane at the side of the villa. It would mean moving fast over rocky ground along the foot of a small gully. But the gully provided cover for almost its entire length.

He settled himself against the metal of the silo and smoked two cigarettes, his eye on his wrist watch. When he had finished each cigarette he carefully placed the stub in his pocket. Nothing was to be left lying around.

He let himself relax; his hands were steady and, apart from the growing heat of the day, he was comfortable. The rifle, still wrapped in the towel, lay beside him. It would not be unwrapped until he climbed the silo. There was always an outside chance of someone passing, one of the locals, a farmer or a labourer on some errand. All they would see, should they come near the silo, would be a tourist resting in the shade, a towel at his side.

At ten minutes to twelve, after assuring himself that there was no one in sight, Fraser climbed to the top of the silo, the towel and its contents under his arm. He settled himself at first on the top of the metal tower on the side away from the villa. Here he unwrapped the rifle and carefully loaded it with the three bullets in the magazine. Only after he had done this did he crawl across the slightly curved dome and settle himself facing the villa.

Below, in the garden he had crossed only the day before, there was considerable activity. Two long trestle tables had been erected and were covered with spotlessly clean white table cloths. On each table were platters containing sandwiches, cakes, fruit and all the necessities for a garden party. At each table too were liveried servants waiting to assist the guests, standing, it seemed to Fraser from his distant vantage point, at attention in almost military fashion. A third table, against the wall of the villa, held a variety of bottles and rows of glasses, some long stemmed for champagne or wine, others, tumblers, for spirits. Three local musicians under large sombreros were playing guitars. Fraser could hear the inconsequential music faintly despite the distance. Or did he simply imagine it?

Already the garden was beginning to fill with guests. Although many of the men were dressed casually in slacks, light blazers and sports shirts, there was a sprinkling of uniforms, officers with a surfeit of braid on their caps and on their shoulders. The women were in chic summer dresses, some with bare shoulders and all with the sparkle of jewellery under the risen sun. They formed small groups around the garden, chatting, laughing, gesticulating and with each new arrival there were, among the women, embraces, the kissing of cheeks; among the men, profuse and hearty handshakes.

All this Fraser viewed through the telescopic sights of the sniper's rifle. His vision ranged around the garden, searching each group, studying the faces which, with the powerful sight, he could see with amazing clarity. There was no sign of Scherer.

He glanced at his watch again. Four minutes to twelve. Scherer would obviously make an entrance with his host, probably exactly at midday.

Fraser waited.

It was three minutes past twelve when Scherer finally appeared on the patio. At his side was a small portly figure exquisitely dressed in grey flannels, a grey silk shirt and a grey scarf. The grey man was obviously the Duke of Porto Christo. Beside the vision of plump greyness, Scherer was dressed as he had been the day before, except that now he was wearing a lightweight blazer.

The two men hesitated on the patio, shaded by the red slate roof. In the dim light Fraser could just make out that the Duke was introducing Scherer to one of the guests. They stood in shadow for some moments talking, the Duke, voluble, gesticulating with enthusiasm.

Fraser moved his telescopic sight lower, focusing on the centre of the stairs from the patio. Another minute past and then Scherer came into vision strolling down the stairs into the sunlight, the Duke at his side. Fraser now had Scherer in his sights and he followed him as the tall German moved to the first group of guests. Hands were shaken and it occurred to Fraser that the whole affair was like a royal garden party in miniature.

Then Scherer was still, in the centre of Fraser's sights, standing motionless, listening to one of the group. Fraser aligned the sights until the hairline cross in the centre was over the forehead of the target.

Gently he squeezed the trigger.

The sound of the shot seemed to Fraser to echo around and around the silo, reverberating against the metal. Somewhere amid the bougainvillaea a bird cried out and soared into the sky.

Below Fraser, in the garden of the villa, Alexander Scherer seemed to stumble, hesitate, and then fall backwards onto the grass. And for what seemed a long moment those around him stood like statues, unmoving, frozen in time.

Fraser waited only seconds to view the reaction of those around the fallen German. Then he slid backwards out of sight of the villa and, twisting the towel quickly around the rifle he lowered himself onto the topmost rung of the steel ladder and descended to the ground.

As he did so, faintly, in the distance he could hear excited shouts and one short sharp scream from the garden below.

He ran swiftly to the gully and, stumbling once, regained his balance and moved off towards his car.

TWELVE

At the front of the villa of the Duke of Porto Christo was a large expanse of tarmac which served as a car park. By ten minutes to midday every available parking space was occupied by a variegated collection of cars, ranging from Rolls-Royces, two Silver Ghosts and an elderly black model, to Mercedes, Citroens, and at least one Cadillac.

As the occupants of the rear seats of these vehicles disappeared into the villa, their chauffeurs congregated at one side of the tarmac where a small table had been set up and a light beer was being served to them. Mingling with this congregation, one as variegated as the cars they drove, was a tall slim figure who spoke to no one and seemed more interested in the villa itself than the amount of beer he could obtain.

Jurgen Haussmann had arranged to be engaged on a part-time basis when needed by a car hire firm in Marbella. This was patronised by certain local dignitaries who preferred, on certain occasions, to hire a rather more expensive car than the one which they actually owned. Money had passed between Jurgen and one of the drivers who had agreed to be ill on that particular Friday. Jurgen had been called in as his replacement.

He had no fear that there would be any repercussions when the police started investigations. Outside the villa he had another car waiting and, once he had ascertained that Fraser had carried out his mission, Haussmann would move towards that car and drive off. Two guests, a local politician and his wife, would find to their surprise that their chauffeur had disappeared. Should any police investigation go further, then the driver who had received money from a young unknown foreigner, possibly German, would have awkward questions to answer. Meanwhile Jurgen Haussmann would have disappeared.

It was not long after midday when Haussmann heard the sound of a shot followed by shouting and a scream. In company with the assembled drivers he moved towards the door of the villa. Two minutes later the door opened and a Spanish manservant, obviously someone in authority, came out and addressed the chauffeurs.

Haussmann's Spanish was rudimentary but he managed to make out something of what was said.

An accident . . . serious . . . they were to be ready shortly . . . the garden party would not last now as long as expected . . . nothing must be said . . .

The manservant turned, about to withdraw into the villa. One of the chauffeurs, an elderly man, who happened to be closest to the entrance to the house, muttered a question. The manservant turned back, seemed to recognise the elderly man, and replied to his question with a slight, regretful shrug. He then went back into the villa. Jurgen sidled up to the elderly man who was talking volubly now to his companions.

'Dead! That is what they say. The German visitor. Dead. Shot dead. Now the police will come . . .'

The rest was lost in a burst of excited chatter from the others. Jurgen's lips tightened into the beginnings of a smile but he knew he had to restrain himself from giving any visible signs of how he actually felt.

It had been done. Fraser had carried out the mission and with success.

It was time for him to go.

Mark Fraser was driving back towards the El Rodeo. He had reached his car with only a slight shortness of breath, deposited the rifle, still wrapped in the towel, in the boot of the car under the spare wheel, and driven off, unhurried now, almost casual, a tourist who had accidentally driven off the road.

As he drove into the town, he mentally cursed himself

for the necessity to return to the hotel. He had left his few belongings in his small case in the hotel room. He could have left these there but it would only have incurred some suspicion. That is, if anyone was going to be suspicious of a British tourist travelling light. And of course there was Frank Lloyd. He would be subjected to questions from Frank Lloyd which, it occurred to him, was ironic. He, Fraser, still had questions to ask of Lloyd, or the man behind Lloyd. Mackeson, sitting comfortably in London, might have some answers.

While he had been sitting waiting in the shade of the silo, he had had a little time to work out some possible answers. Yet each time he did so, he was left with more questions. The KGB had been trying to protect Scherer from assassination. Why? That was still the first question. But there were others. How much did the Department know? What was Mackeson's involvement? Were they really afraid that Fraser's past activities on their behalf would prove an embarrassment and therefore were they trying only to help him find his wife and keep out of trouble? That was Lloyd's story and Lloyd believed it. But it was too easy for Fraser, too naïve.

Under that silo he had worked out his next move. And if his suspicions were justified it would be a move that now would produce results. He prayed only that the results would not be too late. The matter of Scherer was over. He could only pray that the matter of Jill Fraser was not.

Lloyd was sitting on the patio outside the entrance to the El Rodeo when Fraser drove into the hotel car park. He was sipping coffee and across his face was an expression of extreme irritation.

'Mark!' he barked out as Fraser ran up the steps to the hotel entrance. Fraser paused reluctantly.

'Mark, where the hell have you been?' Lloyd went on. 'And what the hell did you think you were doing locking me out on that damned balcony?'

Fraser, despite his impatience, could not resist a smile. 'Thought you needed some air, old man. Doesn't seem to have done you much good.'

'I had to shout down to some ruddy porter to let me out!' Lloyd explained, his face red.

'You can get too much sun in this part of the world,' Fraser replied and continued into the foyer of the hotel, Lloyd following him angrily.

'What the devil is it all about?' he demanded of Fraser as they entered the elevator.

'Now you're asking the right questions,' Fraser replied. 'But at the wrong time. Perhaps you're too late, Frank . . .'

'For what, for God's sake?'

Fraser looked at him as the elevator shuddered and started to move upwards. 'Mackeson didn't brief you very well, did he?'

'Look, I've told you before, I was sent here to look after you. To help you.'

Fraser grinned. 'Help me do what?'

'Find your wife.'

The elevator rattled to a halt and the doors slid open. Fraser stepped onto the landing and turned to face Lloyd.

'I'm going to do just that now. But I don't want you around, Frank. So keep out of my way. Otherwise, I'll roll over you.'

So saying, he gently pushed Lloyd back into the lift and pressed the descend button on the outside. The doors slid shut, separating them.

Rolf Gruner was pacing up and down between the pillars of the castle's inner courtyard. Occasionally he strolled to the outer gate, stared long and hard down the winding road across the plain, and then returned to the shade of the inner yard.

Elisa Toth appeared at the open door of the castle.

'How long?' she asked.

'For Jurgen, about two hours' drive,' he replied. 'Maybe two hours and a half.'

'Do you think Fraser will have . . .?'

'I think nothing,' Rolf interrupted her, irritably. 'I wait until I hear!'

He turned away from her with ill-concealed impatience. He had to know whether Scherer has been killed or not; whether months of planning had come to fruition. Yet he could not bear to see his own impatience reflected in another. He walked again to the outer courtyard, stared for a moment at the road, still devoid of traffic, then, on impulse, glanced up at the ramparts of the castle.

He could just make out the figures on the roof, the two captive women leaning against the battlements. They were his next and final problem.

Final problem? Was the phrase only too appropriate? It would be the one remaining problem if Scherer was indeed assassinated. To dispose of the women. And indeed the other occupants of the castle. The neat answer was obvious, the final solution, that was the apposite phrase. The loose ends would be tidied up, dangers removed. They would no longer be able to identify him.

He frowned. There had been the meeting with Fraser; the identification there. He should have sent Jurgen to do that. Yet he had been uncertain of Jurgen's ability to remain calm and direct while giving Fraser instructions. No, he had had to do that himself. Therefore, apart from the women, Fraser was another problem. Of course, with some luck, the Spanish authorities might take care of Fraser if they caught him. And if they didn't then he could be taken care of in other ways. How were these ways described? Not taken care of; removed with extreme prejudice. There were others who could remove Fraser with extreme prejudice. Meanwhile his immediate task would be the women.

It might have seemed, like Hamlet, that his thoughts flew upwards. The two women on the battlements were discussing the very subject he was considering.

'You believe they will kill us, don't you?' Jill asked, feeling the stone of the wall warm under her touch.

'I think so,' Louisa nodded.

'Then it will be today?'

Another nod of agreement. 'There is also my husband and our two servants. Still, I suppose, to people like these,

169

the risk is the same. If you kill two, you can kill five.'

Jill felt calm, emotionless now. They were talking dispassionately of their own deaths. She was surprised at her serenity. It was probable, she thought, that despite the words, despite the meaning of the words, the reality had not actually penetrated.

She stared out across the plain at the far Sierras. What were the words of the old hymn?

I lift mine eyes unto the hills from whence doth come my aid.

Nothing moved on the plain or the hills but a ripple across her vision, a haze of heat distorting momentarily the distant vista.

Lloyd had watched Fraser come down from his room and pay his bill at the reception desk. As Fraser came out of the foyer into the sun, Lloyd had stepped forward, about to speak. But Fraser froze him with a look.

'I told you, Frank, to get out of my way. If you come between me and my search for Jill, then I'll kill you.'

Lloyd opened his mouth and then closed it again. The man was serious and indeed possibly unstable because of his concern for his wife. There was no use reiterating that he had only come to help. Fraser had already ignored that statement and indeed, Lloyd himself had, on repeating it, found an uncertainty in himself that he had refused to acknowledge before. It was true Mackeson had said that he was to aid Fraser but there was something more behind what Mackeson had said. There was always something more behind what that man said. In his world nothing should be taken at face value, that was something Lloyd had learned during his years with the Department. Even when most of that time had been spent behind a desk in Whitehall, there was always the knowledge that what the agents in the field appeared to be doing often resulted in quite the reverse result from that which he had expected. And his master, whether it be Tarrant or Mackeson, would in general expect the surprise outcome. Years ago, when he had first joined the Department, the Firm, call it what they might, he had been warned to acknowledge nothing was what it seemed. And the warning had come from two past-masters in the game; the first, Philby, and the other a man called Skardon.

He watched Fraser climb into the Capri and drive out of the hotel grounds. He noted that Fraser had turned north. It was at least an indication of direction. He could be going to Malaga, Granada or even further; and he could be followed. But Lloyd knew Fraser would not allow himself to be followed.

Returning to the foyer, Lloyd lifted the public telephone and dialled the number he had been given in London. To be used if he had problems or emergencies, that was the instruction that had gone with the number. He had nearly used it when he had been released from the balcony of Fraser's room, but he had decided to hold off as he had known Fraser should return for his belongings. At least he had been right in that small assumption. Where Fraser had gone and what he had done, Lloyd could not even guess at.

The receiver was lifted at the other end of the line.

'Yes?'

'Fraser's left the El Rodeo. He's heading north.'

'You've no idea where?'

'None. I could have followed him but . . .'

'Yes?'

'I think he would have prevented me doing so. And my instructions were to help him but avoid incidents.'

'I am aware of what your instructions were.'

Lloyd took a deep breath and decided it was time to be daring. 'One thing, though. What is this all about? There's obviously more to it . . .'

The voice, which seemed vaguely familiar, if distorted by a bad line, cut him off abruptly.

'You will wait at your hotel until you receive further instructions.'

He heard the receiver being replaced and he duly replaced his own. The questions were still in his head but he had been trained to know that he should not ask them. He walked out on to the patio still asking them of himself.

The radio in the sitting-room of the castle was a large, old-fashioned, box-like creation of wood. Rolf bent over it, adjusting the knobs until he found himself listening to the local Spanish news announcements. It was the first item that he wanted to hear.

'An unconfirmed report from Marbella indicating that a prominent foreign national has been assassinated has just been received,' the newscaster's voice droned out in Spanish. 'The suggestion that Basque terrorists may be responsible has not been denied by the police . . .'

He switched off the radio and turned from it, his mouth twisted into a facsimile of a smile. He found himself staring at Elisa who had entered the room behind him.

'Is it true?' she asked, eyes gleaming with a barely suppressed excitement.

Rolf shrugged. 'We will have to wait for Jurgen . . .'

The sound of a car engine reached them through the open window.

'Come!' Rolf ordered her. 'In case it is not Jurgen, you will cover me.'

The car was drawing to a halt in the outer courtyard as they came out of the castle. Jurgen eased himself from behind the driving seat and came towards them.

'He did it!' he said exultantly.

Rolf nodded. 'There was an unconfirmed report on the radio . . .'

'I heard the shot,' Jurgen went on. 'And then there was a kind of commotion . . .'

'You saw the body?'

Jurgen became exasperated. 'How could I? They wouldn't let us in. But there was the shot and then they came out and told us. And there was a police siren when I left.'

Rolf kicked the dust with his foot, thoughtfully. Elisa stared at him and then at Jurgen.

172

'For God's sake, he wants a death certificate!'

'No!' Rolf looked up and again there was the attempt at a smile. 'Fraser has done it. He had to.'

Elisa looked up at the ramparts of the castle. 'So now we can get rid of them and go?'

The smile dissolved on Rolf's face. 'Not yet! We have to wait for instructions.' He glanced at Jurgen. 'I want you to reconnect the telephone now, please.'

He turned and retraced his steps into the castle. Elisa stared at Jurgen, frowning. 'Instructions from whom?'

Jurgen shrugged. Such questions held little interest for him. Rolf knew what he was doing and he trusted Rolf. And he was distracted by Gudrun who appeared at the door and ran towards him. There was a sense of security in the warmth of her embrace. But after accepting it with an awkward grin, he disentangled himself from her arms.

'You are all right?' Gudrun asked, as if to reassure herself of the evidence of her eyes.

'I'm all right. And it is done,' he replied allowing a little kindness to creep into his voice. Normally he did not believe in being kind to his women; it gave them proprietory inclinations. However now, the job being nearly over, he could afford a small degree of generosity.

'Now I have to reconnect the telephone for him,' he explained, allowing her to take his arm as they went into the castle. Elisa followed them, the frown still on her face.

Half an hour later, Jurgen finished reconnecting the broken telephone wires. It was a simple task for him, a return to a past when he had been a telephone engineer's apprentice in Bremen. He worked quickly but despite his speed Rolf stood over him impatiently, fingers drumming on the edge of the table. Elisa lolled in one of the deep armchairs, eyebrows raised as she stared at Rolf.

'You said you had to await instructions?' she asked, affecting a casualness she did not feel. She was intrigued and concerned as to who was giving instructions on an operation she had presumed belonged to the Group alone.

'So?' Rolf said, avoiding her look.

'Instructions from whom?' she pressed on.

He swung round irritably. 'Do you really think we set this up on our own? Do you think we had the money to hire Santos before he was killed? He only worked for money, you know, not for any love of a cause. Do you think we could fly to Scotland and get Fraser's wife out without help?'

'Who is helping us?'

'We are not the only people who wanted Scherer dead.'

Jurgen stood up and nodded to Rolf. The telephone was reconnected.

'I want to know who we are working for?' Elisa insisted, cold anger in her tone.

'Damn you!' Rolf shouted. 'There are other revolutionary groups. Now don't just sit there. Get a meal prepared for all of us!'

She rose with deliberate slowness. 'You sound quite the male chauvinist, Rolf. But this is a democratic group. Should we not all know aims, intentions, background to every militant action?'

Rolf stared at her, struggling to keep his irritation under control. 'If we agree a course of action which meets with all our approval, such as the elimination of Scherer, does it matter to whom I have to go for financial help? And when that person, a sympathiser, prefers to remain anonymous, then I find it simpler to keep quiet. After all some of us allow ourselves to fall into enemy hands. Don't we, Elisa?'

Elisa reddened, seemed about to say something and then turned and walked from the room. Rolf looked at Jurgen, as if expecting further questioning from that source, but Jurgen was testing the telephone. Satisfied, after a moment he returned the receiver to its stand.

'You can phone whoever you want from now on,' he said.

Rolf nodded but made no move towards the phone.

Rocas's shop was even dimmer than it had been on Mark Fraser's first visit. Fraser attributed it to the brightness of the sun during the drive from Marbella. At the same time, hot and damp with sweat, he was grateful for the coolness of the shop.

Fraser had driven fast without stopping and during the drive his mind had been active. Rocas was the one contact he had, and Rocas had been given to him through Bartlett from British Intelligence. Therefore now, in his mind, Rocas was suspect. That is, if his ideas were correct. Now he was going to find out. As he shut the door behind him Rocas looked up, eyes accustomed to the gloom. He seemed startled as he recognised Fraser.

'Señor Fraser! You . . . you reached here . . .?'

'Why shouldn't I have reached here?' Fraser asked, Rocas's question the beginning of a confirmation of all that was in his mind.

'I thought . . . the police . . . the road would be blocked.'

'They weren't. That surprises you?' Fraser replied with an assumed serenity he did not feel.

'No matter,' said Rocas, mopping his brow, which had suddenly broken out in a profuse sweat. 'Your wife . . . I am very hopeful that soon I will have some word . . .'

'Not soon. Now!' Fraser's voice was steady. He stepped forward and reached out, grabbing the little man by the lapels of the light jacket and pulling him across his own counter.

'I've been working it out, Señor Rocas. The only possible explanation. From Bartlett to you, all along the line I had all that help to get me to Marbella. Even Frank Lloyd turns up to help. Although, like Bartlett, I don't think he knows what he's doing.'

'I do not know myself, señor,' Rocas squirmed under Fraser's grip.

'Somebody had to know what was going on. Someone who knew the country, who knew I was going to Marbella even before I told him. You, Rocas, you knew that.'

'I only take orders . . .'

'Of course. But from whom? Anyway now you take orders from me. Tell me where my wife is!'

'Why should I know? I am no terrorist . . .'

'But you were told to help me. And helping me meant helping me to complete the mission the terrorists set me. I am therefore hoping that help extended to knowing where they are with my wife. After all they're young Germans. Someone had to suggest safe houses for them. Where is Jill?'

Fraser tightened his grip and Rocas spluttered, coughing nervously.

'They will release her now. The mission is carried out. They will bring her to the Café dos Palmas . . .'

'So you even know all the arrangements? You're really letting it hang out now, Rocas.'

'Yes, *si*, I know the arrangements . . .'

Fraser pulled the little man closer. 'The trouble is I don't think they can afford to let Jill go. Just as you and they might be hoping I would be arrested by the Spanish police at one of the road blocks they must surely have set up around Marbella. That would have eliminated me. And then if they eliminated Jill it would appear I simply killed Scherer off my own bat. One miscalculation. I saw no road blocks.'

Rocas took time to frown. 'I don't understand that . . .'

'Where is my wife?' This time the question was asked with some force. Rocas stared at the tall Scot. The man was coldly angry and he was a former killer; indeed to Rocas, a very recent assassin. And Rocas was no hero. He saw no need to play games when, in the end, this man could make him talk.

'The . . . the Castello de Triana. Near Guadix. They have taken over the castle. It is very easy. The Duke is paralysed and there is only his wife and two very old servants . . .'

Fraser was silent for a moment, considering the disposal of Rocas. Free, the man could contact Lloyd or Mackeson; he could contact anyone involved, perhaps even warn those at the castle. The alternative was to immobilise Rocas for a time. But there was no guarantee for how long he could be immobilised. And then of course he could kill Rocas.

The thought was there, very definitely there. It could be

done silently here, in the darkened shop and, with the shop locked, it might take days before the body was found. Only British Intelligence could link Rocas with Mark Fraser.

It was as if Rocas knew what he was thinking. The small man started to tremble visibly. And, watching him, Fraser felt the man's fear. And his own thoughts made him feel suddenly sick. He had done enough killing. It might be necessary later when he freed Jill. But not now, not without necessity.

'Listen to me,' Fraser said, releasing the man's lapels from his grip. 'If you want to come out of this alive, do nothing. No phone calls, no contacts. If anyone comes, you haven't seen me. Otherwise, I'll be back, and if I haven't got my wife with me, unharmed, I will kill you.'

Rocas nodded vigorously, relief spreading over his mottled complexion. Fraser turned on his heel and went out. The door rattled behind him.

Climbing into his car, he found himself wondering whether he had been right or not to hope that the fear he had instilled in Rocas would be sufficient to prevent him making contact. It had to be; and yet, if it wasn't, he could have endangered Jill's life. Not that there wasn't enough danger already.

He switched on the ignition and as the engine started, he rammed the car into gear. There was little time left.

He drove north from Granada, heading towards Gaudix.

Yet even as he had sat in the car considering whether he had made the correct decision regarding Rocas, he had not noticed the large black sedan parked on the other side of the street and the interest shown in him by the occupant of the rear seat of that car. Only when Fraser had driven off did the door open and the man, left arm in a black sling, step onto the pavement. With a muttered instruction to his driver he walked to Rocas's shop and entered.

Rocas was behind the counter gulping cognac nervously from a large tumbler. He looked up as the man entered, seeing only a shadowy outline. At least Fraser had not come back. And the telephone was in front of Rocas, his free hand on the receiver.

'You were going to telephone?' To Rocas's ears the voice was foreign, guttural; and yet, in its tone, not unfriendly.

'It is not important, señor.'

'I think it might be,' said the shadow, stepping forward. As it came closer Rocas saw the right hand was stretched out and was holding a heavy automatic.

'Mr Fraser is too soft-hearted,' the voice went on. 'So soft-hearted he becomes careless. I think we have to allow him to rescue his lady without warning those who hold her.'

Fear gripped Rocas again. '*Si, si,* we do that!' I do not know such people . . .'

The voice cut in again. 'Unfortunately Mr Fraser leaves so much refuse, so much rubbish behind him. He doesn't clear it up.'

The voice hesitated for a moment before going on. When it did go on again, the tone was almost sad.

'You are the refuse, Señor Rocas. You are the rubbish in this affair. You see, you are rubbish because you do what you do for money. You say you do it for ideals but that is not so. You work neither for belief, or a cause or even love of country. Simply for money. So sordid. So much rubbish.'

Even with a silencer on the gun, the sound of the shot, a noise like the bursting of a paper bag, echoed in the small shop. Rocas, however, heard nothing. The bullet made a small entry hole, flecking his shirt front with blood. Its force threw him back against the wall behind the counter which was festooned with leather goods. Its exit hole was twice the size of a man's fist and the wall and two shining brief cases hanging on the wall were splattered with blood, part of the heart muscle and small fragments of shattered rib. Rocas's face, still with the nervous frown on it, sank down behind the counter.

Colonel Grigor replaced the automatic in his pocket, wincing slightly from a twinge of pain that came from the wound in his left shoulder. Then, with a glance behind the counter to assure himself Rocas was dead, he turned and quietly left the shop.

THIRTEEN

Jill Fraser was again lying on the bed. But this time she was wide-awake, alert and waiting.

Any time now she knew they would be fed. They would hear the door at the foot of the stairs being unlocked and footsteps on the stairs. Then one of the Germans would enter carrying a tray prepared by the two servants who were still being held in the kitchen. And if this time one of the group did not come to feed them, then they would still come for another reason. It was now well into Friday afternoon and Jill knew whatever was to happen to them would happen soon.

The plan of course had come from Louisa. Not that Jill had not been contemplating a plan of her own but it came from the Marquisa first; perhaps because the castle was her home and the violation of it paramount in her mind. And Jill was of course grateful to have an ally.

They heard the door open and shut below. Now it was time to put into operation what could be their last attempt at freedom.

They could hear footsteps on the stairs and then the bedroom door opened. Elisa entered carrying the tray.

She saw only Jill sitting on the bed and she hesitated, looking around for Louisa.

'Where is . . .?' she started to ask when Louisa stepped from behind the door wielding a large ornamental brass salver which had recently decorated the wall in the corridor outside.

The salver rose and fell. It struck Elisa on the side of the head with the sound of a small gong. The tray of food the girl was carrying fell forward with a clatter onto the floor. Elisa herself fell sideways without a sound.

Jill was on her feet at once and beside Louisa. They both stared down at the German girl.

'God!' Louisa exclaimed. 'Have I killed her?'

'I doubt it,' replied Jill and was surprised at her own callousness. She knelt down and searched the unconscious girl. With a satisfied smile she stood up holding Elisa's gun in her hand.

'You didn't hit her hard enough to kill her,' Jill said. 'But when she comes around she'll have a very sore head.'

Louisa gave a nervous grin. 'I wasn't sure I could do it.'

'My husband would be proud of you,' Jill replied matching her grin. 'And now we have this . . .' She showed Louisa the gun.

'I don't think I know how to use those things,' Louisa said apologetically. 'You keep it.' She had an afterthought, 'Can you use it?'

'I think so,' Jill replied, not at all sure that she could. She looked at the gun, decided that the small lever on one side was the safety catch, and slipped it along. Now it should be able to be fired, she thought hopefully. Now all I need is the courage to use it.

Unaware of the onslaught on one of his group Rolf sat alone in the lounge staring at the telephone, waiting for it to ring. He had been waiting ever since Jurgen had reconnected it, and, as he waited, he became more and more impatient. They should have phoned by now. What the hell were they playing at? If he knew Scherer had been assassinated, and there had been a report on the radio, then his prospective caller must now also be satisfied. Yet Jurgen had been back well over an hour and he had heard nothing.

Then the telephone rang.

Rolf stood and lifted the receiver.

'Yes, yes,' he acknowledged his identity to the speaker at the other end of the line. 'Yes, you were right. With the correct pressure Fraser did the job.'

He paused as the voice went on from afar. The speaker was pleased and Rolf felt his pleasure giving him assurance.

180

'Yes, of course we cannot permit any leaking of information,' Rolf took up the conversation. 'The Spanish police should take care of Fraser if they have not already done so. That leaves us to take out his wife.'

The voice cut in again briefly. Rolf found himself nodding as if the speaker could see he was in agreement.

'Of course. Not simply Fraser's wife,' Rolf agreed. 'The others as well. All of them. And then I make contact with you as arranged.'

A terse assent was followed by the click of the receiver being replaced at the other end of the line. The young German replaced his own receiver and, crossing to the sofa, sat down, permitting himself a small satisfied smile. Rolf Gruner could see the end of a successful operation in sight.

It was then that he heard the gunshot from upstairs.

The moments leading up to the gunshot had seemed of interminable length to Jill and Louisa. Stepping over the unconscious body of Elisa Toth they had crept along the corridor leading to the stairs. At the head of the stairs they hesitated. Below they were faced with a locked door. It would be unlocked by whichever of the terrorists was guarding it only to let Elisa Toth out. This would be their one opportunity of getting to the ground floor of the castle.

Jill looked at Louisa. 'You all right?'

'Yes.'

'We'll have to deal with whoever's behind the door.'

Louisa acknowledged the fact with a nod. Then she looked around. At the head of the stairs was a small table on which was a brass candlestick with one candle in it.

'We keep that in case the electricity fails,' Louisa explained. 'It happens out here now and then. But now I think it could be useful in another way. More effective than the salver.'

She lifted the brass candlestick, pulled the candle from the holder, and gripped the candlestick at the top.

'You've got the gun. I'll have this,' she said as if regretful that it might be inadequate.

Jill smiled encouragingly and walked slowly down the stairs. Louisa followed. When they reached the door at the foot, Jill took a deep breath and knocked heavily on the door assuming a confidence she did not feel.

The key turned in the lock and the door swung open.

Jurgen had been dozing when Elisa had brought up the tray and he had let her through the door. He was still tired, the heat of the afternoon and the drive from Marbella having taken their toll. Now, as he reopened the door, he barely glanced at the woman who came through. It was only when he felt the gun press into his side that he turned to face Jill and, behind her, Louisa.

Despite his fatigue his reaction was immediate, his reflexes functioning quickly. His right hand descended on the gun in his side deflecting it outwards, away from his body. At the same time he reached out with his left hand attempting to circle Jill's neck.

The act of firing a gun was not one to which Jill was accustomed; and firing it at close range into the body of a human being was something she could barely bring herself to do. Yet, as she felt his hand twisting her wrist, her finger closed on the trigger and the gun went off. But, pointing away now from Jurgen, the bullet whined across the corridor gouging a scar on the plaster of the wall.

Still struggling, they fell against the skirting board, Jurgen loosening the grip on her wrist to grasp at the weapon. Jill, breathless and frightened that he would reach the gun, let go her grip on its butt and it fell from her fingers into the clutching hand of the German.

Louisa, who had come through the door behind Jill, stood in the middle of the corridor staring uncertainly at the struggling figures. Like Jill, violence was foreign to her nature, and at first she seemed frozen into immobility by the vicious struggle in front of her. But when she saw the gun fall into Jurgen's hand she realised that unless she acted speedily the German youth would turn the gun into Jill's body and fire.

She lifted the heavy brass candlestick and brought it down with all the force she could muster onto the wrist of Jurgen's right hand. Behind the blow was the strength of an arm accustomed to lifting the dead weight of her paralysed husband. There was a distinct cracking sound as the brass connected with the outstretched wrist.

Jurgen uttered one long howl of pain; the gun fell to the floor and slithered towards Louisa's feet. At the same time the stabbing agony that ran up the nerves of his right arm as the bone of the wrist shattered, caused him to release his grip on Jill and fall back against the corridor wall.

Jill tried to regain her footing but slipped on the polished floorboards and fell back onto the body of the German. Despite the pain in his right arm Jurgen now clutched at her head with his left hand and his fingers entangled themselves in her hair.

To Louisa it seemed that despite his broken wrist he was still attempting to hold the girl in his grip. Bending down she lifted the gun from the floor and pointed it vaguely in Jurgen's direction. For a second his body was obscured by Jill's but, as Jill flailed around attempting to disengage herself, she slipped down to Jurgen's side leaving Louisa with a clear view of him.

Louisa fired, screwing her eyes shut as she did so. The thought had gone through her mind that she must wound this man and allow Jill to be free of him. Yet she had no idea of how to aim the gun and simply fired in the general direction of the terrorist. The bullet hit Jurgen at the top of his forehead just below the hairline. On a downward trajectory it ploughed through his brain and exited at the base of his neck. He died instantly.

Jill twisted free and stood up. The corridor ran to the main staircase that lead down to the hall of the castle and, at the top of this staircase, Rolf, who had heard the first shot, appeared. He took in the scene at once and fumbled for his own revolver.

'*Alte!*' he shouted as if the pitch of his voice would cause the two women to submit instantly.

Startled by the shout Louisa turned to face him, gun still clutched in her hand. As she did so she squeezed the trigger, spraying the corridor with bullets. Fortunately for Rolf she fired without aim and the bullets splattered wildly around without hitting him. He threw himself back onto the stairs where he was shielded by the heavy balustrade. Plaster and dust from the walls where the bullets had struck filled the air at the top of the staircase.

Jill, realising that Louisa would soon have emptied the gun of ammunition, knelt down beside Jurgen's body and felt in his pockets, sure that he would have another weapon. She was right. She produced a heavy automatic and entangled with the trigger guard was a set of car keys. Her mind registered the fact that she had now access to one of their vehicles and, pocketing the keys, she rose, still holding the automatic.

Louisa, dazed and close to a state of shock, was standing, a stone statue, in the centre of the corridor facing the head of the stairs, gun in hand. She was aware only of one thing; that if anyone appeared at the top of the staircase she would have to fire the gun again. She was unaware that there were only two shots left in the chamber of the gun.

Jill grasped her by the arm, digging into the flesh as hard as she could to arouse the woman from the state of shock. She had recognised at once the glazed eyes, the somnambulistic stare.

'He's blocked the main stairs,' she gasped, conscious that her statement was self-evident. 'Is there any other way down?'

Louisa stared at her, struggling for comprehension. Then as Jill's fingers dug again into her arm, awareness began to filter into her eyes.

'Please!' Jill begged her. 'We have to get out of here.'

Then, at once Louisa snapped out of shock. She nodded towards a door half-way along the corridor which Jill had presumed led to another bedroom.

'That door!' Louisa stammered. 'Back stairs to the kitchen.'

Almost dragging the older woman with her, Jill ran towards the door and wrenched it open. She was faced with a small spiral stone staircase leading downwards. Pushing Louisa ahead, she shut the door behind them and they began a breathless descent.

Rolf, crouching behind the balustrade, heard and saw nothing of their disappearance from the corridor. He was trying to work out the best course of action, believing that at least he had the two women trapped, when Gudrun appeared at the foot of the stairs. She had been in the kitchen and was only aroused into motion when Louisa had let loose the fusillade.

'What's happening?' she called to him in German.

'Those damned women have got out and they've got a gun,' he shouted back at her. Then, as she climbed the stairs to join him, he eased himself forward to try and see along the corridor. But for the crumpled body of Jurgen, looking like a large sawdust doll from which much of the sawdust had leaked, there was no one in sight.

Carefully he straightened up and, followed now by Gudrun, he advanced slowly along the corridor, gun in hand. Oblivious of the door to the back stairway, he reached Jurgen's body. One glance told him Jurgen was dead. Blood and greyish matter stained the wall behind his head. Rolf turned away. The idea of death intrigued him but the sight of it offended his susceptibilities. He stared now at the open door leading to the upper corridor. He assumed that the Fraser woman and the Marquisa must have retreated back towards the bedroom.

As he stepped towards the door Gudrun received her first clear view of Jurgen's body. Her face became ashen.

'*Gott!*' she exclaimed, horror rising within her. Kneeling down she reached out tentatively to caress his head.

Rolf was aware at once of the movement behind him.

'He's finished!' he said harshly without bothering to turn around.

'No! No,' Gudrun moaned and reaching out, cradled his head in her arms. She felt dampness soaking through the thin sleeves of her blouse and, pulling her arms away, stared with a sudden disgust at the obscene stains of blood that patterned the cloth. She choked back the nausea that arose in her throat but could no longer control the tears that came to blind her eyes. She had loved Jurgen and now, it seemed, this bloodstained, inanimate doll was all that was left to her.

Ignoring her, Rolf brought his gun up as he heard stumbling footsteps on the stairs above. He had no need to use the gun. Elisa came into view, ruefully rubbing the side of her head where she had been struck. Her eyes were still trying to focus as she tried to dispel the pain in her head.

'Have they gone back up there?' Rolf demanded.

Elisa stared at him for a second uncertainly. 'No . . . no, there's no one up there now.'

Rolf turned as if searching the corridor with his eyes, expecting to find his quarries pressed against the wall. As he did so, Elisa saw Jurgen's body, Gudrun crouched beside it. Her only reaction was a widening of the eyes.

Below, at the foot of the spiral staircase, Jill and Louisa came out into a narrow passageway, a door on either side. Louisa indicated the door to her left. Jill opened it, gun ready in her hand.

They were in the kitchen of the castle, a large vaulted room with whitewashed stone walls, a long trestle work table in the centre of the room and, beyond it, a door leading to the kitchen garden. One wall of the kitchen was taken up by an enormous old-fashioned kitchen range, massive oven doors on either side of an open fireplace. Shelves lined another wall, filled with rows of pots and cooking utensils. In the centre of the kitchen, at the top of the trestle table the Marquis sat in his wheelchair, dark eyes staring angrily towards them. The look however melted as he recognised them. Standing beside him was a large fat woman in her sixties. Under a white apron she wore a voluminous black dress. Jill assumed at once this was the cook, José's wife.

José himself stepped from behind the door, with a nervous look, tentatively threatening; but at the same time his hands were trembling.

'Ah, madame, you are safe and alive,' he spoke in Spanish, excitedly. 'We heard shooting and we thought . . .' He ended with an expressive shrug.

'We are all right,' Louisa replied also in Spanish. 'How is my husband?'

José looked over at the figure in the wheelchair. 'He is greatly angered but we calm him.'

Crossing the room, Louisa embraced her husband at the same time murmuring words of consolation. Jill meanwhile turned and contemplated the door they had just come through.

'Can you lock this door?' she asked in English of José.

'*Si*, señora,' he replied and reaching up to one of the shelves produced a large, antiquated key. 'But . . . but the lock is very old.'

'Lock the door!' she ordered and he did so, with some strain and much grinding of rusty metal.

'What do we do now?' Louisa said, addressing herself to Jill.

'That door?' asked Jill. 'Where does it lead to?'

'The kitchen garden.'

'Can you get around to the courtyard from there?' Jill demanded, aware that the geography of the castle was a mystery to her.

'Yes!' Louisa replied. 'Just around the corner to the right and you're in the inner courtyard.'

'We can try for the cars then?'

Louisa frowned. 'No, we can't. I can't leave my husband and it would take too long to get him to the outer yard and the cars.'

Jill held the car keys she had taken from Jurgen's pocket in her hand beside the automatic. They had to fit one of the two cars outside. Yet she knew Louisa was right. With the Marquis in the wheelchair the four of them could not hope to reach the cars quickly.

'It's not you they want,' she said. 'It's me. There's only three of them now and if I run they'll come after me. With luck I'll have them follow me away from here and you'll have time to get out.'

Louisa nodded agreement.

'You still have the gun?' Jill asked as an afterthought.

'Yes. But you can have it . . .'

'I've got this gun,' Jill held up the automatic. 'You keep that one. If they try to break in here or come back after

I've gone, use it.'

'They could kill you if you try to get to the cars,' Louisa exclaimed, suddenly aware of the danger beyond the kitchen, once Jill was in the open.

Jill made a feeble attempt to smile. 'Or I might kill them. I'll go now . . .'

She hesitated, her eyes on Louisa. The Marquisa gave a brief nod of comprehension.

'Yes, you have to try.'

'Goodbye and . . . thank you,' Jill said and turning quickly walked to the rear door and threw it open. The heat of the late afternoon struck her face and the sun, low on the distant sierras, filtered a dying yellow light into the garden of the castle.

Hesitating momentarily, Jill half turned towards José. 'Lock this door behind me and, if you hear shooting, pay no attention.'

The old man nodded. Jill stepped outside shutting the door behind her. Her eyes took in the oblong of the garden. A neat lawn occupied half of the oblong and was bisected by a gravel path. Next to the lawn was an area of brown earth from which green stalks protruded. But it was the gravel path that Jill's eyes followed. It led to the castle wall, along the side of the wall and round a corner. Pressing herself to the stone Jill edged her way to the corner, treading as lightly as she could on the gravel.

Beyond the corner of the castle wall was an archway leading to the sheltered side of the inner courtyard. There was no one in sight. She moved silently to the shaded path around the courtyard. Faintly behind her she heard sounds of voices from the kitchen and beyond.

In the kitchen, Louisa faced the door leading to the hall of the castle. Through the thick wood of the door a voice was raised, shouting angrily. Rolf Gruner had found the back stairway and the locked kitchen door.

Beckoning José to wheel the Marquis out of any possible line of fire coming through the door, Louisa raised the gun, pointing it at the wood just above waist level. Her hand trembled slightly and aware of this, she frowned with irrita-

188

tion at what she considered her own weakness.

'Open the door and no one will be hurt!' Rolf called, his words belying his intention as he gripped his gun in his hand. Behind him stood Elisa, pain from her head now ignored, her eyes smiling with anticipation. Excitement charged her body like some kind of physical electricity.

Rolf shouted again, hoarsely, his words indistinct.

There was no reply from beyond the locked door.

With deliberation he raised his gun and fired at chest height into the centre of the door. There were two sounds, that of the shot and that on top of it, of the wood cracking as the bullet ploughed through.

On the other side of the door, Louisa jumped at the sound of the gun firing. It seemed to echo around the stone walls of the kitchen, reverberating in her ears. As she reacted to the sound she knew the bullet had missed her, smashing through the door and whining across the room to flatten itself on the stone. Splinters flew from the door, jaggedly slashing the air before falling at her feet.

She was about to return the shot when she realised that her weapon might be nearly empty. Resisting the temptation to fire back she moved out of range of the door. She was prepared to use the gun but only when the lock was broken and someone entered the room.

Then she was surprised by another shot, this time not from outside the door but from beyond the garden.

Jill, at the edge of the inner courtyard, had heard the shot from the kitchen. She knew Louisa could not for long prevent the terrorists breaking into the kitchen and, once inside they would not hesitate to shoot the four occupants. They must be distracted from breaking into the kitchen. She raised her own weapon and fired into the air. And then she ran towards the outer courtyard.

Her shot had the desired effect. Rolf turned to Elisa. 'They're outside!'

They turned away from the kitchen door and ran back through the corridor, through the great hall and out of the front door. They were in time to see Jill running from the inner yard towards the two cars.

Rolf came to a stop, his lungs drawing in air painfully. Steadying himself, legs apart, he raised his automatic, sighted it on the running figure and fired.

The bullet ploughed up stone and sand in front of Jill. She swerved and, reaching the nearest of the two cars, wrenched its driving door open. She threw herself into the seat fumbling for the key.

Behind Rolf, Elisa, still in the grip of an inner exultation at the violence in which she was participating, fired at the first car. Her excitement was not conducive to accuracy and the bullet went high, scraping the roof of the car with a harsh metallic rasp.

Jill, desperately trying to find Jurgen's car keys, and aware that she was a prime target, half turned in her seat and fired one shot in the general direction of the castle door. The bullet, even more inaccurate than Elisa's shot, ploughed into the stone lintel above Rolf's head, and despite its inaccuracy, caused both Rolf and Elisa to duck down behind the heavy stone balustrade.

Jill at last found the keys, seconds seeming like eternities as she thrust them to the ignition lock. They were too large to fit. She was in the wrong car.

Rolf jerked his head and arm over the stonework and fired another shot towards the car. The clang of lead on metal and the vibration caused by the impact sent a shudder through both Jill and the car. She pulled herself across the front seat and, with effort opened the offside door.

Rolf twisted his body round towards Elisa. 'Get Gudrun! One of us can cut the girl off at the castle arch!'

Elisa's pang of disappointment at having to leave the scene of the action was overcome by her sense of obedience. She had been taught to obey orders. She obeyed. She sidled back into the doorway of the castle and, as she did so another possible area of action occurred to her.

'What about the other woman and the cripple? And the two servants?' she asked, breathlessly.

'Forget them! We have to get Fraser's wife!'

Elisa ran into the castle.

Rolf turned back to catch a fleeting glimpse of Jill run-

190

ning now from the first car to the second. He fired again and a puff of dust appeared behind the heels of the running woman.

Jill threw herself down beside the door of the second car. As she did so a second bullet punctured a neat hole in the bodywork of the car just above the rear wheel. Twisting her body Jill fired back and heard her bullet ricochet off the stone steps. Rolf ducked as it whined over his head and this gave Jill the opportunity to reach up and open the driving door of the second car.

Again she found herself pulling her body into the driving seat. This time the keys of the car were in her hand and she reached out at once to insert the principal key in the ignition. It moved in easily and a click released the steering lock.

Rolf fired again, scraping the roof of the car. Then, to his disgust, he heard the car engine splutter to life. He stood up, knowing Jill would be concentrating now on getting the vehicle moving.

As he anticipated the car suddenly jerked forward, came to a stop and jerked ahead again. This time it kept moving.

Lifting his automatic, Rolf permitted himself the luxury of taking careful aim. As the car moved around heading for the archway and the road beyond, he sighted on the front tyre. He would have preferred to aim at the girl but she was an indistinct blob behind tinted glass and, as the car moved forward, was hidden by the headrest. He thought, hit the tyre and she won't get far.

He squeezed the trigger.

This time his aim was deadly accurate. The sound of the shot merged with the sound of the exploding tyre. The car wobbled and weaved in a dry skid.

Behind the steering wheel, Jill struggled to control the car which bucked like a wild horse. She knew the front tyre had gone but was determined to drive as far as she could even if it meant the wheel rotating on the metal rim. She was convinced now, an utterly certain conviction that, even if she was taken again by the terrorists alive, they would kill her.

The car came under control although, as it moved, it was shuddering, a wounded mechanical beast.

Rolf fired again, this time at the rear wheel, but his aim was high and his target was now increasing its speed. The bullet shattered the offside rear light fitting, throwing red and yellow glass into the air.

Jill slammed her foot on the accelerator and steered towards the archway entrance. Despite the bumping, uneven pace as the car lumbered forward on the rim of one wheel it seemed to be gathering momentum.

She drove under the arch, with the beginning of a feeling of relief. Once on the road there would be a chance of escape, and, despite the inevitable pursuit, she was better in the open than penned inside the castle.

The other car seemed to come from nowhere. As Jill's vehicle emerged from under the shadow of the arch it leaped into vision, and, with a screeching of brakes, spun, sideways on in front of her, effectively blocking her way to the road and freedom.

FOURTEEN

Mark Fraser seemed to have been driving for hours since he left Granada; although in fact, it was only late afternoon when he came down the foothills of the Sierra Nevada and saw, standing on a hill above the plain, the outline of the Castello de Triana. Against the sky the rounded turrets and heavy walls appeared as some giant prehistoric creature squatting above the earth, casting an elephantine shadow on the ground below.

Fraser accelerated. The goal was in sight and he erased from his mind any thought that he might be too late. He drove eagerly now, ignoring the weariness and discomfort that he felt in his body. His eyes were red-rimmed, his throat dry and raw from the dust that had seeped into the car from the twisting mountain roads.

He had no plan in mind as to a course of action when he reached the castle. He told himself he was going to play it by ear, play it as it came. Yet he knew that without a plan he was leaving himself dangerously vulnerable; risking being picked off by one accurate gunshot as he climbed from the car. But he had to press on, take chances in order to be sure of arriving before any action might be taken to harm Jill.

The car rattled and bucked over the ill-surfaced road dipping into a hollow. As it came out of the hollow he saw the arched entrance to the castle dead ahead. He felt his hands damp on the steering wheel.

It was as he reached the archway that the other car appeared driving straight at him. His first thought as he twisted the wheel round was that whoever was driving might get away; and he had come too far to let anyone escape until he found Jill.

He swung his own car until it was side on to the approaching vehicle. The car, its front tyre flat, came to a halt in a flurry of dust and only then did he see through the dust the face of the driver.

Jill!

The relief of tension is almost as shattering as a sudden build-up of tension. Momentarily he felt himself become limp as he sat behind the steering wheel, drained of strength. Then with an effort he reached out and threw the door of his car open.

Jill, at first, could not see the face of the driver. All she knew was that this gold Capri was blocking the road and her chance of escape. In her desperation she was prepared now to use the gun in her hand to get past the obstacle. She came out of the driving seat, weapon at the ready.

Then through the haze she saw the face of the driver of the Capri. Her relief matched her husband's. She stumbled towards his car, still gripping the gun, waving it in an almost hysterical gesture of greeting.

'Mark! Mark, thank God!'

A sense of the reality of their situation came to Fraser. Her former captors would not be far behind her.

'Get in!' he shouted, throwing the offside door open. Jill ran around the bonnet of the car and, as she threw herself in beside him, he switched on the ignition and the engine roared again into life.

Without a word he reversed the car until the entrance to the castle was behind him. Changing gear violently, he drove off down the road towards the plain and the Sierra Nevada. Only then did he allow himself to speak.

'I'm glad you came out to meet me,' he said with a reassuring smile. 'I might have had problems getting into that place'

'They'll be coming after us, Mark. There's three of them now . . .'

'Not bad odds,' he assumed a flippancy he did not feel. Three behind them; how many in front?

'How did you find me?' Jill asked, lying back in her seat. Exultation was giving way to exhaustion.

194

'Long story,' he replied. 'For later.'

He was concentrating on driving now, pushing the car to the maximum speed he could achieve on the rough surface without losing control. They would be following and he had to keep as much distance as possible between himself and them. Now, at least, he thought, it had all come together. He and Jill against the rest, if necessary, that's how it was now. He could not look for or expect allies. If they appeared, well and good; if not he had Jill beside him.

He glanced at the rear-view mirror. In the distance he could see the car Jill had abandoned outside the entrance to the forecourt of the castle. The light was dying with the day but it seemed as if he could make out figures around the car. Then he found himself driving into the hollow and the sight of the castle disappeared.

He had been correct in what he thought he had seen. Rolf had driven the other car out of the forecourt to find Jill's abandoned vehicle blocking the road. As he got out of his car Elisa came running from the castle door followed by Gudrun.

Cheeks streaked with tears, Gudrun followed at a walking pace. When she reached them they were pushing the abandoned car off the road.

Rolf turned to face her. 'We have to catch them!'

Gudrun stared, the dazed expression on her face. 'Why?' she asked dully.

Elisa glared at her, as always irritated by signs of weakness.

'What does it matter now?' Gudrun went on, the words uttered in a monotone.

It then occurred to Elisa that she might be right. What did it matter? She put the thought into words, facing Rolf now.

'Because they are still dangerous to us all!' he said, unable to control the impatience in his voice. 'Both of you, get in!'

Elisa obeyed orders and slipped into the front passenger seat of the second car. Gudrun shook her head.

'I want to stay with Jurgen,' she explained, her voice

breaking as she did so. More tears carved deltas of salt on her cheeks.

'Jurgen is dead!' Rolf insisted with direct callousness. 'Dead and cold, with his brains all over the wall up there,' he nodded towards the castle. 'You'll come with us now!'

Gudrun still didn't move. Defiance had crept into the cold eyes. Recognising it, Rolf was tempted to leave her. Yet three of them against Fraser and his wife was an advantage he was not willing to forgo. He brought his automatic out, holding it at waist level, pointing at Gudrun. Then he leaned forward and slapped her across both cheeks with his left hand. She staggered back a few paces, her face flushing, eyes wild.

'Get into the car!' ordered Rolf. 'Or you will be as dead as Jurgen.'

He pushed the automatic towards her threateningly. She stared at it for a moment then looked up at his face. And in his face she saw an icy determination. She shuddered.

'Inside now!' he insisted.

Until that moment she had thought she wanted to die. She thought she would like to be, indeed was desperate to be, with Jurgen. Since seeing his body she had been in love with death. Now, faced with it; knowing that Rolf would shoot, her desperation dissipated. She was alive and she felt fear as she faced his gun. Did she want to be a broken rag doll, blood stains turning rust-coloured in the ugly image of death?

She climbed into the rear of the car.

Rolf started the engine. The car ahead of him had vanished into the distance. He knew that the man driving it, though barely glimpsed, was Mark Fraser, and he thought now, if he could catch them, the whole operation could be tidied up at once. It did not matter that Fraser had a head start. There was only one road over the mountains.

He accelerated away from the castle.

Fraser, a distance ahead, had now reached the foothills of the sierras. The dim half-light before darkness had begun to surround him and he switched on his headlights.

He was determined not to slacken speed despite the difficulties of the terrain.

Jill stirred beside him. She had, for a few moments, closed her eyes and he thought she had fallen asleep. But now she peered up at him, straining to reassure herself of his presence in the dim light.

'Darling, it's . . . it's so good to be with you.'

'You're all right? They didn't hurt you?'

'I'm all right.'

'Fine,' he said and there was a world of relief in the one word.

Jill frowned. 'Mark, the Marquisa and her husband . . . they own the castle. They're still back there . . .'

The distress was obvious in her tone. Yet he had no intention of going back.

'They should be all right. We're the main target . . .'

He felt her move beside him. It gave him reassurance.

'Yes. Yes, I said that to her. But . . . she did help me . . .'

'We'll thank her another time. If we go back we won't live to thank her.'

The car took a hairpin bend with a squealing of brakes. Fraser remembered there was a village in the mountains he had driven through. They could lose themselves in that village for the night. The car continued to climb steadily.

Jill started to shiver violently. 'Oh, God, Mark, I'm so cold . . . so very cold.'

The chill of the night filled the car but it was, so far, only a mild temperature drop. Fraser knew it would get colder the higher they climbed. He had seen snow on the peaks of the high sierras on his way along this road before. But Jill's shivering was not to do with temperature. It was a nervous reaction.

'Shock,' said Fraser. 'Delayed. There's a village ahead. We'll stop there for the night.'

'No!' Jill looked terrified. 'We mustn't stop. They'll catch up with us.'

'If we hide the car well enough, they'll go right past . . .'

Some miles behind, Rolf switched his headlights to full beam. Elisa sat beside him peering through the windscreen at the road ahead.

'We may lose them in the dark.'

'Only one road through the mountains. And with his lights on we'll see him miles away. We'll see him and we'll catch him.'

His voice was hard, determined. It gave Elisa a shiver of anticipation.

'And when we've caught them . . .?' she asked.

Rolf shrugged his shoulders. It was an expressive shrug, one which implied the ultimate act. Elisa smiled and glanced around at Gudrun. She sat in the rear of the car, shoulders hunched up, eyes staring ahead into nothingness. She was somewhere else; with them in body but not in mind. Ten minutes later Fraser drove the Capri into the narrow streets of the mountain village. The car bounced and rattled over the uneven cobbles and Jill, who had been dozing lightly, opened her eyes, memory bringing her to nervous consciousness at once.

'There's an inn . . a kind of bodega here. Now if we hide the car we can stay the night,' Fraser said with as much confidence as he could assume.

The bodega was slightly larger than the other buildings, the white stucco walls bleached and peeling around the corners. At the side a narrow lane ran up a slope towards a large wooden outhouse. Fraser swung the car up the lane and brought it to a halt in the shelter of the outhouse.

Two minutes later they were facing the owner of the bodega, a large Spaniard with receding dark hair and a prominent chin which had obviously not seen a razor for twenty-four hours.

'Señor?' he said amiably.

'Do you speak English?' asked Fraser. *'Inglese?'*

The large man smiled, showing a row of discoloured teeth. 'Little,' he replied.

'We need a room for the night. And a place to put the car under cover. It's in the shed at the back . . .'

'Si. It can . . . can be there all night.'

'With the doors shut and locked?' Fraser went on tentatively. As he did so he took out his wallet and started dealing out notes.

The Spaniard smiled. 'I am named Juan. I shut the car away myself, eh?'

'That's fine, Juan,' Fraser hesitated before going on. 'There are people trying to find us. Not the police. The . . . the lady's family.'

The stained teeth came into wide view as a grin spread over Juan's face. 'Ah, *si,*' he said and gave a broad wink.

Fraser went on. 'So, you understand, if anyone asks, we are not here.' He pushed a number of notes towards Juan. 'And if we are still not here in the morning, there will be more money.'

Juan nodded, still grinning. Foreigners, they did mad things, maybe things the church would not approve of, but then they were not of the church. And with the money he was being offered, a part of it, not too large a part, could be given to the church, maybe.

The bedroom was square and small, with white walls, and most of it was taken up by the large antique bed. The only other furnishings were a small wooden table and a wicker chair. On the table was a basin and next to it a jug half full of water. The room was lit by an ancient oil lamp which hung from the ceiling, the flame flickering and casting dancing shadows on the walls.

Jill lay on the bed, eyes closed, for the first time in five days feeling she could really relax. Fraser, having made sure that Juan had locked the door of the outhouse effectively concealing the car, bathed his face gratefully in the icy water from the jug.

Jill opened her eyes, looked across at him and smiled. 'I closed my eyes,' she said as if the obvious needed explanation.

'I noticed.'

'I was almost afraid to open them in case . . . in case it wasn't you and I was dreaming.'

'It's me and you're not dreaming.'

From outside the silence of the village was broken by the deep roar of a car engine. Fraser took out his gun and went to the door of the room where he stood listening. Jill's eyes were on the gun in his hand and he was aware of her gaze.

'Only to be used if necessary,' he explained.

'Will they find us? Will it be necessary?'

'Not unless I've misjudged Juan.'

Below in the narrow street the car engine spluttered to a stop, the sound echoing against the walls of the squat houses.

Elisa peered from the side window.

'Darkness,' she said. 'And no cars.'

'At least none in sight,' added Rolf, stepping into the street.

'They will be miles ahead.' It was the first words Gudrun had uttered since she had got into the car. Rolf stared at her. At least she was coming out of the state of shock she had been in. If there was a need for action she might just be able to function. He turned away and surveyed the wall and the narrow doorway into the bodega.

'Wait here,' he said and entered the building.

Juan, behind his small counter, was all smiles and assumed artifice. No, there was no one staying at the hotel; yes, he had heard a car go through the village some minutes before. He was fluent in his assurances that the car had passed, perhaps too fluent, Rolf thought. Yet even if Fraser and his wife were staying in the inn, an attempt to take them would result in the use of weapons, and he knew he would have the entire village about his ears.

'Have you a telephone?' he asked.

'Ah, *si, si, telefono* . . . is the only one in the village,' Juan replied indicating an ancient upright telephone in the shadows at the end of the counter.

Rolf lifted the earpiece. After he was connected he talked for some minutes in a low voice. Then, hanging up the ear-piece, he pushed some notes towards Juan, nodded and went back into the street.

In the car Elisa stared at him curiously. 'Well?'

'They could be in the village or they could have gone on,' Rolf replied. 'I've made a phone call. There will be a road block on the other side of the mountains.'

This time the question came from Gudrun in the back of

200

the car. 'Who did you phone?'

'We have friends,' Rolf said cryptically, switching on the ignition. As the engine started up he changed the subject. 'I think the innkeeper was lying.'

He drove slowly out of the village. An idea began to form in his mind. If Fraser and his wife were still in the village they would have two road blocks to get through. In the beam of his headlight he began to look for a suitable spot.

At the door of the bedroom Fraser relaxed. He had listened as the sound of the car engine became fainter as it moved out of the village.

'They've gone,' he said. 'Our host has come through for us.'

He crossed to the window as if to reassure himself that he had heard correctly. Then he turned to Jill, smiling.

'Try and get some sleep. We'll leave at dawn.'

But she was wide awake, staring up at him, frowning. 'Mark?'

'Yes?'

'Did you do what they wanted you to do, Mark? Did you kill the man they wanted you to kill?'

Fraser paused, his smile becoming fixed. 'Would you rather I hadn't and they'd killed you?'

'They would have done so anyway,' she said, her frown deepening. 'Why? Why do we have to be killed?'

'It's tidier for them. No loose ends. No one to accuse them . . .'

'But terrorists . . . don't they usually want people to know what they've done?'

Fraser sat on the edge of the bed. 'I married a very intelligent lady. Of course you're right. And that's part of the problem I've been trying to work out.'

There was a knock on the door. Fraser was instantly alert, gun in hand. He opened the door carefully. It was Juan standing holding a battered tray on which were two glasses.

'Señor, I told them, as you said, you were not here.'

'Good. Very good.'

'And for you and your lady I bring this.'

The glasses contained Spanish brandy. Fraser thanked him, genuinely grateful for the thought.

'*Buenas noches,*' said Juan and withdrew.

Fraser handed Jill one of the glasses. 'Purely medicinal. No more questions. After this we sleep. Only until dawn.'

She drank holding his hand. She was still holding it when she fell asleep.

FIFTEEN

At six o'clock in the morning the sun was already casting tentative shadows across the snow fields of the high sierras. The shadows would become shorter as the morning grew on; and the snow patterning the highest peaks would melt fractionally throughout the day. But now, as Fraser stepped out into the morning air with the innkeeper at his side, he could feel the dying chill of the night and the snow touch his face.

'You come back for holiday, eh?' Juan said, fracturing the English language with his accent.

Fraser nodded abstractedly as he paid the large man and walked towards the outhouse and his car. When he drove from the outhouse it was to find Jill waiting at the door of the bodega. She settled beside him, rested, smiling after her night's sleep. Fraser sensed in her a return to her old self; but it was when she saw the sniper's rifle resting, ready for use, on the rear seat of the Capri that she frowned, the memory of their situation back with her.

'An unasked for gift,' he explained seeing her look towards the rifle. 'It might just come in handy.'

She said nothing. During their married life she had learned not to question him on any action or decision of importance. She was used to waiting for him to raise the subject first before she gave an opinion. And now, even more so, she was content to leave whatever problems or dangers they might meet to him. Once they were back in Scotland then the day-to-day ordering of their life would be controlled by her.

Yet she could not help noticing the dark lines under his eyes, the drawn features and the occasional yawn he tried to suppress.

'You didn't sleep?'

'Someone had to keep an eye open. I dozed a bit.'

She looked away. They were driving out of the village along the narrow, twisting mountain road. She gnawed the top of her lower lip, an old habit from childhood which recurred only when a sudden thought worried her.

'Mark, once we're clear of them, will it be over? Will we be able to go home?' She permitted herself the tentative question.

Fraser answered with all the reassurance he could muster. 'Today. It'll be finished today. One way or another. And then we'll go home.'

She lay back in her seat. 'I was afraid they'd come back in the night but I was so tired in the end I just fell asleep.'

'I noticed,' he replied and then frowned. 'The trouble is . . . they should have come back.'

She looked up at him questioningly.

'They must have realised eventually we weren't ahead of them,' he explained. 'So why didn't they come back, looking for us. They should have.'

Ahead of them, steep rocks rose up, sheer embankments on either side of the road. They were now about two miles from the village. Fraser took his foot off the accelerator and easing down on the footbrake he drove the car into a rough lay-by before the road ran into the gully ahead.

'What is it?' said Jill.

'I want you to wait here,' he replied opening his door.

'Mark, I don't want to be left alone any more.'

He considered this for a moment. 'All right. You've been on your own in this long enough to qualify. Come on, but do exactly as I say.'

As she got out of the car he took the sniper's rifle from the back seat. Then he stared at the gully ahead.

'You see,' he said. 'If I wanted to ambush us, I'd pick a spot just like that ahead. The road narrows, the sides are steep, we couldn't even drive off the road. Now, we're going to climb up there . . .' He indicated the left side of the gully. 'That's where we can get a good view of anything on the road ahead.'

A narrow path pitted with small rocks led up to the summit of the rock face above the gully. Fraser led the way, Jill following. It took them two minutes to reach the top, the rocks flattening out and broken by patches of scrub. Jill found herself short of breath, gulping cool air as she followed Fraser along the crest. As the ridge curved with the line of the road a hundred feet below, Fraser stopped stock still motioning Jill to do likewise. Then crouching, he moved forward to peer over the edge of the ridge down at the road.

After a moment he beckoned Jill forward. Aping her husband's crouch she crept up to join him. He pointed to the road below.

'Our friends, I think,' he whispered ironically.

She nodded. On the road Rolf had parked his car under an overhanging clump of rock and gorse, the bonnet facing the rock face. Secured to the rear bumper of the car was a length of cable which lay across the surface of the road and at the other side was tied around a large boulder. Rolf himself stood leaning on the side of his car, cigarette hanging from his lips. Gudrun sat on the ground near him, leaning against the front wheel of the car. Elisa was at the other side of the road apparently checking that the cable was secure around the rock.

Fraser led Jill back some yards until they were well clear of the ridge.

'You knew they'd be there,' Jill said in a low tone.

'I told you it's where I would have waited if I'd been in their place,' Fraser replied. 'I noticed the gully yesterday when I was on my way to the castle.'

'What's that they've got across the road? A rope?'

'Cable. Steel cable. Might have had it in his car. Or nicked it from some road-works site. If he swings his car around and drives a few yards forward it'll stretch right across the road around chest level.'

Jill looked puzzled.

'That's pretty tough cable,' Fraser explained. 'If we came into that damn bottleneck at top speed it would slice the top off the bonnet of our car. Might even slice the car in half and us with it.'

Her face taking on an ashen hue, Jill turned away.

'Not nice people,' Fraser said moving back towards the vantage point above the road, Jill followed him again but as the road came into her vision, she grasped his arm, pointing to a narrow pathway leading from the road up to the summit on which they were standing.

'That girl . . . Elisa . . . she's coming up here. They must have seen us!'

Fraser shook his head. 'No. She'll be the look-out. Just as well we got up early. Earlier than they'd expect. That girl comes up here and she can see the road all the way back to the village. If she sees our car, she signals and he drives his car until that damn cable is taut across the road.'

'What do we do?'

Fraser gave her an encouraging smile. 'We lie down here just out of sight and we wait.'

He turned, searching the uneven surface of the ridge. His eyes lit on a hollow between two large rocks.

'There!' he said, pointing.

Within seconds they were huddled down between the two rocks, invisible to anyone climbing onto the ridge. Fraser eased the sniper's rifle forward, gripping it by the stock. Jill, seeing his hands come forward with the rifle, stared at him, her eyes widening. He gave her a reassuring nod which did little to reassure her.

They lay together, a light breeze stirring and probing at the scrub and the gorse. Then they heard the crunching of feet on broken rock and pebble. Jill felt Fraser tense expectantly. She did not allow herself to consider his intentions. She knew if she did so she would induce in herself a fear she wanted to avoid.

Next they heard a sound of heavy breathing, a scraping sound of shoes on rocks, and they knew Elisa had reached the crest of the ridge. Fraser raised his head and could see her, some few yards from him, standing waving down at her companions on the road below. Then she turned away seeking a vantage point from which she could view the road leading from the village.

Fraser moved as silently as a large cat. It seemed to Jill that one moment he was beside her and the next he had risen and with a few loping steps was behind Elisa. And then Jill saw the rifle rise into the air and fall towards the German girl's neck. There was a thudding sound, metal on a soft surface, followed by a low gasp from the girl as she pitched forward, and was a fallen scarecrow, loose straw arms drooping from the sides of a flat rock surface.

Despite the fact that she had seen Jurgen die suddenly and violently the day before, Jill came to her feet with the sick thought that she had just witnessed her husband committing murder. Jurgen's death through the wild shooting of the Marquisa had almost seemed accidental; but to see Mark kill someone, no matter how much one could believe that person might deserve death, created within Jill a feeling of horror and panic.

Fraser looked across at her as if reading her mind. 'Don't worry,' he said. 'She's not dead. She'll come round with a hell of a headache. I used to be an expert at this kind of thing, remember?'

The relief showed on Jill's face. 'It'll be her second headache. The Marquisa knocked her out with a tray yesterday!'

'Sounds like my kind of woman,' Fraser said, adding with a hint of mockery, 'Next to you, darling.'

Jill looked from the body of the unconscious girl to the edge of the ridge. 'What do we do now?'

'Put the other two out of action.'

He turned away from her and going back to the crest overlooking the road he lay down with the rifle at his shoulder.

'Stay back,' he ordered Jill. 'There just may be the odd gunshot flying around.'

Before Jill had time to feel any recurrence of her fears, Fraser had sighted the rifle and fired.

There were two bangs, the first the cracking sound of the rifle and its echoes against the rock; the second came almost instantly upon it, the sound of the rear tyre of Rolf's car exploding.

Below them, Gudrun jumped to her feet, staring wildly around, unable to identify the direction from which the shot had come. Rolf had straightened up and his automatic was now in his hand. He seemed to have a better developed sense of direction than the girl and his eyes scanned the ridge.

Fraser fired again, this time hitting the bonnet of the car. The bullet scored the top of the bonnet, scraping a six-inch furrow across the metal. Rolf waved his hand in the general direction of the ridge, clutching his gun and shouting something at Gudrun. She hesitated, staring up at the ridge. Rolf brought his automatic up and fired.

The bullet ploughed up dust a good fifteen yards from Fraser's vantage point and it made Fraser realise that, while they knew he was on the ridge, they had not yet spotted where. Carefully he sighted the sniper's rifle again and fired. This time he was dead on target. The bullet hit the side of the bonnet and ploughed into the engine beneath. No way of knowing how much damage he'd done but two or three shots like that and the engine would be wrecked.

This shot caused Rolf to throw himself behind a clump of rocks, uncertain as to whether he was the target or not. Gudrun, still standing in the open, fired upwards towards the ridge. She was a better shot than Rolf; the bullet scraped the side of a rock a few feet below Fraser's hiding place. The girl then ran to join Rolf behind the rocks.

Then there followed a fusillade. Keeping his head down, Fraser checked the rifle and reloaded. The shots from below ceased as there seemed no sign of movement from the ridge. Slowly Fraser raised his head and aimed again at the bonnet of the car. Again he knew he had hit the engine and indeed he was almost certain that, despite the distance, he could see a wisp of smoke curling from underneath the bonnet.

The girl below raised herself above the concealment of the rocks and, with meticulous care, aimed and fired again. Chips of stone gashed Fraser's forehead as the bullet struck rock this time only inches from his face. Damn it, he thought, the bitch was bloody good with a hand gun. She had to be stopped. He squinted down his sights again, moving away from the car. She was now behind the rock again but, on her next appearance, he knew he could kill her.

He waited.

He calculated that below, the German with the young old face would be assessing his situation. His road block had been discovered but, if the car was still mobile, then the road could yet be shut, the wire tightened against any car that attempted to drive through. At the same time he would realise that should he try to move the car, to get to it he would have to break cover. Even if he reached the car without Fraser hitting him, the flat rear tyre would make moving the car at best a slow and hazardous operation. Fraser could still snipe at him in the car. And if the engine was damaged and the car immovable then the attempt to block the road had failed.

So Rolf would have to shoot it out with Fraser from an inferior position. Nevertheless his female companion seemed to have spotted Fraser's position and she was an accurate shot. If he had been in Rolf's place he would be relying on the girl to try and kill or wound the sniper. It was the immediate, practical tactic.

Below him Fraser saw Rolf suddenly move, head and shoulders over the rock as far from where the girl had last appeared as he could get. A burst of firing came from Rolf's automatic. Of course he would be giving the girl covering fire when she appeared. Time to take aim. Ignoring bullets which were still several feet from him Fraser did not move but kept his rifle aiming at the spot where the girl should appear.

If he was right, with the immaculate sight on the rifle, he knew he could accurately put a bullet in her head. Waiting, he suddenly shivered and phlegm rose in the back of his throat. Damn the sick feeling of death! He knew he could easily kill in rage, kill to protect Jill. But Jill was safely behind him and rage had given way to calculation. Yet he had only seconds in which he had to decide whether to kill the unknown girl below.

Gudrun rose, sighting her gun with care. Her head was in his sight, the forehead in the centre of the cross hairs. He moved, taking the sight down to the neck and then to the shoulder of her arm, the arm that held her gun. In the second it took him to move he knew she could have sighted her own gun on him and fired. But she wasn't ready. He could almost imagine he was seeing the muscles of her arm tighten as she put pressure on her trigger. He fired.

A fraction later the girl must have fired although the bullet from the sniper's rifle had already ploughed into the soft flesh of her upper arm, fracturing bone and tearing muscle apart. She was thrown back onto the road and her automatic went off uselessly, the bullet projected upwards high over the ridge. As she fell into the dust of the road Gudrun screamed, a high pitched tonal reflection of pain.

Rolf disappeared behind the rock cover but Fraser moved the sights over the rock and again onto the bonnet of the car. He fired two more shots and was rewarded by a distinct if thin line of black smoke curling out of the radiator.

Fraser was satisfied. He rolled back from the crest of the ridge and turned to face Jill. She was sitting, her back towards him, against a rock, her arms across her breasts, as if nursing pain.

'You all right?' he asked, surprised to find himself breathless.

Jill turned to look up at him. 'Did you . . . did you kill any of them?'

'No.'

'I wanted . . . wanted you to kill them. When you were shooting . . . I . . . wanted them to be dead.'

'I know,' Fraser replied, gripping her arm and forcing her to her feet. 'Don't worry about it. We had to make sure we could get past them. We can now. So let's move.'

It took them three minutes to climb down to their car. For the entire three minutes, Fraser held Jill's arm in a firm grip, so firm that much later she was to wonder at the bruising on her arm.

Back in the narrow gorge Rolf, after some time, tentatively came out from behind his cover. There was no answering sound of gunfire from above. He turned back to face Gudrun who had crawled into the shade of the rocks and sat, eyes dull with shock, staring at the dust at her feet and clutching her right shoulder. Her thin shirt was torn at the shoulder and soaked in blood which, on one side, had spread down the entire sleeve, and, on the other, covered the light material over her right breast, outlining even the nipple in scarlet.

Rolf turned away without concealing an expression of disgust on his face. He went over to the car and climbed into the driving seat. The pungent, acrid odour of petrol mixed with burnt rubber pervaded the interior of the car. Rolf switched on the ignition and there was a momentary grating cough from the engine, followed by a metallic rattle and then silence. He turned the ignition key again but this time there was nothing. Although the black smoke seen by Fraser had dissipated, a further small wisp of smoke seeped from the radiator. With a muttered curse Rolf climbed out of the car.

As he did so, Fraser's car came through the gorge at speed. Seeing it, Rolf made the only attempt he could to try and stop it by bringing his automatic up, sighting it, and firing. But the car was moving too fast and the shot merely grazed the off-side wing. Then the car was over the cable and disappearing around the bend in the road. Rolf tried ineffectually to sight his automatic on the rear window, realised he would merely be wasting ammunition and turned away with a frustrated scowl.

There was a sound of small stones and rocks slithering down the side of the gorge and he looked up to see Elisa, swaying as she stumbled down towards the road.

'Where the hell have you been?' he shouted.

She did not reply until she'd reached the foot of the incline. Then, massaging the back of her head, she replied. 'I've been asleep. Not from choice.'

She stared towards the bend in the road where the car had just disappeared. 'So they got through,' she went on. 'Does it matter?'

'Of course it matters!'

Elisa frowned. 'Fraser did the job we wanted him to do. So he and his wife get away. I don't see how it matters. It's over and we can leave Spain now.'

Rolf smiled at her, a smile that was meant to indicate agreement. Of course she'd think it was easy just to go, get out of the country. But then she didn't know the whole story. She never would know it. As long as he was trying to stop Fraser and his wife, Rolf had to acknowledge he had needed the two girls. Now, someone else would take over and stop Fraser. Now, an impatient girl who only wanted to run and a wounded one, how badly he didn't yet know, they were no longer assets, no longer necessary. Indeed they were now a liability to Rolf Gruner.

Elisa was still staring at him with an expression of mild perplexity. Why was he hesitating? What was there to think about?

Rolf straightened his shoulders, aware then that he was still stooping, cowering from Fraser's bullets. As he did so he felt the metal of the automatic, hard and damp in his hand.

'We *can* leave Spain now, can't we?' Elisa demanded. 'Now that it's over we're allowed to get out?'

'Allowed?' he replied admiringly. 'How very perceptive of you, using the word, allowed.'

He raised the automatic and fired from the hip. He was so close it was impossible to miss. He fired two shots and the first hit her just above the heart. The force of it caused the gun to jump and the second shot took her in the centre of the forehead. She fell without uttering a sound.

As the echo resounded around the gorge he turned towards Gudrun. She was staring up at him, eyes twisted with pain, face ashen, and the shirt, obscene to his eyes with its patches of damp scarlet. As he brought the automatic up again, he doubted whether she was aware of what was happening.

212

And now, he thought, it would be so much easier to back-track to the village and, alone, hire some form of conveyance to get down to the coast again. By that time others would have dealt with Mark Fraser and his wife.

SIXTEEN

As they drove down from the sierras into the foothills, Jill slept. It was a nervous reaction to the events at the gorge and Fraser was pleased that she was able to sleep despite the uneven road and the ever-increasing heat. He was glad he did not have to talk but could concentrate on questions, so many questions, which he was still trying to define in his own mind. Answers he would think about later. And he could also keep a sharp eye on the road.

The immediate question was their course of action on reaching the coast. His first thought was that they should drive to the airport at Malaga and fly immediately back to the UK. Yet he knew the business was not over. Would they be able to get out of Spain? And who would try and stop them? He had his suspicions about the answer to that question and yet could be sure of nothing. Nothing, that is, except that the end had not yet been reached.

Then, quite suddenly as they rounded a bend in the road, beyond which he could actually see the coastline on the horizon, he saw the car directly ahead.

The car was blocking the road effectively and the figure of the man was standing in front of the car, waving him down.

Fraser applied the brakes gently but the car still shuddered on the primitive road surface, and the brake drums, overheated, squealed indignantly. Jill woke up.

'What . . . what is it?' she asked wearily.

'Nothing. Back to sleep. Just spending a peso.'

His eyes flickered momentarily and then she seemed to go back to sleep.

Pulling on the handbrake, Fraser got out of the car, aware that he had a revolver in his pocket. He decided it was not enough, that he must be seen to be armed, and so he reached into the back of the Capri and came out holding the sniper's rifle. He then turned and walked slowly towards the figure in the middle of the road.

'No need for artillery, Mark. It's only me,' Frank Lloyd called nervously as Fraser approached.

'You know, I thought it might be,' Fraser replied.

'You've to come with me, Mark.'

'Really, Frank. Now why should I do that?'

Lloyd smiled awkwardly, an embarrassed small boy struggling to get out. 'Mackeson's here, in Spain. Flew from London. Wants to see you.'

'And if I don't want to see him?'

'Mark, for God's sake, don't rock the boat.'

'Not my boat.'

Lloyd's feet shuffled in the dust. He stared down at them, frowning that the patent leather should be soiled by foreign earth. 'Don't be a bloody fool, Mark!' he went on. 'I know what you've done now. The Spanish police don't like assassination of foreign nationals on their soil by other foreign nationals. Especially when the victim is one of the big boys.'

Fraser was staring at him without expression. 'Mackeson told you all about it of course?'

Lloyd shrugged, still staring at his shoes. Fraser suddenly felt they must look like two characters in a western movie facing up to each other in the street. He had the sniper's rifle and his revolver and he could see the bulge under Lloyd's well-cut jacket. He knew he had the advantage, doubting that Lloyd had ever fired a gun in anger in his entire career.

He decided to ease the tension. 'I could use a cigarette, Frank. Haven't had much time to do any shopping.'

The tension was not eased. Lloyd shrugged. 'Sorry, I've given up smoking. Mark, I was sent out to help you, I told you . . .'

'And to help me find my wife,' Fraser interjected. 'But then, unfortunately I beat you to that.'

Lloyd nodded his head impatiently, a nervous puppet

whose string was being agitated. 'Okay. You found her and I'm glad . . .'

'Should I say I'm glad you're glad?'

'Damn it if you hadn't flattened my tyres and . . . earlier, locked me out on that balcony we could have found her together without your having to shoot Scherer.'

Fraser rubbed his hand over his chin thoughtfully. 'No, I don't think so. Scherer's . . . killing had to come first.'

Lloyd peered at him, eyes screwed up. 'I don't understand that . . .'

'You will in time. We both will.'

'Anyway, now you've found your wife Mackeson can get the two of you out of Spain.'

'Why should he bother?'

Lloyd flushed, irritated. 'You are an *ex-British* agent . . .'

'Oh, I see, not just an agent, though. Ex-sandbagger. Ex-dirty tricks, ex-assassin. An embarrassment to Her Majesty's Government.'

'That's what Mackeson said,' Lloyd assented quickly.

Fraser could not resist smiling. 'And yet I wonder . . . if the Spanish police had got me after . . . after the Scherer business, would Mackeson have cared? I was an ex-agent. I could be working now for anybody. I could be simply the hired killer. To be written off. Perhaps he might even have assisted the Spanish police if they had put out road blocks to trap the assassin. But they didn't put out road blocks, Frank . . .'

'I . . . I don't know about that,' Lloyd responded with a puzzled frown.

'Poor old Frank,' Fraser said. 'You believe everything Mackeson tells you. You believe without question. I'll bet you even believe everything you read in the newspapers.' His smile was broad now. 'Tell me, where is Mackeson?'

'I've to take you to him. He's in Malaga.'

'Where exactly?' Fraser pressed the question.

'Villa Circe. Calle Moreno Monroy,' Lloyd replied. He suddenly became aware of Fraser's fixed smile, a cynical smile containing elements of disbelief. 'What's bothering you, Mark?' he added.

'You. Here. Waiting for me. Doesn't that bother you?'

Lloyd gestured, exasperated. 'Mackeson simply got word that your wife had been taken to this castle . . . the Castello de Triana.'

'From where? The little man in Granada? Rocas?'

Lloyd stammered. 'Not Rocas . . . no . . .'

'Why not? He knew where Jill was being held,' said Fraser, his voice hardening, the smile having disappeared.

'Someone shot Rocas,' Lloyd explained. 'We did think it might have been you.'

'It wasn't. But Rocas could have told Mackeson. Before he even told me. He knew. That's what I find interesting.'

'I'm sure it wasn't Rocas,' Lloyd insisted, his face soaked with sweat. 'Someone else. Mackeson has other agents in Spain.'

'I suppose he has,' Fraser responded thoughtfully. 'Interesting though that Rocas knew, and you have confirmed he was one of Mackeson's people.'

'For God's sake, Mark, I only know what I'm told!' Lloyd protested. 'And none of these local people are completely reliable. Anyway what does it matter? Mackeson got word and sent me up here . . .'

'That's the other thing that worries me,' Fraser pressed on. 'Your orders were to wait here for me. Not to go to the castle . . .?'

'I did question that . . .'

'But nobody enlightened you?' Fraser cut in. 'Nobody explained it to you, Frank. And you accept that . . .'

He stopped in mid-speech, his eyes catching something behind Frank Lloyd.

'You're going to have to move your car, Frank. You're blocking the traffic.'

Lloyd turned around to see a plume of dust moving along the road from the direction of the coast towards them. The dust resolved its shape into that of a large powerful Citroen.

'Damn it!' Lloyd exclaimed. 'Look, Mark, I'll have to move my car. You have to come with me so don't try . . .'

He stopped, his eyes widening. The Citroen came to a

halt some feet from his car and both the driving and the passenger doors opened. A large man in an ill-cut dark suit of some inappropriately heavy material got out of the driving seat. The figure coming from the passenger door was instantly recognisable to Fraser, especially when he saw the left arm was in a sling.

To Lloyd however the occupants of the Citroen were obviously strangers. 'Sorry!' he called out. 'I'll move my car . . .'

But the two figures kept coming towards them. Then the large man in the dark suit veered towards Lloyd's car. He opened the driving door and, reaching inside, released the hand brake and proceeded to push the car towards the side of the road.

'What the hell . . .!' Lloyd exclaimed. 'I'll do that . . .!'

The other figure with the left arm in the sling, dressed in a light-coloured suit, kept moving towards them.

'I don't think you've met Colonel Grigor of the KGB,' said Fraser. 'Colonel, this is Frank Lloyd of British Intelligence.'

Grigor nodded as he came up to them. Lloyd flashed a furious look at Fraser.

'For God's sake, Mark . . .!' he almost shouted. 'Have you gone over?'

Fraser shrugged. 'Not to my knowledge. But perhaps someone else wants me even more than you do.'

'That might be exactly right, Mr Fraser,' said Grigor, smiling amiably at Lloyd. 'Now, you will have to accept my apologies for some inconvenience, my dear sir.'

He had an automatic pointing at Lloyd's midriff. The large man in the black suit, having pushed Lloyd's car to the side of the road, now joined them.

'Maxim will attend to you now, Lloyd,' Grigor went on, his amiability unlessened.

The large man gripped Lloyd's shoulder with his right hand and spun him around. His left hand flicked over Lloyd's jacket, frisking him expertly.

'Now, look here . . .!' Lloyd started to protest but

stopped as Maxim produced a revolver from under Lloyd's jacket.

Fraser couldn't help smiling. 'I didn't know you knew how to use one of those.'

Lloyd glared at him, tight-lipped. He was trembling slightly and Fraser recognised the kind of fear that came from uncertainty and lack of experience.

'Do not concern yourself, Mr Lloyd,' Grigor interjected, obviously aware of the fear in Lloyd. 'We do not intend to harm you. The unnecessary elimination of a British Agent is counter-productive unless essential to the operation.'

He nodded to Maxim who had pocketed Lloyd's revolver. Still gripping Lloyd by the shoulder the large Russian propelled the Englishman towards his own car. After a few ineffectual twitches Lloyd realised he was powerless, indeed immobilised, from independent action by the man's grip. When they reached the car the Russian produced a pair of antiquated handcuffs. He wrapped one cuff around the steering wheel and the other around Lloyd's left wrist. Then with determined force he impelled Lloyd to sit on the driver's seat. Finally he removed the car key from Lloyd's pocket, turned, nodded to Grigor and walked back to the Citroen.

'Very efficient,' Fraser commented. 'What now?'

'I will come with you and your wife in your car now,' Grigor replied affably. 'Maxim will follow.'

They walked with a casual air back to Fraser's Capri. Jill was standing beside the car, having observed everything that had occurred. She wore an anxious look.

'Mark, what's happening . . .?'

'We're in demand,' he replied as lightly as he could. 'Jill, this is Colonel Grigor . . .'

Grigor gave a minuscule bow. 'I am pleased you are unharmed, Madame Fraser.'

He beckoned them to climb back into the car and when Jill had done so, he stepped into the rear of the Capri, indicating that Fraser should drive.

'Now you will go where I tell you, Mr Fraser,' he said, settling back in his seat.

Fraser drove off aware that the Citroen was reversing and following them. They were coming now out of the hills heading for the coast.

'How did you find us?' Fraser asked Grigor without turning.

'We learned that the British had an agent in Marbella,' Grigor replied. 'We too have sources of information in Spain. We simply followed him. Your Mr Lloyd. We felt he would lead us possibly to you. We were right.'

Fraser found himself believing the Russian. He hadn't believed Lloyd but then Lloyd had not been let into the whole picture. At least that's what he had gathered from Lloyd's stumbling explanations.

He glanced in his rear driving mirror. Grigor had settled back comfortably into his seat. There was no sign of any weapon to implement the route he wished them to take. No compulsion of a physical kind. But then Fraser knew in himself that Grigor did not consider it necessary. Fraser, Grigor was assuming, was willing to follow his instructions. And Fraser knew Grigor's assumption was correct. To fill in the missing pieces of the jigsaw he had to go with Grigor.

'Marbella, my friend,' Grigor said. 'That is our destination. You will know the house when we arrive. And Mrs Fraser, do not concern yourself. You are both under my protection.'

Jill nodded although, within herself, she could not pretend an assurance of safety she did not feel.

When they reached Marbella it was just after midday. They drove out to the north of the town and Fraser realised where they were going. It was no surprise to him. As they drove through the gates it was Jill who stared with curiosity at the front of the large villa.

'Mark, whose place is this? Do you know?' she asked nervously as the villa gates closed behind them.

'Oh, yes, I know,' Fraser replied.

He brought the car to a halt outside the main door and they got out.

'Leave the car here,' Grigor said, leading the way into the villa of the Duke of Porto Christo. As they went in

Fraser noticed the Citroen driven by the large Russian, Maxim, had drawn up outside the gates of the villa.

The same silent phantom of a manservant led them through cool, elegant rooms, the walls decorated with yellowing family photographs and flamboyantly executed portraits of past members of the Porto Christo lineage. They came out onto the patio at the rear of the villa. To Fraser it seemed so much more than two days since he had sat on this same patio drinking coffee with Alexander Scherer.

'Please, both of you, sit down,' Grigor said, pleasantly. 'I think, something cool is called for.'

He turned to the wraith-like figure of the butler. 'Lager, I think. Iced.'

Fraser almost imagined the butler creaked as he bowed and then withdrew silently into the house. Grigor settled himself facing Fraser and Jill and smiled politely.

'You will be unfamiliar with this house, Madame Fraser, although your husband knows it. It is the Marbella villa of the Duke of Porto Christo, the . . . scion . . . I believe you would say, of a very old Spanish family. It may strike you as incongruous that I, a colonel in the Red Army, should be so at home here. But then shortly you will understand. More important this villa was the holiday residence of Mr Alexander Scherer of whom you may have heard.'

Fraser heard Jill distinctly catch her breath. She looked across at him, alarm in her eyes.

'Scherer!' she said. 'The man who . . .'

Before Fraser could reply, Grigor cut in, an icy smile on his face. 'We thought you would like to return to the scene of your crime, Fraser.'

There was a movement behind them. Jill half-turned, uncertain. The tall man came out of the shade of the house into the light of the patio.

'And we felt you deserved some explanations in view of all you have both gone through,' said Alexander Scherer, sitting down languidly beside Grigor.

SEVENTEEN

Mark Fraser leaned forward, smiling reassuringly at his wife. He had greeted Scherer with a nod of acknowledgement and showed no surprise as he made the introductions.

'Jill, I have to introduce you to Alexander Scherer.'

Jill stared without comprehension at her husband. Her previous anxiety had changed into a feeling of absolute bafflement. And with the heat of noon surrounding her, she felt disorientated, as if the length of the patio had turned to liquid and was undulating before her eyes. Then she was aware that the man called Scherer was holding out his hand towards her in greeting. She took the hand limply, held it, and let it go almost immediately. She wasn't trying to understand but rather to bring herself back to earth, to stop the patio from weaving in front of her eyes.

'Yes, Frau Fraser,' said Scherer softly. 'I am the man your husband assassinated. Or rather he appeared to do so. And I believe when he came to me two days ago he would have done so if there had been no other way of freeing you. Indeed he told me this.'

'He would have done it too,' Grigor joined in. 'And if to stop him we had to kill him, then these people would simply have found someone else. So we did not kill him.'

Scherer leaned back in his seat expansively. 'Fortunately your husband came up with an alternative plan.'

The ghost-like servant reappeared and large glasses of iced lager were placed in front of them. Until the man withdrew there was a silence. It was finally broken by Fraser.

'Alternative plan? I suppose it could be called that,' he said, addressing himself to Jill. 'It was simply assassination with a blank cartridge.'

'And I agreed to seem to fall dead the moment I heard the bang of the rifle,' Scherer took up the story. 'We agreed to it two days ago. I even supplied the blood as I fell. A nice touch. Tomato sauce, your husband suggested, Frau Fraser. Of course we didn't notify the police of a killing. We simply let the guests spread the rumour. And to re-assure your captors we arranged for police sirens. Very efficient, we were. The rumour of my death seeped out.'

The tall German took a sip of lager and then continued. 'I even had that rumour reach a friend of mine in the Spanish radio service. So he put it out on radio. I made sure it was never retracted, although then we did have en-quiries from the police. We had to reassure them too, but discreetly. But then I have influence.'

Fraser broke in, this time talking to Scherer. 'I was lucky only Rocas questioned the fact that I got through the road blocks. There should have been road blocks had I really assassinated you, Scherer. We slipped up on that one.'

'Rocas!' Grigor cut in. 'We made sure he didn't ask any more questions, Fraser. Just after you left him.'

Fraser felt suddenly cold. He had found himself respect-ing the neat, light-suited, pale Russian; it was a wary respect that had grown over the last days. But now there was, in Grigor's tone, his dismissal of the problem of Rocas and his implications, something that Fraser recognised. Looking at the Russian he could see his own reflection just over two years ago, and he didn't like that reflection. Bartlett and Rocas, their deaths had helped to make Grigor in Fraser's image. He had to force his mind away from the thought. And there were his questions to be asked.

'Since we are here at your invitation, I hope you'll pro-vide us with some answers,' Fraser said turning his thoughts to words. 'For instance I'd like to know why the KGB has worked so strenuously to protect a rich German who is not only the typical capitalist reactionary of their own fables but actively conducts a McCarthy type witch-hunt against Communists in West Germany?'

Scherer and Grigor exchanged smiles. Fraser took the opportunity to gulp a mouthful of lager, content to let them take their own time in replying.

It was Scherer who leant forward to answer. 'Fraser, think of two things. First, as the great anti-communist, I am trusted by the Western establishment. Positively courted by the Americans, and admired by your Conservative Party. I am allowed access to much information, not perhaps the secret details but opinions which I know will have weight.'

'Friend of presidents and prime minsters?' Fraser enquired quizzically.

'Exactly so. Now, secondly, answer me on this. How much damage did the late Senator Joseph McCarthy do to American democracy, do you think?'

One side of it was clear to Fraser now. He had imagined something like this but until now he could not be sure.

'Quite a lot of damage,' he replied. 'McCarthy put a lot of good patriotic liberals out of action.'

'Exactly!' Scherer went on. 'Like McCarthy I attack the intellectuals, the scientists, the technocrats, all the liberals. Attack them as communists and they cease to function. They are anathema. Rendered impotent, their careers ruined, destroyed. That and the information gathering, that was my mission.'

'So you're a Russian agent and I claim the ten-pound prize . . . or is it merely a free pair of sunglasses?' Fraser said lightly, glancing at Jill who was listening, round-eyed.

Scherer gave a small shrug. 'I have been a Russian agent for many years.'

'If it hadn't been for those idiotic Red Action people forcing you to assassinate a man they considered a Fascist menace, this whole affair would never have happened,' Grigor said with a mild trace of irritation.

'But was it only the Red Action Brigade who wanted you killed?' Fraser said, trying to keep his voice on an even tone. This was the key question.

Another exchange of glances between Scherer and Grigor. The German answered. 'Perceptive of you. You think there is more to this than a group of insane children?'

'There has to be!'

'You may be right. Like your Kim Philby . . . or should I say our Kim Philby . . . my cover may be blown,' Scherer said studying the palms of his hands. Small lines of perspiration flowed along those lines. 'It is time I retired.'

'I am taking Comrade Scherer out tonight. We fly to East Germany,' Grigor added.

'And then, home. To Russia,' Scherer smiled. 'Otherwise I will be rendered useless anyway. When they realise, if they have not already done so, that I am not dead, there will be another assassination plot.'

'Someone's very persistent,' said Fraser, watching a petal fall slowly from a clump of bougainvillaea. 'I wonder who.'

Scherer drained his glass of lager and shot Fraser a nervous glance, the first time he had revealed anything other than a cautious bonhomie.

'You would not attempt to stop us leaving for East Germany?' he asked.

Fraser took his time in replying. He swallowed a mouthful of lager, rubbed the back of his hand across his mouth and stared intently at Scherer before he replied. They were still playing games, he thought, these two and the others. Deadly games. He could play games too, especially now Jill was safely beside him.

'If I had wanted to stop you,' he finally replied, 'I would have put a real bullet in the sniper's rifle. But we did make an arrangement that I would fire a blank cartridge. I've no reason to change that arrangement now. Anyway, as I told Colonel Grigor, I'm retired. I'm finished with your type of games.'

Scherer visibly relaxed. 'Of course. I was actually paying you a compliment, Herr Fraser. We were genuinely afraid of your professional abilities. That is why we asked you to come here. We felt that if we explained that my work is now finished you would see there is no longer any point in these people trying to kill me.'

Fraser nodded as he rose. 'You've explained, then. And I still have no interest in your . . . your affairs or your life. Now if we may go . . .?'

Scherer insisted on shaking hands with them both. Grigor disappeared into the villa to make sure, as he said, they would have no difficulty in leaving. And when Scherer walked them to the car, the gates of the villa were open though Grigor himself was nowhere in sight.

They drove onto the road past the figure of the large Russian, Maxim, who had his back towards them, busying himself loading luggage into the rear of the black car.

'Is it over now?' Jill asked, nestling her head against his shoulder.

'Not quite.'

She stiffened. 'What now . . .?'

Fraser tried to reassure her. 'It's finished as regards the Russians. But not our own people.'

He was confident he was right about the Russians. Grigor would get Scherer out to East Germany, there would be a furious scandal in Bonn and another undercover agent would have finished his work. He was right on all counts but one. They hadn't seen the last of Lieutenant-Colonel Grigor.

'What about our own people?' Jill was asking for the second time. They were driving through Marbella now and he realised he had been lost in his own thoughts. He searched through his pockets for a cigarette without success.

'Mark! I asked you . . .'

'I know. Look, we're going to Malaga. We'll find out if I'm right when we get there,' he said with a tired smile. He felt suddenly desperate for a cigarette.

'Anyway it's on our way to the airport,' he added by way of consolation.

Jill was inconsolable. She sat away from him now, her face petulant, staring out of the window. It seemed all too complex to her, the whole business. The game, as Mark called it. She hated the expression. It was a game where too many people got killed, as casually as counters got knocked from a board. A game she had hoped they were both out of; and yet she knew she shouldn't blame Mark. Yet there was no one else in sight she could blame.

'I think I've worked it out,' he broke into her thoughts. 'But I want to be sure.'

He took his eyes from the road to glance at her briefly. He was concerned by her silence. 'I promise you, it's nearly over.'

She accepted the promise with a nod. After all he had rescued her, been willing to commit murder in order to do so. And he had been clever enough to avoid having to do so. She knew she was being childish in her petulance. What more could she expect from him? She simply wanted it to be over now. Must he hang on; must he insist on knowing it all?

His voice broke in on her again. 'I'm hungry. In fact I'm starving. And I need cigarettes.'

They ate on the verandah of a small hotel outside the town of Calahonda. The Mediterranean lay below them, a blue haze stretching to the horizon, warm and beautiful. Jill was beginning to hate such beauty. During their meal Mark, who'd bought some cigarettes, chain-smoked as he covered several sheets of paper taken from the hotel reception desk in small neat handwriting.

'What is it?' she asked as he finished writing and placed the sheets in a large envelope.

'Insurance,' he replied. 'The whole story as I see it, to be sent now to our solicitor in Edinburgh. To be released to the press if anything happens to us.'

'Would they allow it to be published?'

'They might try slapping a "D" notice on it,' he admitted. 'But the European press will get copies too and they'll print. That'll do the damage. We can now walk into the Villa Circe without worry.'

'The Villa Circe?'

'Lloyd wanted to take us there before the Russians arrived. A safe house, I think, for the Department. Mackeson's there. Sir James, Tarrant's successor. He'll tell us it all but I want to walk in there, in my own time.'

'With me, please,' she insisted.

'With you.'

'Circe? Wasn't she the witch who turned men into

swine?'

Fraser looked up from sealing the envelope. 'I hadn't thought of that,' he smiled. 'How very appropriate.'

He paid their bill and posted the envelope in the hotel. As they drove off Jill sensed he was more relaxed. It was infectious. She rested on his shoulder as he drove.

An hour later they were on the Calle Moreno Monroy. The gates of the Villa Circe were decorated by a motif of entwined dolphins and the rear of the villa faced the sea and a small jetty. At this jetty was moored a large motor cruiser, the type that took two or three wealthy tourists on deep-sea fishing trips. All this Fraser noted as they swung through the open gates and along a curved driveway to the villa itself.

The villa was of a more modest scale than that of the Duke of Porto Christo. Nevertheless, Fraser thought, it was an expensive establishment, unlike the safe houses he had been used to when he had been in the field. He remembered a small, damp, Swedish farmhouse, an apartment in Vienna with only the bare necessities in furnishings, and a hut on the edge of the Black Forest. Mackeson did himself well. The Villa Circe, apart from its jetty which constituted a miniature marina, had half an acre of rolling lawn discreetly hidden from the road by thick bushes. And, Fraser estimated, at the rear of the house there had to be another half acre between the building and the beach.

As they left the car he took Jill's arm and together they approached the front door. The bell, to his surprise was a ghastly series of chimes. This man Mackeson was obviously a different type from his predecessor. Tarrant's safe house would have been a low-priced hotel room. But then Tarrant, apart from qualities of ruthlessness towards his country's enemies, had always revealed elements of timidity in his nature when it came to justifying the budget of the Department; as if he had a fear that the taxpayers of the country might find him out.

The door was opened by a tall man with thinning hair and a broken nose. He stared at Fraser with a glint of recognition in his eyes.

'Basle, Switzerland, 1973,' said Fraser. 'Tarrant sent you and another heavy out to get me out of the hands of the two Albanians. Jimmy Baskcomb, isn't it?'

Baskcomb nodded. 'I thought you were out of this until the chief told me you were expected.'

'I thought I was out of it too,' Fraser replied. 'Jill, this is Jimmy Baskcomb who once saved my life. Don't be encouraged by that. If he was told to end it, he would do it just as expertly.'

Baskcomb ushered them through a small hallway into a large cool lounge, one wall of which had wide French windows opening on to a stone patio, beyond which Fraser caught the blue sparkle of a swimming pool. Baskcomb indicated they go through to the patio but made no move to follow them further.

'I'm restricted to household duties now,' he explained with a trace of bitterness.

'The new man will appreciate you one day,' Fraser said with mock sympathy. 'By the way who broke your nose? It wasn't like that in the old days.'

He was surprised to see Baskcomb actually blush. 'Bloody CIA character thought I was a Russian. Amateurs, all of those CIA goons.'

Fraser and Jill crossed the patio, descended five stone steps and were at the side of the swimming pool.

Sir James Mackeson was lolling in a deck chair at the pool side. In a pair of blue and white trunks his body was fleshy, running to fat. In his left hand he held a long glass filled with colourless liquid topped by fast melting ice. His legs were stretched out, feet on the edge of the pool. In the pool, swimming with considerable and deliberate grace, was a bronze young man with lank black hair. He was wearing the smallest of pink trunks, the colour of which, apart from obvious visual omissions, gave the impression that he was swimming in the nude.

Hearing their footsteps, Mackeson heaved himself to his feet to greet Jill and Fraser. Incongruously, Jill noticed, he was wearing a large pair of plaid carpet slippers.

'Ah, Fraser, isn't it?' Mackeson greeted them, hand outstretched. 'And Mrs Fraser. I'm Mackeson. Would have recognised you anywhere, Fraser, from your photo in our files.'

He glanced towards the young man in the pool who had stopped swimming and was clinging to the edge of the concrete.

'Exactly like his picture in the files, eh, Cater?' Mackeson went on. 'And of course, Tarrant once talked to me about you, Fraser, so I feel I know you.'

'I feel I've been getting to know you,' Fraser replied with an edge of irony.

'Oh, yes, really. Now do sit down, both of you,' Mackeson gesticulated expansively towards two empty deck chairs facing his own. Jill sat nervously and uncomfortably on the crossbar of the first chair. Fraser placed a hand on the back of her chair but did not sit.

Mackeson waved his hand towards the figure in the pool. 'That's Cater. New since your day, Fraser. Good marksman but not in your class. Actually he's better with a hand gun. But he's a nice lad.' He suddenly looked around, vaguely apprehensive. 'But where's Frank Lloyd? He was bringing you . . .'

'We brought ourselves. Frank was . . . tied up.' Fraser shrugged.

Mackeson laughed. 'I'm sure he is quite securely tied up. My dear man, you are inimitable. You must know, Mrs Fraser, your husband is a character, really a character.'

Jill said nothing. She simply watched him, curiosity in her gaze.

'I'm so glad you came,' Mackeson continued. 'So very glad to see both of you.'

'We came to be flown home,' Fraser said coldly. 'Or did you have other plans for us?'

'To be frank, I did have other plans,' Mackeson admitted. 'If you had done what I had hoped you would do, I would have had to put those other plans into operation.'

'You mean, if I had killed Scherer?'

'You've guessed. You've worked it out. Very clever,' Mackeson beamed with the amiability of a smiling cobra.

230

'I don't think Frank Lloyd worked it out,' Fraser pressed on. 'He really thinks you were trying to help me find Jill. Just as he thinks you would naturally get us out of Spain.'

Mackeson took a sip from his glass. 'I really was sorry about the whole thing. But I had to use the best weapon to hand. After Santos was killed, you were that weapon. Of course you had to be pressured, hence your good lady's kidnapping. And I would have regretted that neither of you could have been permitted to get away. But you will appreciate it was all for the greater good of the old country.'

'Rocas knew what was going on, didn't he?' Fraser asked, maintaining the cool quality in his voice. 'Your man in Granada, he knew the whole thing. Including where Jill was being held.'

'His instructions were simply to make sure you got to Marbella in time to kill Scherer,' replied Mackeson, and then a frown crossed his face, a small shadow in the fleshy sun. 'By the way, did you kill Rocas?'

'Not guilty. The Russians. You know, you might have got away with it, only I couldn't understand why the Russians were protecting Scherer.'

'I gather you now know he has been one of their people for many years. A mole burrowing his way into the confidence of the Western powers.'

'Which is why you wanted him killed,' Fraser said, his eyes suddenly on the figure of Cater who was hauling himself out of the pool.

Jill, too, had noticed Cater. Until then she had followed the conversation between her husband and Mackeson with a sick fascination. They were talking about murder, as she might have talked to Mrs McCrae in the little shop at Craigallen village about shopping. This plumpish middle-aged Englishman, who was one of the heads of British Intelligence, was also talking about the possibility of having to kill both Mark and her; and she knew Cater, this tall, startling looking young man, might well be the chosen instrument of their deaths.

Fraser was still talking over her thoughts. '. . . of course

231

you couldn't openly make Scherer's murder a British Intelligence operation. It would be an admission that you'd been taken in, fooled by Scherer for years. Another Burgess and Maclean scandal,' he shook his head in mock pity. 'You might not even have been believed. You might have seemed to be killing a wealthy West German by mistake.'

'A fair assessment of the situation,' Mackeson agreed.

'So you struck upon the idea of using a terrorist group. Of course they were hardly experienced assassins. Oh, they could rob banks, spray innocent civilians with bullets from automatic weapons; but a planned assassination needing an expert marksman, that was something else. They recruited Santos . . . with your approval, I presume . . .'

Mackeson interrupted him. 'Unfortunately Santos was a marked man and the Mossad killed him. It was then I suggested you. I was honestly hoping we might not have to get rid of you afterwards, I assure you of that . . . but, had you killed Scherer I could see you would have known too much. You would have put it all together, as you have done.'

Footsteps on the stone, coming from the villa. Jill turned. A slight, slim figure came into the sun, the young old face, creasing as the eyes were screwed up against the glare. Jill caught her breath.

'Mark!' It was almost as if she was uttering a warning as well as an exclamation.

Fraser faced the new arrival.

Mackeson stepped forward, a modestly massive white whale effecting introductions. 'Your wife has of course already met Herr Gruner, Rolf Gruner.'

Rolf affected the easy, relaxed smile of the friend who has called in for afternoon tea. 'And Mr Fraser has seen me a few hours ago in the mountains at the other end of his rifle sight. Before that, of course, we met at Mijas.'

He turned from Fraser back to Jill and continued. 'How nice to see you again, Mrs Fraser. I did my best to make you comfortable under the circumstances. Mind you, it was difficult at times to control those two terrible young women. However that problem has been now eliminated.'

232

Jill could not restrain the shudder that ran through her body. This was the man who had been responsible for everything that had happened to her in the last week. His urbane smile and the assumption of an easy manner could not eradicate her fear and horror. She turned away to find herself staring at Cater again. He seemed to have no interest in their discussion but was gently oiling his body against the sun. There was something nauseating about his casual disregard of what was happening.

'Of course Herr Gruner is not one of the Department's establishment,' Mackeson continued to explain. 'Not one of our agents as you were, Fraser. Let's say he's a part-time employee. An infiltrator. He infiltrated the Holgar Group for us. I believe the rest of the Group were genuine terrorists. Sincere, idealistic murderers. Not like Gruner. Rolf does it for money. But he has such qualities of leadership he easily rose high in their counsels. All for money, all for us.'

At once, as if, as host he had forgotten his manners, Mackeson turned to a small table some yards from the pool side which was liberally stocked with bottles.

'But I am forgetting myself. I have not offered anyone a drink. Mrs Fraser . . .?'

'No, thank you.'

He turned to Fraser who declined with a curt negative. Fraser's face retained its impassivity but his eyes were wary, flickering from Gruner to Cater and back.

'You may help yourself, Rolf,' Mackeson said to Gruner and then faced Fraser again.

'It was very complimentary to you, Fraser . . . may I call you Mark . . .' Mackeson went on. 'Choosing you as assassin. Cater there wouldn't have been good enough.' An aside to Cater. 'No hard feelings, dear boy.'

'You knew I'd been finished with the Department for two years?' Fraser cut in.

'I couldn't think about that. I could only think of what would persuade you to do the job. Hence Mrs Fraser's abduction.'

'And afterwards, who would have eliminated us?'

Mackeson glanced from Rolf to Cater. 'One of the two. However I learned only this morning you didn't kill Scherer. Very clever of you to have arranged with Scherer your little fake assassination. I admire it so much. But then of course we did train you in deception And even cleverer of you now there is no need to eliminate you and Mrs Fraser.'

To Jill, Mark's eyes seemed to flash in the sunlight as he replied, not without a trace of satisfaction. 'If you had still considered our deaths a necessity, you would have been in trouble, Mackeson. I mailed the whole story to my solicitor this afternoon.'

'Cleverer and cleverer, as Alice might have said. Or was it the White Rabbit?' Mackeson replied. 'Of course it would never have been published in the UK. A "D" notice can be very effective. And even the news of your deaths would have been suppressed.'

Jill could contain herself no longer. The sickness growing within her required some kind of release. 'You . . . you can even smile while talking about murder . . .!' she burst out.

'My dear lady . . .!'

She ignored his attempted interruption. 'What kind of animals are you? How many people have been killed because of you? And of course, you usually sit in Whitehall without ever having to fire a gun. You're a bloody murderer just the same!'

Mackeson allowed a small silence before replying. 'But you are perfectly correct. I am a murderer. So is Gruner. And so is Cater. And so, too, was your husband, Mrs Fraser. We do it for Queen and country. And sometimes we make mistakes and innocent people suffer. But we consider that in the light of the greater good.'

'The end justifies the means,' Fraser muttered.

'Exactly.'

'You're no different from the Reds then?'

'We think we are. But the old days of . . . as Hollywood said it . . . the good guys and the bad guys . . . they're over. We're no longer black and white. Simply grey. Of course

I look upon myself as a patriot,' Mackeson ended on a smug tone, as if confession and admission permitted and excused all that went before.

'You have to believe you're some sort of patriot,' Jill went on, passionately angry. 'Otherwise how would you sleep at night? But when I look at you and your patriotism . . . and the Russians and theirs . . . perhaps I understand those . . . those sick children you used, those Red Action children. Oh, they're murderers all right . . . but you, Sir James Mackeson, you made them in your own image.'

Mackeson's face reddened and he cleared his throat loudly.

'It's an opinion, Mrs Fraser,' he said. 'Not that I can afford to subscribe to it. But I can say that now there is no need to harm you or your husband.'

'Would another killing or two really worry you?' Jill asked, bitterness overflowing.

'As I'm trying to tell you,' said Mackeson with a hint of exasperation that he should be harangued by this young woman. 'No further . . . eliminations . . . are necessary. We have been informed that Scherer is being flown out to East Germany and then to Russia. Although the actual assassination plan did not work, Scherer knows he has been "blown" so to speak. He has effectively been put out of action. So he's being taken out. The mission has therefore been successful, the mole flushed out.'

He was pacing the poolside now, the carpet slippers flapping against the concrete. He brushed up against Cater, frowned at the oiled body, and then faced them again.

'Of course there will be an uproar in West Germany. Bonn has been harbouring a viper. But it will pass. They're rather used to harbouring vipers.' He allowed the frown to dissolve into a smile. Again the smiling cobra, Jill thought.

Mackeson continued to hiss. 'You may fly home today, Mrs Fraser. You and your husband. Mark, I shall make one phone call and your tickets on the night plane will be waiting at the airport. You don't have to thank me.' The last sentence was added blandly without a trace of irony.

Fraser couldn't help his small tired grimace. 'I don't

think we intend to,' he said, and glanced at Rolf Gruner who had poured himself a glass of green liquid which might have been crème-de-menthe but wasn't. 'What about Gruner? Do you pay him for kidnapping my wife, or kill him? The latter course would be more sensible. And more deserving. He just might talk.'

Gruner returned his glance with no expression. But he did lift his glass as if toasting Fraser.

'Oh, Rolf won't talk,' replied Mackeson. 'We pay him enough to ensure that. And we wouldn't kill him. We may need him again. After all he can always claim *he* aborted the assassination of Scherer when he learned Scherer worked for the Russians.'

'And the deaths of his Group? How will he explain that?'

'He can blame those on us,' Mackeson was expansive in his confidence. 'You must realise how valuable it is for us to have a man inside those terrorist gangs. But that need not concern you, Mark. I assure you, you'll not be bothered again.'

'If I am I shall come to London and kill you,' said Fraser.

The statement hung in the air for a second. The tone of Fraser's voice indicated it had not been uttered lightly. For a moment Mackeson was nonplussed. Then again he regained his confidence.

'Now I'll say goodbye to you both. Any expenses incurred will not be questioned,' he said, trying to beam benevolently as if he had not heard Fraser's threat. 'I want you to feel we will not be petty about compensation . . .'

'You know what you can do with your compensation!' Fraser said, gripping Jill's shoulder. She rose awkwardly from the deckchair.

'No,' she said to her husband. 'We will take one thousand pounds to the Marquisa de Triana!'

Mackeson gave a slight bow. 'A very practical woman, your wife, Fraser. Of course I will do what she asks. And now, goodbye.'

Fraser felt Jill's hand slip into his. He knew he should

236

say something more; perhaps shout at Mackeson, anything to destroy the complacency the man so easily regained. But already Mackeson had turned away and was addressing Gruner. As they walked back to the shade of the villa he could hear Mackeson's voice address Gruner.

'The bodies of the young women in the mountains may prove awkward. So Cater will take you across to North Africa in our motor launch. I'll give you your money and provide a new passport. You'll leave in an hour.'

At the French windows Fraser hesitated. He wanted to hear as much as he could.

'And of course, Rolf,' Mackeson went on. 'You'll contact us in the usual way, letting us know where you go to ground. We'll be in touch when we need you again.'

Fraser felt the bile rise in the back of his throat. *When we need you again!* When we need a paid killer to do jobs too dirty even for our own people. That's what Mackeson should be saying. Fraser knew the idea should not surprise him but, after two years, he thought he must be getting soft. Either that or his abhorrence of Gruner was overwhelming. This was the character who had masterminded Jill's abduction; the man who would have killed her had it been necessary with no more compunction than he would have swatted a fly. It was a cliché but a valid one.

He felt Jill's grip tighten on his hand. She sensed his emotions, knew he wanted to go back and smash his fist into that young old face over and over again.

'We're out of it now,' Jill whispered. 'Anything you do would simply make you one of them again.'

She was right. He stepped inside the villa, Jill following. They were greeted by Baskcomb, who, without speaking, escorted them to the front door.

They drove into the centre of Malaga, aware that they had some hours to pass before going to the airport. Parking, they sat for a time in a small bodega and drank Spanish brandy, its rough strength blurring and easing the tensions within them. Later they walked along the promenade and on to the beach by the edge of the sea. They stared at yachts in the bay, clustered together, sheltering as if the

237

calm sea might change its mood, become angry at the wood and fibre-glass intrusions.

Fraser took deep breaths feeling some psychological need to cleanse his lungs. Jill walked at his side in silence, thankful simply to be with him.

'I'll be so glad to get back to Scotland,' she finally broke the silence. 'Oh, Mark I want to see really green hills and feel rain on my face. Just now I hate the sun ...!'

'We'll be home tomorrow,' Fraser replied. 'Out of it. Now that I've seen Mackeson. Now I know he daren't move against us.'

He stared out to sea. A motor launch was moving across the bay, heading south. He thought to himself, yes it must be over and done with; Scherer was still alive and Mackeson had rid himself of the mole. And he, Fraser was out of the game for life. Yet, within him was still fear. Oh, not for their lives, he was sure of that. No, his fear was, would he ever really be out of it? Would he ever be clear of men like Mackeson; cold machines trained to think nothing of method, only of aims. All in the name of patriotism. Was he really free of being one of their creatures? Or would there be another time when somebody remembered that Mark Fraser had an acquired talent that could be utilised in another set of circumstances? All that would be needed would be the application of a degree of pressure and they would believe they could always bring him back. They would never hesitate to apply that pressure, he knew; just as they would not hesitate to destroy him if he became a liability or even simply an embarrassment. Was it then simply a delusion that he was retired and out of it?

These were thoughts he had to put from his mind. He must never allow Jill to be aware of them. Otherwise their life together would be lost in some kind of despairing tension, waiting for the stranger to appear, the pressure to be applied.

He concentrated on the motor launch moving towards a hazy, uncertain horizon. It looked vaguely familiar, like the launch they had glimpsed as they drove to Mackeson's

238

villa. Then he remembered the overheard conversation as they left. It could be Gruner *en route* to North Africa. Until the next time.

The boat cast a long shadow on the blue water as the afternoon neared its end, the sun low. Fraser took Jill's arm and was about to turn away when it happened.

At first there was no sound. The motor launch simply dissolved into an orange cloud of billowing flame. Fragments of material, wood and metal, soared into the air above the expanding flame and smoke, curving against the sky and plunging down back to the sea.

Then the sound of the explosion reached them and with it a physical pressure on the ear-drums, a shock wave echoing in their heads. Jill, eyes wide with horror, dug her fingernails into the palm of his hand. They stood staring with a terrible fascination as the flame died, the smoke drifted, the fragments of the launch hit the sea creating a hundred small spouts of water.

The smoke rose higher and dissolved, their sight of the sea cleared and there was no longer a launch but merely pieces of driftwood wide apart, floating on a ruffled greyish surface surrounded by the cleaner blue sea.

'God!' Jill whispered.

Fraser turned away. It seemed as if his hatred of Gruner had been directed towards the boat and become a tangible practical weapon. And it had been used.

Four yards behind them, where the sand met the concrete of the promenade stood Lieutenant-Colonel Grigor. He smiled bleakly at them. He had been watching the launch with binoculars which were still in his hands.

'We believe in tidying everything up, Fraser,' Grigor said. 'Eliminating dangerous refuse like Herr Gruner.'

Fraser nodded dumbly. There was nothing he could say. The game was still being played.

'Go back to Scotland with your lady, Fraser,' Grigor went on. 'Stay retired!'

The Russian paused momentarily, then jerked his head, a slight formal bow. 'Goodbye.'

He walked away from them. To Fraser, his light suit,

receding in the yellow rays of the dying afternoon, seemed now crumpled and shabby.

Jill stared after the Russian and Fraser felt a shudder run through her body. He put his arm around her shoulders.

'We are . . . retired, Jill,' he said.